S0-BZG-624

"No."

It was said quietly but with finality.

"Will you at least listen to my reasons for offering you the protection of my name?"

"My lord…"

"Marc," he corrected her softly. "Marriage is the only way I can protect you. In return for my name and protection you will give me your discretion and children."

"I *cannot* accept!" Meg's voice wobbled. "You…you are offering certainties in return for something I do not know if I can—" She stopped, very embarrassed. But he had understood.

"You do not know if you can have children? Is that it?" Marc smiled wryly. "My dear *that* would be a problem no matter who I married."

"But…"

"Marry me, Meg." His voice was low and persuasive.

She stared up at him. He meant it. He really did wish her to marry him. It would be a bargain between them.

* * *

The Dutiful Rake
Harlequin Historical #712—July 2004

**Harlequin Historicals is delighted
to introduce Mills & Boon author
ELIZABETH ROLLS**

**DON'T MISS THESE OTHER
TITLES AVAILABLE NOW:**

#711 TEXAS BRIDE
Carol Finch

#713 FULK THE RELUCTANT
Elaine Knighton

#714 WEST OF HEAVEN
Victoria Bylin

Elizabeth Rolls

The Dutiful Rake

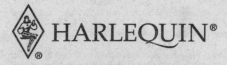

HARLEQUIN®

TORONTO • NEW YORK • LONDON
AMSTERDAM • PARIS • SYDNEY • HAMBURG
STOCKHOLM • ATHENS • TOKYO • MILAN • MADRID
PRAGUE • WARSAW • BUDAPEST • AUCKLAND

If you purchased this book without a cover you should be aware that this book is stolen property. It was reported as "unsold and destroyed" to the publisher, and neither the author nor the publisher has received any payment for this "stripped book."

ISBN 0-373-29312-7

THE DUTIFUL RAKE

Copyright © 2002 by Elizabeth Rolls

First North American Publication 2004

All rights reserved. Except for use in any review, the reproduction or utilization of this work in whole or in part in any form by any electronic, mechanical or other means, now known or hereafter invented, including xerography, photocopying and recording, or in any information storage or retrieval system, is forbidden without the written permission of the publisher, Harlequin Enterprises Limited, 225 Duncan Mill Road, Don Mills, Ontario, Canada M3B 3K9.

All characters in this book have no existence outside the imagination of the author and have no relation whatsoever to anyone bearing the same name or names. They are not even distantly inspired by any individual known or unknown to the author, and all incidents are pure invention.

This edition published by arrangement with Harlequin Books S.A.

® and TM are trademarks of the publisher. Trademarks indicated with ® are registered in the United States Patent and Trademark Office, the Canadian Trade Marks Office and in other countries.

www.eHarlequin.com

Printed in U.S.A.

Available from Harlequin Historicals and
ELIZABETH ROLLS

The Dutiful Rake #712

Please address questions and book requests to:
Harlequin Reader Service
U.S.: 3010 Walden Ave., P.O. Box 1325, Buffalo, NY 14269
Canadian: P.O. Box 609, Fort Erie, Ont. L2A 5X3

Chapter One

Beguiling green eyes glimmered up into cold light grey as Lady Hartleigh circled the crowded floor in the powerful arms of Marcus Langley, Earl of Rutherford. That tall, lithe figure seemed perfectly indifferent to the sylph-like form in its sheath of gold silk. Not the most censorious of Almack's patronesses could have found anything to cavil at in the way they danced. His lordship kept a proper distance at all times, his thighs did not brush against her ladyship's skirts, his hand remained just above her waist as was considered decent and they chatted unconcernedly without gazing passionately into each other's eyes.

For all that, several haughty dames cast outraged glances in their direction, albeit surreptitiously. After all, if the rumours were true and Marcus really was considering marriage at long last, then the last thing anyone wanted to do was offend him. He was one of the richest prizes on the Marriage Mart and it was not only his positively indecent fortune that made him so eligible.

There was the title as well—one of the oldest and most illustrious in the realm. Add to that his lordship's undeniable good looks, prowess as a sportsman and his elegance of dress and it was no wonder that so many lures should have been thrown out to him over the years since he'd returned from serving with Wellington's forces. Lures which had been totally ignored. Until now.

At five and thirty the Earl was marked as a confirmed bachelor. No one could ever remember him showing the slightest interest in any marriageable female. He preferred to live a life of hedonistic pleasure when in the capital, which was only during the spring anyway. The rest of the year he seemed quite happy to spend largely on one or another of his estates, which were scattered around the country.

Tales had drifted back to town about house parties held at those mansions. House parties at which no respectable female was to be seen. For it was not to be thought that his lordship had no interest in women. Quite the opposite. He was a most dangerous and accomplished rake. Husbands might well look to their errant wives when he was around, although, to his credit, it was said that he had no interest in seducing the young and innocent, nor would he pursue any lady whose husband was likely to take a dim view of the matter. Widows, of course, were considered fair game.

Those more cynical, or better acquainted with his lordship, averred that his avoidance of innocent young things sprang not from motives of chivalry, but from a complete lack of interest coupled with a well-developed instinct for self-preservation. He had absolutely no desire to find himself trapped into marriage with one of the fashionable society virgins launched on the Polite World each spring.

Nevertheless, despite his appalling reputation, his title, looks, charm and above all fortune rendered him an eminently acceptable suitor to the highest of sticklers. So to see him dancing with Lady Hartleigh, a widow of somewhat dubious reputation and scanty jointure but unbounded ambition, was enough to send ripples of conjecture eddying around the assembly rooms.

Lord Rutherford's elder sister, Lady Diana Carlton, viewed her brother's interest in the lovely widow with extreme disapprobation.

'Oh, for heaven's sake!' she said in tones of vexation to Jack Hamilton, who was sitting out the dance with her. 'What next will he do? Surely he doesn't intend to marry *her*!'

Hamilton held his tongue but Lady Diana knew her brother's best friend too well to be deflected by his silence.

'Jack, you must know what he intends!' said Lady Diana. 'You even have some influence with him. Which is more than anyone else can boast. Say something!'

Jack Hamilton looked down at her in some amusement and said, 'Oh, I wouldn't say that, Di. After all, you and Lady Grafton managed to get him as far as thinking of marriage. Quite an achievement, that.'

The grey eyes, so like her brother's, snapped fire at this innocent-seeming disclaimer. 'You know perfectly well that Aunt Regina and I never meant him to consider Althea Hartleigh as his *wife*.'

'Precisely,' said Hamilton drily. 'Which is why I have every intention of keeping my mouth shut. Unless, of course, Marc happens to raise the subject with me. If he asks me what I think, then I'll tell him. Otherwise I shall mind my own business.'

There were very few people from whom Lady Diana would have taken that. Fortunately for himself, Jack Hamilton was one of the privileged few.

She sighed. 'I suppose you mean that he is doing this just to vex us. Do you happen to know how far he means to go?' A delicate hand was laid on Hamilton's sleeve. 'You know, Jack, the title must not be allowed to pass to our cousin Aubrey. He is a dear, but quite unsuited to the responsibility. And he doesn't even desire it. Marc must marry! You know he must.'

Hamilton nodded. 'He knows it too. But he has no desire to wed for any other reason than to beget an heir. I fancy he hoped Aubrey might prove a suitable heir. Lord knows the lad's steady enough, but all he wants to do is remain in Oxford with his books and fellowship. Frankly, if I were you, Di, I should leave well alone.' He hesitated and then went on. 'The reason I have some influence with Marc is because I...er...don't beat him over the head with it.'

Lady Diana stared up at him. 'But...'

He nodded. 'Leave it alone, Di. He knows he has to marry. He knew that without you and Lady Grafton descending upon him to demand he secure the succession!'

She grimaced. 'That was Aunt Regina's notion. She favours the direct method.'

'Mmm. Rather like a brace of nine-pounders,' agreed Hamilton.

The grey eyes glared at him unsuccessfully and then twinkled ruefully. 'Thank you, Jack. Your compliments have always the charm of originality.'

He grinned and said comfortably, 'Naturally. That's why I'm still a bachelor.' He turned his head as a tall, exquisitely garbed gentleman joined them. 'Hullo, Toby! What the devil are you doing here? Dancing's a little energetic for you, isn't it?'

Sir Toby Carlton, Lady Diana's husband, shuddered

artistically. 'Perish the thought! Really, Jack—it's exhausting enough just watching Marc whirling Lady Hartleigh around. Let alone hearing Di cursing about it.' He cast his wife an affectionate grin. His lazy, effete pose was just that—a pose. One that amused everyone, himself included.

He viewed his brother-in-law and his fair partner critically. 'Shouldn't have thought he was any more interested in her than any other female he's bedded over the years. Less, possibly.'

'True,' said Jack thoughtfully. 'But if I'm not much mistaken, that is precisely the danger. He doesn't want to care—doesn't want anyone that close.'

His gaze went to the tawny head that towered over nearly every other man in the room. The waltz had just ended and Marc was escorting his lovely partner to the refreshment rooms. He frowned slightly. As little as Lady Diana did he wish to see his best friend throw himself away on Althea Hartleigh.

It was not the fact that he knew her to be Marc's mistress already. If he thought that she and Marc were in love, he would not have given a damn. And he did Lady Diana the credit to know she would have accepted it as well. It was just that he wished Marc could find someone to care for. Someone who could break through that impenetrable wall of reserve with which his lordship held most of the world at bay.

Marriage with a woman who would betray him at the first opportunity was not likely to achieve that. Quite the reverse!

His thoughts were interrupted by Lady Diana. 'Oh, curse it! Here comes Sally Jersey. No doubt she will have something to say.'

The Countess of Jersey sailed up to them. 'How

charming! Old friends having a comfortable cose! Good evening, Di. And Toby! How tiring for you! Dear Jack! To what do we owe the pleasure? Are you on the catch as well as Marc? I vow that would be too good to be true…'

Jack Hamilton eyed her thoughtfully and said simply, 'Sally, bite your tongue.' Again his position as the head of an old, if untitled, and horrendously wealthy family saved him from annihilation.

Lady Jersey pouted and shrugged her shoulders. 'Oh, very well! I dare say the last thing needed is for anyone to tell Marc his business!' She added shrewdly, 'No doubt it would only encourage him!'

She rustled away and Sir Toby heaved a sigh of relief. 'Thank God! She's even more tiring than a waltz!'

Diana giggled and said, 'Darling, you really are dreadful. What if she'd heard you?'

Sir Toby grinned. 'My dear, I'd simply tell her that I'm saving my energies. For later.'

Lord Rutherford, having procured a glass of orgeat for Lady Hartleigh, was idly surveying the assembled throng and wondering how soon he could politely take his leave. Having done what he came to do—namely stir up all the tabbies and give his sister a nasty shock— he could see little reason for remaining.

He slanted a considering glance down at Lady Hartleigh who was sipping her orgeat unconcernedly. No, he could hardly escort her home. That would be going too far, even for him.

'Shall I see anything of you in the next week, Marcus?' Her soft, caressing voice held only idle curiosity, but the green eyes betrayed a whole world of meaning.

He knew perfectly well what she wished to know. When did he mean to take his pleasure with her again? Thoughtfully he gave the question at least half of his attention.

Then, with a shrug of his broad shoulders, he said, 'I have to go out of town tomorrow, Althea. Estate business in Yorkshire. It will take me about three weeks, I should think. Sorry.'

'Three weeks?' She pouted. 'An eternity! Cannot your agent deal with it? I am sure Hartleigh never concerned himself as you do.' Her discontent with his conviction that he must take a personal hand in any and every matter pertaining to his large and scattered properties was obvious.

'Very likely not,' replied Rutherford coldly. He did not consider the way in which the late Lord Hartleigh had run his property to be an example for his emulation. 'And in this case I have to see the property. I have only just inherited it and I understand it to be in a disgraceful state.'

'Then why bother?' Her ivory brow puckered in genuine puzzlement. 'Surely you can just sell it and pocket the proceeds.'

'No, I can't.'

His chiselled lips closed firmly, and Lady Hartleigh recognised at once that he was decided. No amount of cajolery or teasing on her part would change his mind. She might as well accept the inevitable. Besides, he would come back positively eager for her favours and there was no saying what he might not be inveigled into after three weeks of celibacy.

She did not delude herself that he was attached enough to her personally to eschew other women, but she was tolerably certain that if he were engaged on

business he would have little time to pursue any passing
fancy. If, indeed, there were anything to tempt him up
in the wilds of Yorkshire. She could imagine nothing
more unlikely than Marcus showing any interest in a
rustic.

His lordship looked down at her with a faint smile.
'Just so, my dear. And when I return I think we must
have a little discussion about the future.'

'The future?' Lady Hartleigh tried to keep the eagerness out of her voice. Could he possibly mean…?
Despite her hopes she had not seriously believed he
could really be considering marriage. Cold triumph
blazed in her lowered eyes. This would be an achievement indeed.

'The future,' he repeated blandly. Then a steely note
crept into his voice. 'So do…er…look after yourself,
my dear.'

Her eyes flashed up at that and encountered steely
cynicism. So he had noticed! She would have to take
steps to discourage Sir Blaise Winterbourne! If Marcus
were considering marriage, then Sir Blaise would cast
out lures in vain. She was not fool enough to play that
dangerously. She might have known that Marcus would
notice Blaise. After all, the man was reputed to make a
habit of bedding all Rutherford's mistresses. He could
wait. Althea Hartleigh was not going to risk a possible
marriage for the sake of an illicit tumble. No doubt
Blaise Winterbourne would be just as happy, if not
more so, to bed the new Countess of Rutherford.

The following morning saw Lord Rutherford leave
his mansion in Mount Street at the shockingly early
hour of nine o'clock. He was clad in immaculate inex-
pressibles of palest fawn, which clung to his long legs

in a way which displayed their muscles to admiration. His coat of dark blue superfine was similarly moulded to his broad shoulders. His only jewellery was the heavy gold signet ring which never left his finger and a pearl pin which nestled chastely within the snowy folds of his cravat.

He mused on his situation as he strolled around to Brook Street to call on Jack Hamilton. There was little doubt that word of his intentions had leaked out. He had been positively besieged the previous night. Matrons who had never before bothered to accord him more than a passing interest had been assiduous in presenting their virtuous treasures for his inspection.

A cynical smile curved his lips. Usually they were only too careful to warn those same virtuous fillies against the predatory Earl of Rutherford. Quite apart from his physical inclinations, he had encouraged his reputation to a great extent as protection against that sort of thing. He had no taste for simpering, virginal débutantes without two thoughts to rub together in their heads and no idea of how to please a man.

In that regard Lady Hartleigh would suit him very well as a wife. He had ascertained beyond all possible doubt that her ladyship knew to a nicety how best to satisfy his desires.

He was still meditating on Lady Hartleigh's voluptuous charms as Hamilton's elderly valet Fincham ushered him into the snug and extremely untidy chamber that served Hamilton as a dining parlour.

'Lord Rutherford, Mr Jack,' said Fincham and closed the door.

Hamilton waved Marcus to a chair and finished his mouthful of sirloin. He washed it down with a draught of ale before saying. 'Morning, Marc. What brings you here so early? Can't that enormous staff of yours manage a decent breakfast?' His eyes twinkled as he carved a plateful of ham for his lordship and poured him a cup of coffee.

Marcus disposed himself in the chair, stretching out his long legs, and sipped his coffee as he regarded his friend who was calmly continuing with his own breakfast. 'Come on, Jack. Tell me the worst. What are they all saying?'

Playing for time, Jack looked at him inquiringly. 'Saying? About what?' Then encountering an amused lift of one eyebrow, 'Oh, your matrimonial plans! Well, the general consensus is that it's about time you realised your bookish young cousin is neither suited to the position nor even desires it.'

'And Lady Hartleigh?' The grey eyes were suddenly intent. 'What did my dear sister have to say on that head?'

Jack's eyes were sober as he said, 'Not exactly taken with the idea.'

Marcus snorted. 'Perhaps it will teach her not to be such an incorrigible busy head. Not to mention my Aunt Regina!'

'Mmm. It's possible,' said Jack, with a complete lack of expression that suggested that Marcus was indulging his optimism too far.

Marcus sighed and said, 'Say it, then. Come on, don't spare me!'

'You really want to know what I think?' Jack asked seriously. 'You'll think I've run mad.'

'Nothing new in that,' said Marcus grinning at him.

'Very well then.' Jack took a deep breath and embarked upon a forlorn hope. 'I think Althea Hartleigh would be the worst possible choice for you.' He hesi-

tated and then went on. 'Wouldn't say   if you hadn't
asked. But since you do… Tell me, M   …do you really want a wife who can be counted   to entertain
herself with half the men in Londo   she gets a
chance?'

Marcus shrugged. 'Who am I to be hy   ical about
such matters? After all, I have been a   g myself
with such women for years. As long as   enough
sense to provide an heir or two, or at lea   reeding
before she seeks other amusements, I ca   that it
is any of my concern. After all, most of   en of
my acquaintance conduct themselves like   very
convenient I have found it too. And I an   going
live like a monk just because I've taken a wife. It seems
a trifle churlish not to extend my wife the same courtesy.'

Jack grunted. 'No doubt. For God's sake, Marc!
Think to the future. Do you really want to be tied to
Althea Hartleigh for the rest of your life? Don't you
think, if you looked about you, that you might find a
girl or woman to care for?' He saw the amazement in
his friend's eyes and grinned reluctantly. 'Aye, I knew
you'd think I'd run mad.'

'You must have completely slipped your moorings!'
Marcus agreed with alacrity. 'Why should I find someone to care for when all *she* will care for is my wealth
and my title?' There was a bitter twist to his lips.

As bad as that, thought Jack, observing this. All he
said was, 'I think you do yourself an injustice there.
Why should some female not value you for yourself?'
He paused briefly and added deliberately, 'As your
mother valued your father.'

The bitterness around the mouth became even more
pronounced. 'Because I seriously doubt the existence of

such a paragon, Jack! Every female I have ever had anything to do with has been first and foremost concerned with my purse strings.' He ignored the last part of Jack's comment.

Jack was silenced. It was true enough. Mainly because Marc never allowed a woman sufficiently close to see beyond them to anything else. They saw nothing but Marcus, Earl of Rutherford—gazetted rake and confirmed cynic. Very few people ever saw Marc Langley—certainly none of his mistresses did.

So he shrugged and said, 'I admit you have a point, but even if you feel a marriage founded on love or at least affection to be unlikely, might I suggest that one founded on mutual respect rather than lust is more likely to be convenient and bearable?' He looked at Marcus ruefully. 'Sorry, I didn't mean to preach. Have some more ham.'

Marcus helped himself. Jack's last point had hit home. Maybe he was right. And anyway, marrying in a fit of pique to annoy Di would be positively cork-brained. Another thought suddenly presented itself as he sliced ham. Althea had been married to Hartleigh for at least six years and in all that time there had been no children to bless the union. It would be the height of lunacy to marry for the sake of an heir if there were the slightest indication his countess might not be able to oblige.

'I'm going out of town,' he said abruptly. 'Di knows all about it. Our Great-uncle Samuel has cocked up his toes. Since the old miser had no children and was too clutch-fisted to pay a lawyer to draw up a will, the estate comes back to me. And from all I hear it is in an appalling state. I'll have to be gone for several weeks.'

Jack nodded. 'Your father's uncle, wasn't he? The one in Yorkshire?'

'That's him,' said Marcus. 'Apparently he had some connection of Great-aunt Euphemia's to housekeep for him and she's left totally destitute, according to the lawyers, so I'll have to settle some money on her. Uncle Samuel had plenty, so why he didn't deal with the matter himself is beyond me.' He finished his coffee and stood up. 'I just came around to tell you I'd be away. In fact, I'm leaving this morning.'

A friendly grin lightened Hamilton's sombre countenance. 'I'm honoured, my lord, that you deigned to grace my poor table.'

'Oh, go to the devil!' recommended his lordship. He paused. 'Jack, I will give what you said some thought. Oh, not that rubbish about caring for a girl.' The finely moulded mouth tightened slightly, as though in pain. 'Even if it were possible…it's not…not what I want. But I dare say you may be right about the rest of the business. Thanks. And I don't know that you need to tell Di about this conversation.'

'Of course, I always pass on the confidences of my closest friends to their sisters!' said Jack sardonically.

Marcus grinned. 'Sorry. I didn't mean to be offensive.'

He took his departure, leaving Jack Hamilton in a state compounded of concern and relief in equal parts. At least Marc was thinking twice about Althea Hartleigh, but the utter cynicism and contempt for the opposite sex betrayed by his comments did not bode well for a happy union with any woman. Ten to one, even if some female did discover and succumb to his lordship's personal charm, he would find some way to hurt her and ensure that she regretted ever doing so.

Ruefully he wondered if, after all, Althea Hartleigh would be the best choice. At least Marc would know what to expect and there was not the slightest chance of the lady being hurt by his cold humours and likely strayings. There was more to it than straight-out cynicism over the dubious motives which spurred some women to marriage. Still, after nearly twenty years, Marc could not bear to speak of his adored mother. Jack shook his head sadly, remembering the outrageous and delightful woman she had been.

He sighed. No doubt Marc would go his own way to the devil and if it gave him the illusion of happiness then there was not a thing anyone could do for him! Unless, of course, Blaise Winterbourne seduced Althea Hartleigh before she became Countess of Rutherford.

Very few people realised just how deeply Marc disliked Winterbourne. Certainly no one but Jack knew why he did so…and the reason why Winterbourne took such pleasure in seducing Marc's mistresses.

Chapter Two

Three days later Marcus sat in the library of Fenby Hall, wondering if the rest of the house could possibly be in as shabby a state as this room. The wainscoting all looked as though it might as well be torn down; the hangings had obviously not been attended to for years. They hung tattered and faded over windows for which cleaning was a distant memory. When he had taken a volume from the shelves in curiosity, a cloud of dust and several moths had attended it.

The only positive aspect of the room was the fact that it had not succumbed to the atmosphere of damp prevailing in the rest of the house. A phenomenon which Marcus had no hesitation in ascribing to the circumstance of his uncle having used only this room and forbidding fires in any other.

The rest of the house was cold, damp and unspeakably dreary. Rugs were badly worn, although he could see where tears had been carefully mended. Curtains were faded and in many cases ragged. The furniture, he noted, was well dusted except for this room. It was even waxed in the parlour. But everywhere there was evidence of decay.

Certainly the linen was in an appalling condition. He had put his foot through both sheets last night and a brief inspection that morning had revealed that, despite frequent mending and being turned sides to middle, they had long ago reached the point where they would have disgraced a rag-bag.

He sat at the large mahogany desk and perused the estate books. Obviously his great-uncle had taken no interest in his patrimony for years. There was no record of any improvements being made; the wages remained what they had been twenty years ago. Samuel had apparently been content to live on his considerable investments and permit his home and dependents to decay around him.

He had arrived too late yesterday to see anything of the estate, but he'd wager that the workers were housed in cottages he'd be ashamed to see on his land. What the devil had the old man been about to let things come to such a pass? And what was the housekeeper, Miss Fellowes, doing to let the house fall into such a state?

He had not yet had the felicity of meeting Miss Fellowes. When Marcus had inquired for her the previous evening, the old retainer, Barlow, had said apologetically that Miss was laid up with the influenza, having taken a nasty chill at the master's funeral.

'She did tell me to assure your lordship that she would be gone as soon as may be,' explained Barlow nervously. 'Going to Mrs Garsby over at Burvale House as nursery governess she is, but the truth is she ain't too steady on her pins at all. Mrs Barlow did persuade her to stay, feeling sure your lordship would understand.'

Marcus thought sardonically that, from the look of things, Miss Fellowes had been suffering from influenza for the last five years if the state of the house was anything to go by. He hoped his uncle had not paid her a large wage because she certainly hadn't earned it.

Keeping this thought to himself, he nodded and said coldly, 'Inform Miss Fellowes that she is welcome to stay until she is fully recovered. Has a message been sent to Mrs Garsby to inform her of this illness?'

'No, my lord.'

'See to it at once. And where will I find the household accounts?' He would have a look and see just what Miss Fellowes had been doing with herself.

'Miss Meg will have them, me lord.'

'Then ask one of the maids to fetch them, please,' said his lordship firmly.

Barlow opened his mouth, shut it again and left the room.

Some half-hour later a stout, elderly woman wearing an apron entered the library, bearing a large ledger. Marcus looked up frowning from his desk and stared. This was no maidservant!

'Mrs Barlow, your lordship,' she said in answer to his querying gaze. 'Here be the accounts.'

Marcus stared at her and said, 'You're the cook, dammit! Why are you running errands beyond your kitchen? Why did not one of the maids—?'

'Because there ain't none,' was the startling reply.

The hard grey eyes widened in disbelief. 'None? You can't be serious!' A look around the room and the memory of his bed linen served to convince him that she could be serious.

'Then who…?'

Mrs Barlow said, 'Well, Miss Meg does her best, me lord, but since she also gives me a bit of a hand, being as how the master wouldn't hire no help, it don't leave her a lot of time an' it's a big house.' She dumped the book on the desk with scant ceremony and stalked out.

Marcus was horrified at these revelations and mentally made the afflicted Miss Fellowes his apologies. Obviously Great-uncle Samuel had been an even bigger lickpenny than he had thought. A glance at the household accounts confirmed what Mrs Barlow had said. No domestic staff was employed beyond the Barlows. One groom kept the two horses and a couple of carriages in some sort of order.

By the time he had ascertained from the painstaking accounts that the house was run on a budget that would have been laughably inadequate were it quadrupled, he was wondering just why Miss Fellowes had not removed herself years ago. The previous housekeeper had been dismissed four years earlier according to these records, resulting in a saving of twenty pounds a year.

Marcus very much doubted that his economically minded relative had bothered to pay Miss Fellowes a penny. There was certainly no record of it here. Which suggested that she was not, after all, a servant, but rather a dependent that the old devil had used shamefully. And then to leave her destitute! It passed all bounds! He would have to settle some money on the old lady. Marcus began to have a very definite picture of Miss...what was her name? Meg? Margaret, no doubt...Fellowes. Small, in her sixties at least, white hair, an air of nervousness. Probably she had nowhere else to go and no one to turn to and Samuel Langley had treated her like a dog! Damn the old skinflint! How difficult would it have been to leave the poor woman a respectable sum of money? Now he would have to do it as tactfully as possible and try to atone for Samuel's lack of responsibility. Perhaps she would enjoy a stay in London with Di?

Irritably, he dismissed this very minor matter from his mind and turned his attention back to the books. Tomorrow he would have to look over the estate and see what needed doing. Doubtless it was in as bad heart as the house.

A day spent riding around the estate with the bailiff, an individual clearly hired because he fell in with all Samuel Langley's notions of economy, confirmed Marcus in his worst fears. The estate was in ruins, its fields unproductive for much of the year and its tenants housed in conditions that would have shamed their new landlord had they been discovered on any of his other lands.

His face became grimmer and grimmer the more he saw, and Mr Padbury, misunderstanding his new master's cold anger, sought heartily to assure him that there were many more economies that could be made.

Ten minutes later, his face white with shock at the explosion his reassurances had engendered, Mr Padbury was in no doubt that things were about to change rapidly at Fenby. His lordship had informed him that, if he wished to keep his position, he would at once set in train arrangements for the relief of the cottagers and, furthermore, reduce the rents to a more reasonable figure.

Sitting in the library before dinner, contemplating the amount of work needed to bring the estate into order, Marcus wondered if his great-uncle had been merely eccentric or if there had been a hitherto-unrealised streak of insanity in the old man. It was going to cost a fortune to restore the estate. He sincerely hoped the old curmudgeon would spin dizzily in his grave at all the money that would have to be spent.

His cogitations were interrupted by Barlow, who came in and coughed apologetically.

'Yes, Barlow? Is dinner ready?' His annoyance over the ruination around him made his voice rather sharp.

Barlow looked awkward. 'Well, it is, me lord, but that ain't what I came to tell…ask you.'

He hesitated and Marcus, seeing that the old man was actually scared, said more gently, 'Go on, then.'

''Tis Miss Meg, me lord. Just took her dinner up on a tray I have, an' I reckon she's pretty bad. Agnes— Mrs Barlow, that is—saw her this mornin' an' thought the doctor did ought to be called but—'

'Have you done so?' interrupted Marcus, frowning.

'Oh, no, me lord!' Barlow said in soothing accents. 'Not without your permission! An' you was out all day so…'

Sheer disbelief robbed Marcus of speech momentarily. What the hell was going on here? He stared at Barlow for a moment and then said carefully, 'What the devil have I to say to anything? If Miss Fellowes requires or desires the attendance of a doctor, then she is perfectly at liberty to summon one!'

Barlow looked scared and confused and then, his face working, he burst out, 'We told Miss Meg days ago she did ought to have the doctor, but she won't acos she can't pay him. Master wouldn't never let her call the doctor, not even when she broke her arm! Doctor came anyway that time, acos Agnes got a message to him an' the master refused to pay the bill! So Miss Meg won't call him—'

'Enough!' Marcus was horrified. His mental query

about his uncle's sanity was patently answered. The old man must have been next door to a Bedlamite!

He saw Barlow flinch and said, 'Send a message for the doctor at once and assure him that his bills, including the one for Miss Fellowes's broken arm, will be met! I will come and see your mistress at once to reassure her that she need have no fears for the future!'

It was the least he could do. It was not right to leave the poor old lady worrying about her prospects. He had every intention of settling a large enough sum on her to enable her to hire lodgings and live in decent comfort. The idea of her having to go out and earn her living after a Langley had treated her so shabbily was utterly repugnant. Clearly Samuel Langley had not possessed the least idea of what his position entailed.

Barlow stared and said, 'I dunno as it'll do much good, me lord. Right feverish she is. I don't think she even knew I was in the room just then.'

It was Marcus's turn to stare. He said slowly, 'How sick is she?'

Barlow flushed. 'Mortal bad, me lord. I…I haven't been up today on account of Agnes bein' took ill. I been tryin' to help her as well an' now she've took to her bed.' He misinterpreted the look of consternation on his lordship's face and hastened to set his mind at rest. 'Dinner's all ready, me lord,' he said soothingly. 'An' we got Farmer Bates's second girl to come in to help during the day, bein' as how you said this mornin' extra help could be hired.'

'Damn and blast my dinner!' exploded Marcus. 'Conduct me to Miss Fellowes's chamber at once!'

Five minutes later he stood staring down at the feverish occupant of a very large and old-fashioned tester bed, festooned with moth-eaten velvet hangings. Her face was ashen grey in its pallor and sheened with sweat in the flickering light cast by a branch of tallow candles. Thin hands shifted restlessly on the counterpane and her breath rasped harshly. Every few moments the slight frame was racked by paroxysms of coughing.

'Hell!' said Marcus in shock. 'Barlow, get down to the stables on the double. Tell Burnet to harness my bays to the curricle. You are to go with him to fetch the doctor. I don't want him getting lost. Stop! Where will I find firewood?'

The room was pervaded with a chilly damp that seeped into the bones. No wonder she was so ill, thought Marcus. She should have had the doctor days ago. It might have started out as a touch of influenza, but he was willing to bet it was a fully fledged inflammation of the lungs now!

Barlow said, 'I'll send young Judd up with firewood, me lord.'

He was gone, leaving Marcus staring down at Miss Fellowes. He could have kicked himself for not checking on her two days ago. To his admittedly inexperienced eye, she was seriously ill and he felt appallingly responsible. And there was another thing apart from her health to bother him about her.

Miss Fellowes, far from being elderly, was not even middle-aged. He would be very much surprised if she could boast more than twenty summers to her credit. And it was entirely possible, he thought in sinking fear, that she might not live long enough to see this one.

By the time the doctor arrived, Marcus had done a fair bit to make Miss Fellowes more comfortable. A crackling fire was rapidly dispelling the chill of the room. He had bathed her brow and wrists repeatedly with cool water. He had even lifted her slight frame from the pillows when she roused and held a cup of water to her lips, compelling her to swallow some.

She had choked and protested, opening her eyes briefly to gaze at him in mild confusion. Then she had apparently decided he was harmless and said, 'Thank you,' in a faint whisper, before closing her eyes again. Marcus took some encouragement from this. A concern with her manners argued that perhaps she was not quite as ill as he had thought.

Doctor Ellerbeck, a bluff-looking man of about fifty, took one look at Miss Fellowes and said, 'My God! Why the devil didn't you call me sooner?'

Feeling absurdly guilty, Marcus explained. Ellerbeck listened and then turned to examine his patient.

Which presented Marcus with another problem. He definitely ought not to be in the room while the doctor examined Miss Fellowes. It was most improper. On the other hand, it would be even more improper to leave her alone with the doctor. He swore and turned his back. In the absence of Mrs Barlow, that would have to do.

At last Ellerbeck stepped back from the bed and asked, 'Where is Agnes?' And swore when he was told. 'This child needs someone with her constantly. I may be able to find someone tomorrow; but who is to sit with her tonight? I have a woman in labour to attend.'

'I'll sit with her,' said Marcus, feeling that his life had just spun totally out of his control.

Ellerbeck frowned slightly. 'It will be no sinecure, my lord. She'll need the medicine I'll leave with you and a saline draft. That fever is likely to rise before morning and she'll be very difficult to handle.'

Marcus shrugged and said resignedly, 'There's no one else, Doctor. And it's partially my fault. I should have checked on her two days ago. You can't blame the Barlows. They weren't to know I wouldn't behave like my uncle.' He felt sick to his stomach at the thought of the girl lying there, too proud to call the doctor because she couldn't pay him, and too scared to let anyone know how ill she was. To be that alone in the world, to have no one to care for you! An icy band contracted around his heart at the thought. He looked down at Miss Fellowes's ashen face. At least for the next few days she had someone to take care of her.

Ellerbeck regarded him intently and then said slowly, 'I do not mean to offend you, my lord, but it is the sort of thing that will be frowned upon, and while I do not listen to gossip—'

Marcus cut him short, saying ruefully, 'My reputation is disgraceful. You will have to take my word for it, Ellerbeck, that even were I in the habit of seducing the innocent, a girl as sick as this…'

'I was not concerned for Miss Fellowes's safety at your hands, my lord!' said Ellerbeck caustically. 'Rather I was concerned at what the reaction of the local gabsters may be.'

'And do you think I care more for their tattle than for my own opinion if I leave her unattended?' asked Marcus quietly. 'As I said, there is no one else. Frankly, I should not even have been in the house with her; but I was under the mistaken impression that she was an elderly woman. And now, if I put up in the village to save her reputation, she may well lose her life.'

A brief silence ensued as Ellerbeck considered his options. At last he said, 'Very well,' and proceeded to give Marcus his instructions. These were issued with all the authority of a general who expected to be obeyed in every particular. Marcus, who had received orders directly from Wellington himself, was impressed as well as amused. He listened closely, asking questions occasionally.

Finally Ellerbeck was finished. 'I'll send my man back with the medicine and a saline draught. Give her plenty of fluids. It will help to keep the fever down. Oh, try to keep her propped up against the pillows. It will be easier on her breathing.'

'I sponged her face and wrists...' Marcus's tone was questioning. He was starting to feel extremely nervous. The girl looked so ill and she was muttering to herself and moving restlessly.

Ellerbeck followed his gaze and frowned slightly. 'Just the thing,' he said. 'I'll come back in the morning. You can send for me sooner if necessary. My man will know where I am.' He sat down on the bed and took one of those restless hands. 'Miss Meg...Meg. Open your eyes.' His voice was gentle but commanding.

To Marcus's immense surprise the heavy lids fluttered open. Eyes of a deep blue-grey focused confusedly on the doctor, who said kindly, 'Good girl. Miss Meg, you are very ill with this wretched influenza. You need not worry, this gentleman is a friend of mine. His name is...' He looked questioningly up at Marcus.

'Marcus...Marc,' he responded automatically, and then wondered what had possessed him to use the name only his family and closest friends knew him by.

'Marcus. He is going to look after you. I have to look in on Agnes and then help Mrs Watkins with her baby tonight. I have told Marcus just what to do for you. He will give you your medicine and anything else you need. You may trust him as you would myself.' Ellerbeck gave the hand a reassuring pat.

Gradually some of the confusion cleared in the hazy regard and it shifted slightly to include Marcus. A faint smile touched the pallid lips and a weak voice said, 'You were here…before. Gave me a drink…a flannel.'

Surprised that she remembered, Marcus smiled down at her and nodded. She smiled back and shut her eyes wearily. As sick as she was, the smile held a great deal of sweetness.

Ellerbeck stood up to leave and said quietly to Marcus, 'No need for her to know who you are yet. Only worry her.' Shrewdly he looked at Marcus and said, 'Don't you worry too much, either. She'll do well enough now we've caught it. Believe me, little Miss Meg has the constitution of a horse.' Seeing the doubt in the taut face and frowning grey eyes, he said, 'I mean it, my lord. She's a very sick lassie but I'll warrant she'll be up in a few days.'

Left alone with his charge, Marcus wondered what to do. Miss Meg…no, dammit! Meg! If he were going to be her nurse, then there was little point in adhering to the usual rules governing polite intercourse. He'd already broken most of them anyway and was about to break a fair few more.

Meg seemed inclined to sleep peacefully for the time being. Reflecting that this was likely to be of short duration, he pulled a large and battered leather armchair up to the bed and settled down to wait.

A soft knock at the door announced the return of Barlow. 'Brought some dinner up, my lord, and broth for Miss Meg. It ain't just what you'll be used to, but it's better than nowt. Would there be aught else?'

Marcus shook his head. 'Not at the moment, Barlow. But stay…how is your wife?'

Barlow smiled. 'Doctor says she's not too bad. Not

like Miss Meg. He told her to remain in bed for two or three days.'

'Good.' Genuine pleasure warmed his tones. 'Go and look after her, Barlow. I can manage Miss Meg.'

When Barlow had gone he turned his attention to the laden tray. It held a roast chicken, very cold, and dumplings along with fresh bread and a pat of butter. He grinned. There had been times during the war in Spain and Portugal when this would have been considered an extravagant meal for several famished officers in Wellington's army.

Also on the tray was a *veilleuse*, a combination night lamp and food warmer. He could remember his mother using one years ago when she had been ill. Barlow had already lit the oil lamp in the bottom section, its cheerful glow shone through the apertures in the porcelain. On top was the lidded bowl, doubtless containing Meg's broth.

What to do first? Meg was asleep and the heat from the lamp would keep the broth warm. After some thought he decided to let her sleep while he had something to eat. Accordingly he set the *veilleuse* on the nightstand, and addressed his own dinner. He was hungry after a long day in the saddle and made short work of the meal.

Now, he thought, Meg. He had noticed a small curved porcelain sickroom-syphon on the tray, its lower end pierced. Barlow, he realised, was an unexpected treasure. He'd thought of everything. No doubt it would be a great deal easier to let Meg use this, rather than trying to spoon broth into her—a procedure that he suspected might have been more than a trifle messy.

After putting the bowl of broth and syphon on the small bedside table, he followed the doctor's example and sat down beside her on the bed to pick up a small hand. Chafing it gently between his large ones, he spoke her name quietly.

'Meg…Meg, wake up.'

At first there was no response, but then a sigh was heard and the eyes opened. They were very cloudy and wandered around the room before settling on Marcus with a puzzled frown. Gradually recognition dawned and she smiled. 'Marc.'

'That's right. You remembered.' He felt absurdly pleased that she remembered his name and her smile for some unknown reason warmed him. No doubt it was relief to think that Ellerbeck was right, and she was not so ill as he had first thought.

'Oh, yes.' The expression hazed over slightly. 'I don't know anyone else so handsome…nice.' She closed her eyes, patently unaware of having said anything untoward.

Somewhat startled, Marcus tried again. 'Meg…it is time for you to have some dinner. Come.'

Again the eyes opened.

'That's the way,' said Marcus encouragingly. He slipped an arm around her and helped her to sit up. She was pitifully weak and leaned against him, shaking. He could feel her trembling, feel the heat of her fevered body clear through her nightgown as he held her against him. With his free hand he picked up the syphon and presented it to her.

A feeble yet outraged protest greeted this. 'I don't need that blasted thing!'

'Rubbish!' he responded succinctly, firmly suppressing a delighted smile at her intransigence. 'Do as you are bid.'

Rather to his surprise she obeyed without further ar-

gument and took it. He reached out for the bowl and
held it so that the pierced end of the syphon rested in
the broth.

'There you are, my dear, drink it up.' He was conscious of a swell of satisfaction as the level in the bowl
dropped. Half the broth was gone before she shook her
head. Marcus did not insist. She could have some more
later. Thanks to Barlow's forethought, the broth could
be kept warm for hours.

'A drink?'

She nodded against his shoulder. He brought the glass
to her lips and held it for her to take several swallows.
When she had finished, he held her steady while with
his free hand he rearranged the pillows. Carefully he sat
her back against them and drew the blankets up around
her.

Her eyes were shut again, but he did not think she
was asleep. Sure enough, a moment later her eyes
opened and she surveyed him with mild curiosity.

'Who are you?' Her voice was weak and cracked
slightly as though her throat were sore.

'Marc. I'm a friend.'

That seemed to puzzle her. 'Oh. I didn't know.
You're a very nice one. Sorry I was rude.' Then the
eyes fluttered shut again.

As the night wore on she became more confused and
restless. Marcus was kept extremely busy in his efforts
to help her be quiet and comfortable. Once when he
was building up the fire he heard a noise and turned
around to find her getting out of bed. Horrified, he
strode across and lifted her effortlessly in his arms to
put her back. She struggled at first, but submitted when
he spoke.

'Meg, sweetheart—' the endearment slipped out unconsciously '—you must stay in bed.'

'Am I sick?' She clung to him as he attempted to tuck her in. 'Oh, that's right. Ellerbeck was here!' Suddenly she panicked. 'I can't pay him! There's no money for me, Cousin Samuel says.'

It was like a blow over the heart to hear the fear in her voice. What would it be like to face destitution as this girl did? To face your entire life knowing that there was not a soul in the world to care what became of you and to have to go out into that world to earn your living. It must be a nightmare for anyone at the best of times, and must be so for her if it could even penetrate the feverish fog clouding her mind.

Still holding her in his arms, he tried gently to reassure her. 'Don't worry, Meg. The bills are all paid and there is plenty of money. You are quite safe with me. Go to sleep.' His hands automatically stroked the thick dark curls, which felt lank and lifeless to his touch.

Much to his surprise she seemed to accept this and settled down. He found though that when he left her she became upset and scared. Ironically he thought that, although he had spent countless nights with a woman clasped in his arms, this one would stand out in his memory as the most novel of his entire misspent career. Resignedly he climbed back on to the bed beside her and pulled her to him, nestling her into the curve of his arm to rest against his side. He firmly repressed the thought that she felt rather nice snuggled against him.

With a contented little sigh her head drooped on to his shoulder and she slept.

Oddly enough, Marcus found that he got a great deal more rest this way. When she stirred he could recall her wandering mind simply by speaking to her gently. She

district. Told you I'd try to get a woman, didn't I? Well, I did try, and not one of them was willing to come or even send a maid to help the girl!'

'What?' Marcus was aghast. 'Why not?'

Ellerbeck looked self-conscious. 'Er…they seemed to feel that your reputation…'

White hot fury seared through Marcus. His usually cold eyes were blazing with rage and his big frame was absolutely rigid. If this were the case, it made his plans for Meg's future very dangerous. If he settled money on her, then it would be whispered that she had been his mistress. She would be a social pariah. In his estimation she had suffered enough through Samuel Langley's irresponsibility without another member of the family completing the job. He would have to think of something else.

All he said was, 'Charming that they would then leave a sick girl to my care.'

It was not the first time he had been confronted with the hypocrisy of society in general and women in particular. He did not doubt that if he appeared socially and showed the slightest interest in any of the eligible females, that he would be courted and toadied to glory. None of them would have cared a rap for his reputation did they but think his fortune and title were going to embellish one of their daughters.

They would not care if he had ruined Meg Fellowes in fact or merely compromised her technically. Meg's reputation would be mud while he was still a matrimonial prize.

He was still seething on and off and wondering exactly what he should do about it when Agnes Barlow appeared the following morning to remove him from

his position as nurse. Although she looked far from
well, she ejected him from the room unceremoniously,
muttering that things were come to a pretty pass if a
young lady was expected to have a gentleman to nurse
her.

'Not but what the doctor was sayin' you was very
good to Miss Meg an' she ought to be grateful you was
here! But what I say is, the less she knows about it the
better. Now get along with you, lad…me lord…an'
have your breakfast. Farmer Bates's girl Nellie ain't
much, but she can cook ham an' eggs!'

From which Marcus gathered that, despite her disapproval of the necessity that had put him in charge of
the sickroom, Mrs Barlow was far from disapproving
of him personally. He definitely hoped the Barlows
were going to agree to stay on under his management.
Naturally if they wanted to be pensioned off, he would
do so, but he rather thought that it would be preferable
to have two such loyal and intelligent servants remain
here.

Chapter Three

Miss Marguerite Fellowes was very puzzled when she awoke later that morning. Not only was the room warm, but she felt very much better. She felt so much better that she was ready to be curious about the tall and handsome stranger who had been in attendance while she was so sick. A very elegant stranger at that. And so kind.

Except for the Barlows and, of course, the Vicar and Dr Ellerbeck, Miss Fellowes couldn't think of anyone who was kind to her. And that reminded her…had someone called Dr Ellerbeck? She hoped it was just a dream that he had been to see her, because she couldn't imagine how she was going to pay him. Frowning, she tried to remember properly. She was sure he had been… yes…she recalled him introducing Marc to her, saying he was a friend.

Expectantly she looked around for Marc. And found Agnes sitting in the armchair, turning the heel of a sock. Conscious of a feeling of crushing disappointment, Meg realised that Marc must have just been a dream, a fever-induced vision compounded of her deepest romantic fancies. And she had certainly had some peculiar fancies while she was ill. But to think a gentleman had nursed her! She might have known it was a dream. As if any gentleman, let alone one as handsome as that, would ever be so kind to Meg Fellowes. No, only an imaginary man could possibly have held her so safely and soothed her so tenderly.

He had fed her too, she suddenly remembered. Out of that revolting syphon of Cousin Samuel's. And hadn't he helped her when she had to...surely she would not have imagined those sort of things! Not being able to pay the doctor's bill would be a small embarrassment compared to this.

'Hullo, Agnes.' She smiled as Mrs Barlow looked up. 'Have you been there long?'

Caught off-guard, Mrs Barlow replied, 'An hour or so, dearie. How do you feel? Doctor said as how you'd pull up quick once you turned the corner.'

Meg thought that she still felt fairly gruesome, weak and achey. But at least her wits were her own again. And her head didn't feel as though a blacksmith had set up business in it. Nor was her throat still sore. That was something. No doubt she could get up later and do her packing. It would not do to keep Mrs Garsby waiting too long for her nursery governess or she might decide to offer someone else the position.

Then her gaze lit on that beastly syphon, lying beside the bottom half of the *veilleuse* on the nightstand. Her eyes widened. Oh, dear! Maybe she hadn't been dreaming after all! But who...?

Nervously she cleared her throat and asked, 'Agnes, who looked after me while I was sick? Was it you?'

Agnes Barlow shook her head reluctantly and Meg realised from her demeanour that something odd was going on. A deep and mortified blush swept over the pale face and throat.

'Agnes! Who was it?' Meg's voice came out as a startled squeak.

'His lordship,' said Agnes. 'I'm that sorry, Miss Meg, but I was sick too. Not like you was, but I wouldn't have been much good to you. Barlow looked after me and I'll tell you one thing.' She lowered her voice. 'It may not have been what you call proper, but Barlow told me his lordship was that careful with you. And he insisted on paying for the doctor to come out. Cross as anything he was that we hadn't told him sooner.'

'His lordship?' echoed Meg. 'I don't know any lord-ships!' Let alone one she called Marc and who claimed to be a friend.

Agnes elaborated. 'Lord Rutherford, dearie. Turned up t'other night. Right put about he was when Barlow told him about you...'

Meg stared in horror. She had fully intended to be out of the house before Cousin Samuel's horrid heir arrived! And she would have been if the Barlows hadn't practically forced her into bed and told her to stay there. She had heard *all* about the Earl of Rutherford and he hadn't sounded at all the sort of person she wanted to know...or, for that matter, the sort of person to nurse a stranger through an attack of influenza. Especially a girl with her history.

All she could find to say was, 'Did someone send over to Mrs Garsby? She...she was expecting me.'

Agnes pursed her lips in evident disapproval. She had voiced her opinion of Miss Meg's proposed employment at Burvale House often enough for Meg to have it by heart. Despite all the gossip and nastiness of some people who called themselves ladies, Miss Meg was a young lady and ought not to be cast out on the world like an unwanted kitten, and so on, and so on.

She opened her mouth, clearly intending to say it all again, but Meg said, 'Oh, Agnes, please don't! I have to live after all. What else can I do? I can't remain here any longer. Was a message sent?' There was real fear in her voice.

Agnes nodded with obvious disapproval. 'Aye. Barlow sent a message, sayin' you was took sick.'

Relief flooded through Meg. It would never do to lose her situation before she had even started. She was determined never to ask for charity or assistance again in her life. She would starve rather than ever be someone's poor relation again. She reflected that, after Cousin Samuel's pointed lessons in economy, she would be able to save a great deal for her old age out of the twenty pounds per annum that her prospective employer had offered.

To Meg, who had never had any money of her own, it seemed a fortune, but she was wise enough to realise that her wages must be husbanded carefully against times when she might be without a job and particularly against the time when she was too old to work.

A knock at the door presaged the entrance of Nellie Bates with a tray.

'Nellie! What are you doing here?'

'Temp'rary 'elp, Miss Meg,' said Nellie proudly. 'To 'elp Mrs Barlow. Just days, mind. Me mam won't let me stay o' nights. On account of 'is lordship's reputation. Real wicked, they say 'e is!'

A snort from Mrs Barlow as Nellie left the room suggested that her help was not entirely appreciated. She softened it by saying, 'She means well, I'll say that for her. Not but what some folks 'ud do a sight better to worry 'bout their own beams afore they goes looking for motes in other folks' eyes.'

Meg thought things were definitely taking a turn for the better. If Marc…Lord Rutherford was hiring help, then perhaps he was not such a shocking lickpenny as Cousin Samuel, who had given new layers of meaning to the term, 'of a saving disposition'. That would mean better times for everyone on the estate.

Agnes bustled over with the tray, placing it on her lap. It held a plate of bread and butter and the bowl from the top of the *veilleuse*. Suspiciously Meg raised the lid. Ugh! More broth! Well, at least this time she had been provided with a spoon rather than that horrid syphon. She could not recall how many times she had carried the thing to Cousin Samuel after he had bought it. He had agonised over the purchase price and consequently had been determined to get his money's worth out of it, so he had used it every time he had so much as a head cold.

Meg remembered the time she had suggested that, at four pence, he could afford to keep it for special occasions. The old man had practically had a seizure, moaning that she was a wanton, extravagant hussy, just like her mother, and would bring him to ruin with her spendthrift ways!

And now she had used it! She had a very clear memory of Marc…his lordship, giving it to her…she was very much afraid that she had sworn at him. Blushing once more as she spooned up the broth, Meg realised that she would have to see his lordship again, if only to thank him for his care of her and to apologise for trespassing on his hospitality. She hoped he would not think she was angling for a handout.

* * *

In the event, Meg did not see his lordship for several days. Her voiced intent of getting up to pack and remove herself to Burvale House to take up her duties there, was dealt with summarily, if vicariously, by Marcus. Having been informed by Mrs Barlow of the patient's plan, he had charged her with the message that if Miss Fellowes was such a pea goose, he would personally strip her, put her back to bed and tie her to it if necessary, until the doctor gave her permission to get up.

While deprecating the blunt nature of Lord Ruthford's graphic threat, Mrs Barlow relayed it faithfully and was bound to acknowledge that it had its effect. Nothing more was heard from Miss Fellowes about getting up for another five days, by which time the doctor was perfectly satisfied with her progress.

Inwardly fuming over his lordship's high-handed attitude, Meg had to admit that she didn't really want to get up all that much. Certainly not enough to risk calling his lordship's bluff. If indeed he was bluffing, which she thought extremely doubtful. So she remained in bed, happily reading, for five days.

Having been informed by Ellerbeck that in his opinion the patient was recovered enough to leave her bed, Marcus sat waiting at the desk in the library to inform Miss Fellowes of her future. He had it all sorted out. She was most definitely not going to take up that position at Burvale House. It would be quite ineligible for a young lady, which she undoubtedly was.

First off, she could go to stay with Diana. He would send her to London post. That would get her out of this neighbourhood, where there might be some spiteful whispers about her sojourn under his roof. After a decent interval he would settle some of Samuel Langley's money on her, which was what the scaly old nipcheese ought to have done in the first place. He would tell her that Samuel had desired him to do so when the extent of his obligations and debts should be known. No need for her to think she was being handed charity. He would write to Diana tonight and send a note over to Mrs Garsby in a day or so, informing her that she would need to find another nursery governess.

He smiled to himself in anticipation. He simply couldn't wait to see her face. She would be disbelieving at first, would probably demur. Then she would be excited, happy. Her face would be flushed with pleasure, anticipation.

A tap at the door informed him that Miss Fellowes had arrived to be told of the change in her fortunes.

'Come in.'

Meg heard the deep rumble and trembled slightly. His voice was just as she remembered it, dark and velvety…it was the sort of voice that made you want to stroke it…like a big cat. Nervously she opened the door and went in, wondering if her eyes had remembered as well as her ears.

They hadn't. She really must have been quite out of her wits with that influenza. Marc—faced with him she had trouble reminding herself to think of him as Lord Rutherford—sat there at Cousin Samuel's old desk, looking even more lethally handsome than she recalled. His frame looked impossibly large and powerful, the shoulders too broad to be contained in any coat made for a normal human being. His hair was, as she remembered, a rich tawny brown. The eyes puzzled her. She had thought them warm and kind. Now they were cold and impassive, the sort of eyes that held their own counsel and gave nothing away.

Perhaps if she concentrated on those chilly eyes she might be able to remember that this was Lord Rutherford—that Marc was a dream.

Marcus was delighted to see that Miss Fellowes—he must remember to call her that—looked so much better. She was still far too pale, in stark contrast to the shadows under her eyes, but she looked as though she had put on a little weight in the last few days since he had seen her. There was actually some colour in her lips, which were, he noticed, quite beautifully cut, soft and full. Just the sort of mouth, he caught himself thinking, which begged to be kissed. Frowning, he reminded himself that kissing was not on his agenda for Meg... dammit! Miss Fellowes!

Seeing the frown, Meg quailed inwardly and flushed; no doubt he thought her dress shabby, not at all the thing to wear for meeting an earl. Well, it was the best she had and if he didn't like it then that was too bad. She didn't like it either, being tolerably certain that dull black was not calculated to make her look her best. And it must look so dowdy to one used to women in the highest kick of fashion. She knew the crossover bodice was years out of date. So she held her head high, determined not to be flustered. From all Agnes had said, he did not have the slightest idea who she was. Fellowes, after all, was a common enough name.

'Good morning Miss Fellowes,' said Marcus politely. 'I trust you are recovered.' He noted the slight flush. Better not to say she looks much improved. No need to rub her face in the fact that I nursed her.

But Meg was made of sterner stuff. 'I am very much better, my lord. For which I am given to understand I must thank you.' Not for worlds would she have admitted that she could remember in detail all that he had done for her, including holding her in his arms for the whole of one night.

Very embarrassed, he waved her thanks aside. 'It was nothing, Miss Fellowes. A trifling service. I could wish Barlow had informed me earlier of the severity of your illness. You might then have been spared my very inexpert assistance.' He thought he had never heard himself sound like such a pompous jackass, so cold and uncaring. Yet this was the face he always presented to the world.

Meg thought he sounded bored, as though she had been a complete and utter nuisance. Which, she admitted, she probably had. Still…perhaps she ought to hold on to her memory of Marc…so kind and tender…yes, that would be a better memory to cherish in the lonely years ahead. Even if it had been a dream, it was better than the icy reality before her.

Marcus cleared his throat. What on earth had brought that odd smile to her face? It was perhaps the loveliest smile he had ever seen, shy and considering, as though she smiled at something inexpressibly dear and private.

With a mental snort for this whimsical flight, he said, 'I am informed that you had the intention of taking up a post as a nursery governess in this neighbourhood.'

Acutely Meg picked up his use of the past tense and replied firmly, 'Yes, my lord, the Vicar arranged it for me. That *is* my intention.'

Just as acute, Marcus heard the slight stress on the tense. Flatly he said, 'It will not do. You are unsuited for such a position and I will not countenance it.' As soon as the words had left his mouth he wondered if he had made a serious tactical error.

Meg's eyes widened and she could practically feel her hackles rise. Having just buried one loathsome guardian, she was not about to submit to another. Especially not one who had not the slightest right to wield authority over her. She opened her mouth to administer a blistering snub and reconsidered. Had he, after all, found out who she was? Was that why he considered her unfit to have charge of children? Better to find out what he meant without losing her temper. If she riled him, he could make it impossible for her to find employment.

'What then, my lord, do you recommend for me?' Her voice was sweet and reasonable, her eyes modestly downcast. Meg had learned long ago that it was generally best to find out the lie of the land without giving the least hint of her own thoughts, leave alone her feelings.

It took Marcus in completely. Phew! He had thought she was about to rip up at him. Doubtless she was just surprised. Relieved, he outlined his plans for her, dwelling on the pleasure it would give his sister to entertain her indefinitely, pointing out that, with a respectable sum settled on her, she might even make a creditable marriage.

She listened, unbearably tempted. To visit London, be able to buy a pretty dress, perhaps marry and have her own babies rather than easing her longing in caring for another woman's children. But it was not possible. Despite his lordship's kindly untruth—yes, he was kind after all under the icy exterior: in telling her Cousin Samuel had asked him to settle money on her, he had tried to spare her pride—she knew it for a lie.

And she seriously doubted that his lordship's sister would wish to have a stranger foisted on to her.

Certainly not one with no pretensions to fashion, wealth or even beauty. Certainly not once she knew just who Miss Marguerite Fellowes was. Obviously his lordship could not possibly know or he would never have suggested such a thing. And once he knew then she would be out on her ear. Even her own family had kicked her out. No, Miss Fellowes preferred to remove herself voluntarily.

For a moment the thought occurred to her that she could take the money and run before he found out the truth, but she instantly dismissed that as dishonourable. She could not take advantage of his kindness and ignorance so shamefully.

Resolutely she stifled her longings and said very calmly, 'No.' Then, as an afterthought, 'No, thank you.'

Had she protested angrily Marcus would have believed she was merely making a token resistance, trying to make him think she couldn't possibly accept such generosity, when all the time she intended to capitulate at the right moment. The quiet, unemotional voice in which she had uttered her carefully polite refusal told him at once that she was deadly serious.

Throttling the urge to issue a series of autocratic decrees and carry her position by storm, Marcus asked equally quietly, 'Will you tell me why not?'

Meg thought about that, frowning slightly. It was none of his business, after all, what she chose to do with her life and the habit of keeping her own counsel was strong. But perhaps, having made such a kind offer, he deserved better than to have it flung back in his face without any explanation. She owed him part of the truth.

Drawing a deep breath, she said, 'To start with, I cannot possibly accept money from you. People would think—'

'Rubbish!' said Marcus. 'I told you—'

He was interrupted in his turn. 'My lord, Samuel Langley didn't give a damn for me! He made no pretence of that, to me or to anyone else. He died intestate because he was too miserly to pay a lawyer to draw up his will and the only reason he permitted Cousin Euphemia to take me in was because he saw in me a potential housekeeper he wouldn't have to pay!' She hadn't meant to say that, but once she had started it seemed some of the anger she had kept leashed for years had come spilling out. Gritting her teeth, she forced herself to take a deep breath, reaching for self-control. He must not know the truth…Marc she might have been able to tell…but not this cold, dictatorial earl.

Seeing that she had silenced his lordship's charitable lies, she went on more temperately. 'So you see, I cannot take your money. And I most certainly will not impose upon your sister. I have not the least claim on her and, to be frank, sir, I do not wish to continue as a poor relation, dependent on another's charity. I thank you for your kindness, but I will do as I had planned.'

Silence hung between them for a moment. Marcus could definitely see her point. Obviously her position had chafed her, but he failed to see how it could possibly be better as a governess. Indeed it might, depending upon her mistress, be even worse. He knew of many fashionable women who treated their children's preceptresses with undisguised scorn and the contempt of the strong for the weak, using them as underpaid drudges, blaming them for every piece of misbehaviour and overturning any attempt made to discipline their high spirited darlings.

He couldn't permit it. It was unthinkable. Something icy seemed to contract around his heart at the idea of

Meg at the mercy of one of those women. He didn't say what was going through his mind. His emotions were far too confusing. Which was in itself confusing. Lord Rutherford always kept his emotions under strict control!

So he fell back on issuing commands, using storm tactics. 'Very well. You have made your point. Now that is said, I will send a message over to Mrs Garsby in the morning informing her of my decision. We will remain here for another week to allow you to recuperate, then I will take you to my sister. That is all. There is no more to be said on the subject.' The firm lips clipped together and his eyes were as cold and impersonal as his voice had been

'Oh. Very well, then.' Again her eyes were downcast, her voice unassuming.

He eyed her narrowly, suddenly suspicious of her meek demeanour. All at once her submissiveness seemed out of character. And he couldn't put his finger on why.

'You have nothing more to say, Meg?'

Her Christian name slipped out unconsciously. He clenched his fist slightly. The name brought back all the intimacy of her illness. His body tingled at the memory of how she had snuggled up to him so trustingly. At the time he had not felt any physical interest. But now he was burningly aware of it. His estimation that she would be attractive when restored to health had not been wrong. Even now, when she was still out of sorts, her slender, lissom grace could not be obliviated by the shapeless excuse for a dress which hung on her.

'No, my lord. Good morning.' She dropped him a small curtsy and left the room.

She went back to her room with her head held high.

So his lordship thought that she would dance to his bidding, did he? Well, if he thought that yet another Langley was going to ride over Marguerite Fellowes roughshod, then he had another think coming. There might be nothing more to be said on the matter, but there was certainly something to be done!

Heavy grey clouds were pressing in ominously from the west at four-thirty as Meg jumped down from the gig at the front door of Burvale House and held her hand up to young Tom Judd who had driven her over.

'Thank you Tom. Goodbye. And please ask Barlow to give this to his lordship.' She handed him a sealed letter with a hand that trembled slightly. His lordship was going to be furious, but she couldn't help that. She couldn't accept his offer and he had to know why, but she couldn't bear to see him turn away and withdraw his offer, or worse, swallow his disgust and renew it.

Tom touched his cap and said cheerfully. 'Aye, Miss Meg. Good luck to ye.' He turned the cob and shook up the reins. 'Walk on there!'

Meg watched the gig bowl away down the avenue. It seemed to go very quickly, leaving her cut off from the past to face the future alone. She lifted her chin in an oddly gallant gesture and clutched her scarlet woollen cloak more closely around her. Nothing had changed really, she had always been alone. It was just that now that fact seemed harder to face, doubtless because for one blinding moment she had thought that it might be different.

Blinking to clear her eyes, she told herself angrily that the best thing to do now was to banish all thoughts of what could never be and concentrate on what must be. Especially she must banish all thoughts of her friend

'But I *was* ill!' she protested. 'You may ask Dr Ellerbeck!'

Mrs Garsby snorted her disbelief. 'Even so, to remain in the house once his lordship had arrived! No doubt you thought to entangle him, you presumptuous little slut! Take yourself off at once! No doubt his lordship can find a more suitable position for you. One in keeping with the colour of your cloak. I should be failing in my duty as a Mother were I to permit your contaminating influence anywhere near my family!'

Ten years ago Meg had heard similar words. Then she had not known what they meant, only the tones had struck home into the heart of a confused, grieving little girl. Then she had turned away in mortified hurt, but now she was no longer that defenceless, ignorant child. Now she understood what was being said to her, and the injustice of it enraged her. Despite years of hiding her feelings under a meek façade, Meg's temper began to rise and Mrs Garsby's next words were all that was needed to fan it into fiery utterance.

'My sister said I would regret my generous impulse to accede to the Vicar's suggestion that you would suit. What is bred in the bone will come out in the flesh!'

'Will it, Mrs Garsby? Will it indeed?' Meg's voice was low and bitter. 'Then I thank God that I am not to have the charge of your children!' Her voice rose in passionate fury. 'For I have not the slightest doubt that they would be just as unchristian and mean-spirited as their mother! I hope that you are proud of casting the first stone. Good day, Mrs Garsby!'

With that she picked up her portmanteau and walked proudly to the front door. Opening it, she stepped out into the now-blinding rain and slammed the door as hard as she possibly could. Behind her she could hear the crash echoing through the hall with a most satisfying resonance.

The crash was promptly followed by another as a peal of thunder rolled overhead. Meg raised her dripping face and realised that there was not the slightest prospect of the rain clearing. She might as well start walking.

Buoyed up by her fury and satisfaction at having finally told at least one of the local matrons exactly what she thought of her, Meg did not at first realise just what was before her. By the time she had traversed the avenue and had reached the road again, reality had broken around her ears with greater force than the thunder and bucketing rain. Grimly she faced her situation. She would have to go and see the Vicar. Perhaps he could help. Even if it was only entry into the nearest Magdalen. Miserably she thought that indeed that might be her best course. At least they would provide her with some training and she would be placed with charitable people who would not throw her past up in her face too much.

She would go straight to the Vicarage…no, it was fifteen miles. Fenby Hall was only ten. Even if she got a lift part of the way, she couldn't possibly go to the Vicarage tonight. She would go home and slip into the house for the night. No one need know that she was there. She could go to the Vicar tomorrow.

Plodding on down the increasingly muddy road between the dry stone walls, she gradually became aware that she was crying, her tears mingling with the rain on her cheeks. Never in a life of loneliness had she ever felt quite so abandoned. At least this morning she had had the prospect of employment in a respectable household. Now she was literally out on her own.

Briefly she considered going to Lord Rutherford, only to reject the idea. No, she had refused his offer of assistance. She could not now go back and beg. Besides, in the past ten years she had not confided in anyone. She wouldn't even know where to start. A sensible little voice suggested that she was being rather silly. After all, she liked Marc…he was kind…gentle…he would look after her… Perhaps he wouldn't care about her history…her parents…?

She thrust the thought away. How could he not care? Besides, Marc was really Lord Rutherford. He did not exist beyond her feverish imaginings. She plodded on, pretending that the salt mingling with the rain was seawater. She had never seen the sea…but she had heard it was salty.

A yell from behind her broke in on her gloomy reflections. She swung around hopefully and saw a farm cart with a familiar field hand driving it. At least she wouldn't have to walk the whole way home.

Marcus came in late from his day's business, his heavy frieze cloak dripping. It had kept out the rain, but he was definitely chilly. He went to the parlour and rang the bell for Barlow, thinking that he would have a bath and then see Meg. Try and talk some sense into her. He'd been too abrupt with her earlier, too dictatorial.

A fire had been lit and he stood in front of it, warming his hands. Meg's determination to make her own way impressed him as much as it surprised him. Not many girls in her situation, he thought, would have refused what he had offered. Cousin Samuel must have really rubbed in her status. Parsimonious old curmudgeon!

Barlow appeared and started talking immediately. 'Thank God you're back, me lord! It's Miss Meg!'

A chill stole through Marcus's heart. What the hell was wrong with Meg? Was she ill again?

'She's gone.'

'Gone!' Marcus exploded. 'What the devil do you mean? Where has she gone?' Then he realised. He'd thought she was just a bit too meek this morning. Obviously she had decided to act before he could inform her employer of any change in her plans. She had thought thereby to forestall him, putting herself beyond his reach. Well, she would learn her mistake! And then, stealing through his anger, came a surge of admiration for the little vixen. She'd hoaxed him completely with her agreement that there was nothing more to be said on the matter of her future. Little devil, he thought ruefully.

Barlow watched him in some trepidation. 'Aye. Gone to Mrs Garsby. Agnes and I knew nowt. She slipped out and got young Judd to drive her over in the gig. I'm that sorry, me lord! She sent this back for you.' He held out the letter.

Marcus took it. 'Thank you, Barlow. Is the water ready for my bath?'

'Aye, me lord. Shall I draw it?'

Marcus had already opened the letter and simply nodded, beginning to read as Barlow withdrew.

Dear Lord Rutherford,
I hope when you read this letter you will understand why I did not feel capable of fully explaining myself this morning and the reason why I must decline your generous offer of assistance. When I tell you that I am the daughter of Sir Robert

Fellowes and his wife Lady Caroline, I think you must realise why. You are old enough to recall the scandal of my parents' deaths. My mother was a connection of Cousin Samuel's wife, which was why he took me in afterwards. My father, in the light of my mother's behaviour, had completely disinherited me in favour of my cousin Delian. I believe, had he lived long enough, he would have disavowed me. My cousin Delian and his wife refused to house me in case I should pollute their children.

I should have told you this, but I was too cowardly to do so. Thank you again for your care of me while I was ill. I shall never forget it.

Sincerely, Marguerite Fellowes

Marcus stared at the letter, his emotions in turmoil. Robert and Caroline Fellowes's daughter! Good God! No wonder none of the good ladies would have anything to do with the chit! He remembered the scandal quite well. Sir Robert's suicide after catching his wife and a lover *in flagrante delicto* and murdering the pair of them had been the talk of the town for months ten years ago. He had never heard there had been a child, though. Certainly Sir Delian and Lady Fellowes had never mentioned it. And she had been here with Samuel the whole time.

He shook his head, dazed. What to do now? He considered his options. He would have to go after Meg, of course; but should he leave it until morning or go at once? Little fool! Why the hell hadn't she told him? Surely she hadn't thought he would turn his back on her! He grimaced. Perhaps she had. He'd purposely been cold with her as he was with most people. And no doubt plenty of people did shun her. Indeed, her own cousin had refused to assist the orphaned child. This must be the reason that no one had come to help her.

Blast old Samuel! If he had done the right thing by the girl, then her story need not have been such a liability. As it was, it had been allowed to take hold in the popular imagination until it had assumed ridiculous proportions.

He read the letter again. Too cowardly? He shook his head. That was the last thing Marguerite…no… Meg…Fellowes had to reproach herself with. Too proud was more like it. Too proud to accept his offer made in ignorance of the truth and too proud to tell him and perhaps have to see him turn away in disgust, or worse, pity her. And the letter itself! A more unemotional, *uninvolved*, explanation of a tragic situation, he never wished to see. The most personal part of the letter was her brief acknowledgment of his care of her!

He thrust away the thought that this was his own usual way of dealing with the world. That he had, in fact, tried to deal with Meg in that way—with disastrous results.

Now what to do? Go after Meg in the morning or have his bath and go tonight? He thought hard. He hated the idea of leaving her until morning, but the weather would make going at once impossible. Besides, she was probably exhausted and would be the better for a night's sleep. If he fetched her tonight, she would not be in bed before midnight. No, he'd go and fetch her in the morning.

Well, now that all that was taken care of, he could go up to his room and enjoy a nice luxurious soak. After dinner he would write to Di, warning her to expect an indefinite houseguest. Surely between the pair of them they could launch Meg and get her safely established. What the girl needed was a husband. Someone who didn't give a damn what people thought. Someone who would treat her kindly and make sure others did so. Someone she could trust.

As he went up the stairs, Marcus vowed that he would take a close look at anyone who wanted to marry Meg. He was damned if he'd have her used as a drudge again! He was running over possible *partis* in his mind, and dismissing them all out of hand, when his attention was caught by a sudden rustle.

He stopped just at the head of the stairs and looked around but could see no one. Yet he was sure someone was there. All his senses were on the alert, screaming that he was being watched. Had someone slipped into a room? He didn't think so. All the doors squeaked and creaked atrociously. The curtains over the window at the far end of the hall caught his eye. There was an embrasure behind them, deep enough to hold someone.

Determinedly he walked towards it.

Terrified, Meg stood as still as possible, watching through a small rent in the curtain as that tall, leonine figure stalked towards her hiding place. He mustn't find her now! He had her letter in his hand! He would think it was all a take in! That she was trying to engage his sympathy! Worse, he might think, given her parentage, that she would welcome another sort of offer. The sort to which Mrs Garsby had referred.

He was coming closer. His powerful frame loomed nearer. She couldn't think straight, she was so bitterly tired and cold and her cloak was so horribly heavy. All she could think was that Marc might hold her again, comfort her, perhaps let her cry on his shoulder. In her exhaustion, she could not imagine what else such broad shoulders could possibly be for. But no, it was Lord Rutherford, not Marc. He would be disgusted, would inquire coldly just what Miss Fellowes thought she was doing in his house.

She would not be found cowering like a frightened cur! She wouldn't! With her head held high, she stepped out from behind the curtains, clutching her sodden portmanteau, to meet his startled gaze.

'Meg!? What on earth are you doing here?' He strode forward and caught her in his arms. 'My God, you're soaking! You silly child! They told me you had gone, gave me your letter.' His keen eyes took in her exhaustion, her muddied cloak and the even muddier hem of her dress showing beneath it. 'You did go! Meg, what happened?'

It was Marc! Not Lord Rutherford. It was Marc who had found her. Marc, whose worried eyes held that look of tender concern. She could tell Marc what had happened. At least...no, she couldn't! Not all of it. If he found out what had been said, then he would feel obliged to offer for her—at least Marc would...she wasn't so sure about Lord Rutherford. Confusion fogged her mind.

'She had already...filled the position. She couldn't wait...' It was probably true; Meg consoled herself with the thought that it wasn't an outright lie. And he was holding her again, enfolding her against his big frame, warming her, his arms a barrier against the world and its bitter chill. She leaned against him, barely conscious.

'And you walked home? Ten miles!' Horror stabbed through him at the thought. Ten miles in the pouring rain! She had only got out of bed for the first time that morning. What sort of woman would kick a girl out like that? Mrs Garsby was going to be the recipient of a very nasty letter on the morrow. And if she ever showed her face in London, he would have very great pleasure in letting her know exactly what the Earl of Rutherford could do to anyone who crossed him!

In the meantime he yelled loudly for assistance. None was forthcoming. The Barlows were well out of earshot. Increasingly worried, he scanned Meg's face. Her teeth were chattering and there was a blue tinge about her mouth. Her slight frame sagged against him helplessly and her flesh felt stone cold through the soaking garments. Damn it! She shouldn't even be out of bed! She was still sick and if he didn't get her warmed up quickly, she was going to suffer a relapse! Swearing under his breath, he swung her up into his arms. Desperate straits called for desperate remedies.

Meg's brain began to function again as he lifted her. She must be soaking him. And it was Lord Rutherford, after all. His eyes had gone icy again. She must not call him *Marc* in that familiar way.

'Please, my lord, I must change.' She would feel better once she was dry. Warm would be nice too but she'd settle for dry. She did not think that she would ever be warm again. Unless, of course, Marc continued to carry her down the hall like this. That might warm her up… Carry her? What on earth was he doing? And this was his room! Why was he carrying her into it?

Suddenly frightened, she began to struggle. And discovered that Marc's powerful arms were more than sufficient to subdue her efforts to escape. They were like iron bands clamping her to his chest. She heard the door bang shut behind them and panicked. It must be Lord Rutherford after all! He had a dreadful reputation… Where was Marc?

'Take your clothes off.' She was standing on her own two feet again.

'N…no!'

'Meg…' Lord Rutherford was beginning to sound like Marc. Or was Marc sounding like Lord Rutherford? Whichever it was, he sounded exasperated. 'Meg…take your clothes off and get into that bath at once! Before you catch your death of cold!'

Stupidly she stared at him. She couldn't undress in front of him! She might be ruined in an academic sense, but she wasn't *that* dead to shame.

With a muttered curse Marcus caught her to him and began to undress her. Shocked, she tried to push him away, but she was feeling far too weak and confused. One large hand caught both her wrists and held them imprisoned behind her back while his free hand continued to make short work of the buttons of her high-necked spencer and then the ties of her gown.

Despite his efforts not to touch her as he stripped her, his fingers inevitably grazed across her soft skin, searing into her and circumventing her struggles more surely than his grip on her hands. Bemused, she stood helpless as his light, accidental caresses burnt into her trembling body. Indeed, she was no longer sure whether she was shaking with cold—or pleasure at the tantalising touch of his long fingers.

In no time the gown was off, landing on the floor with an audible splat, and she stood shivering in her chemise and petticoat. Marcus found to his horror that his body was showing definite signs of interest in the procedure. And in her undoubted response to his unintentional advances. She was staring up at him with a completely bemused expression, her delicate lips slightly parted, presenting him with an appalling temptation. In addition, the soaking undergarments revealed what he had suspected, and steadfastly managed to ignore, for two long nights. Namely, the manifold charms of Miss Marguerite Fellowes.

Stifling a groan and shackling his sudden desire, he shut his eyes momentarily to block out the sight. And then opened them again. Good God, the girl was literally soaked to the skin, her cotton chemise and petticoat clinging to her slim body; every curve, every nuance was laid bare to his heated gaze. He swallowed hard. Two creamy, rounded breasts, their peaks puckered with cold, thrust from under the thin material. A sinuous waist and the long lovely line of her thighs! God, she was beautiful! What would she be like to lie with? To taste? To love? He could imagine it…soft… yielding…utterly entrancing…

What the hell was he thinking of? He was supposed to be giving her a bath to warm her! Not thinking about taking her to bed! Although the way he was feeling, that would certainly warm her… Swearing audibly now, he picked her up again and strode towards the bath.

'Marc? What are you doing?' She was terrified, not least by the fact that she couldn't force her body to struggle any more. If Marc were about to ravish her, then she… Her fears were put abruptly to rest as he dumped her with an unceremonious splash in the hip bath.

'Oh! Ooooooh…' Her gasp of shock was transmuted to a sigh of pleasure as warmth began to steal back into her body. Beyond caring about the impropriety of her situation, she closed her eyes in utter bliss and leaned back against the bath. A moment later she felt water being tipped over her and opened her eyes. Marc was kneeling beside her, soaking up water in a sponge and squeezing it over her shoulders and breasts.

It felt simply marvellous. Not only was she actually getting warm, but Lord Rutherford seemed to have disappeared completely, leaving Marc in his place. She smiled at him, the horrors of her afternoon receding into the haze of steam rising from the water. Later on she would have to face the ghastly reality with Lord Rutherford, but just at the moment she had Marc to care for her and she might as well sit back and enjoy it. Blissfully she allowed her mind to drift away with the clouds of steam.

Marcus shut his eyes to block out the sight of that trusting, endearing smile. Not to mention the sight of her body with the soaking, transparent cotton clinging to every contour, except for her legs. The petticoat floated around them, revealing the long slender limbs in a teasing, shadowy way. Grimly he thought that if Mrs Garsby ever heard about this, then the only place for Meg would be the nearest Magdalen. Despite Meg's gallant lie, he had absolutely no doubts as to why she had been turned away.

He cleared his throat. 'Are you warmer now, Meg?'

'Oh, yes!' Her response came on a sigh of sheer sensual delight which seemed to ripple through her entire body. Marcus didn't like to think about the devastating effect such a sigh would have on his already beleaguered senses in other circumstances. His own body was already rebelling furiously against his brain which was keeping the reins tight. *For God's sake, she's little more than a child! She's still sick and she's in quite enough trouble without you getting her into more!*

Abruptly he stood up. He couldn't trust himself to dry her. Long strides took him to the bellpull. He would send for Mrs Barlow, as in fact he should have done ten minutes ago. He couldn't imagine what had come over him not to do so. He had just been conscious of an overwhelming tenderness and desire to look after her himself. It had not even occurred to him to summon other assistance. It had seemed perfectly natural and right to do it himself.

Now, as he stood shaking with his back to her, he realised his mistake. Lord! And he'd thought that youth and innocence held no allure for him. He couldn't have been more wrong. A knock at the door interrupted his churning thoughts. Barlow. He went to the door and opened it a fraction.

'You rang, me lord?' Barlow looked very puzzled to see that Marcus had not yet availed himself of the bath. 'Is something wrong?'

'Yes,' said Marcus baldly. He hesitated and then said, 'Miss Meg has returned. I've dumped her in my bath. Mrs Garsby refused to take her in and she walked home in that storm. Could you please ask your wife to come up and dry her and help her get into some dry clothes?'

Barlow's jaw dropped and his lined old face worked for a minute. All he could say was, 'That *bitch*!'

'Quite,' said Marcus in savage agreement. 'In fact that...' He added a number of colourful epithets to describe Mrs Garsby which left Barlow in no doubt that his lordship was quite as angry as he himself was.

'I'll fetch Agnes right away, me lord. An' she walked home? In that storm? Poor little lass.'

Barlow was gone and Marcus turned back into the room. Meg's portmanteau caught his eye and he opened it. And swore violently. It was soaked through and everything in it. She didn't have a stitch to wear thanks to Mrs Garsby's callous disregard for common human decency.

Cursing under his breath, he went to his chest of drawers and found a nightshirt. It would swamp Meg's slight frame, but at least it would be warm. His dressing gown of heavy red silk lay across a chair. That would help too…and… He cast his eyes about the room…ah, yes! His driving coat…and a couple of blankets, and she could sit up and have something to eat in reasonable modesty. From his point of view, the more clothes she had on, the better! He studiously avoided looking too closely at Meg as he went back and forth.

Agnes Barlow entered the room without even bothering to knock. 'My lord! Just what—?' She broke off as she caught sight of Meg dozing in the bath. Her gentle old eyes seemed to blaze. For a moment Marcus thought she was going to say something, but she just went and dropped to her knees beside the bath and shook Meg's shoulder. 'Come along, dearie. 'Tis time to get you dry, afore you gets all wrinkly!'

Marcus felt his heart turn over at the gruff tenderness in her voice. Was this the only kindness Meg had known in the last ten years? And she had been lucky. He shuddered to think what might have been her fate in a more fashionable household where the servants took their tone from their employers. At least here she had been in the care of the Barlows, dour, independent country folk who thought for themselves and formed their own opinions on the evidence before them.

Agnes turned to him. 'I'll get her out now, me lord. If so be you'll remove yourself! Which I'll take leave to say you should have done in the first place! A bath might be just what Miss Meg needed, but you had no call to strip her!' Her voice echoed with indignation at his lack of propriety.

'Her…her things are all wet,' said Marcus awkwardly. It was a measure of his embarrassment that he felt no annoyance at having his actions called to account by one of his servants. 'You can put these on her.' He held out his peculiar collection. 'If her bed is still made up, put her in there. Otherwise she can have my bed and another bed can be made up for me.'

He paused at the door. 'Tell Miss Meg that I will see her in the morning to discuss her situation. I will tell Barlow to send up some dinner.'

'Aye. You do that, me lord,' said Agnes absently as she helped Meg out and wrapped a blanket around her.

'You'll stay with her tonight?' Marcus asked hesitantly. The damage was already done, but he was damned if he wanted to make things worse for the child. As it was, he could only see one solution to Meg's problems. In any case he didn't want her to wake up alone and scared during the night.

The glare which sizzled from Agnes Barlow's eyes suggested that he would have received short shrift had he attempted to make any other disposition. She softened the glare by saying, 'She'll do well enough, me lord. An' I'm sure I beg pardon if I spoke out of turn, but I'm that worritted about the lassie…an' what's to become of her now?'

She finished softly, as though speaking to herself, but Marcus found his thoughts echoing her question. What, indeed? He went down to his own dinner in thoughtful contemplation of the way in which the fates had arranged his future.

Over a meal consisting of a raised rabbit pie, a baked trout and a duckling served with a platter of vegetables and removed with an apple pie, he considered the options before him carefully.

He could settle money on Meg as he had originally planned and trust to his sister's influence to establish the girl creditably. Or he could ask Di to find her a new position if she were steadfast in refusing to accept money from him. The only problem was that if Mrs Garsby could turn Meg away, then so could others. No doubt the tale was all over Yorkshire by now that he had seduced the daughter of Robert and Caroline Fellowes. And it would travel, no doubt about that. If she had been anyone else, they might have been able to carry it off. Unfortunately her background, not to mention his reputation, made that impossible.

Which left marriage. To himself. Looked at dispassionately, the idea did not disturb him in the slightest. From the social viewpoint he had no qualms. He was Rutherford. His pre-eminence in the fashionable world of the *ton* would be sufficient to protect Meg. And as far as her background was concerned, he couldn't have cared less. People had ridden out worse scandals. And he would derive immense, if cynical, satisfaction in forcing the fashionable world to accept his choice. Especially Sir Delian Fellowes and his top-lofty wife.

On a personal level he was as happy to marry Meg as any other female. He actually respected her. Liked her gallant determination to stand alone. Liked the outrageous way she had tried to circumvent his dictatorial management of her future. His little Meg hadn't wasted time on arguing with him, she had just quietly gone ahead with her plans as though he had nothing to do with them. In which she was completely and utterly mistaken, of course, but that did not cancel the determination and courage.

As for the physical side of things…no problems there. He would positively enjoy undertaking Meg's education in her marital duties. Her beauty was not the obvious sort, but rather a subtle elegance tempered with an engaging innocence. Her face had character with its deep blue-grey eyes and the strongly marked brows. She dressed appallingly, but that was doubtless due to necessity not inclination and could be remedied easily enough. Marcus knew enough of women to be tolerably certain that she would be only too happy to be let loose amongst the fashionable modistes and milliners of London. The thought of Meg sheathed in shimmering, clinging silk had a very definite appeal to what he freely admitted to be his base masculine sensibilities.

He spared a brief thought for Lady Hartleigh and shrugged as he helped himself to apple pie. No doubt she would be a trifle disappointed, but it was not as though she needed to marry or fancied herself in love with him. Theirs would have been a marriage of convenience.

As would, of course, his marriage to Meg.

The fact that he did not know her terribly well did not concern him. Except for his mother and sister, he had never known any woman terribly well, apart from in the biblical sense, and he did not intend to start with his wife. No, a marriage of convenience, in which they would pursue their fashionable, separate lives, would suit the Earl of Rutherford to a nicety.

There was little point in pretending that he was in love. She would never believe it even if he did know how to counterfeit an emotion he was not entirely sure he had ever indulged in. No, she was an intelligent girl, to judge by the varied reading matter he had found beside her bed. Better just to put it before her as a business transaction. In return for heirs and her discretion he would give her the protection of his name and all the indulgence she had so far been denied in her barren existence. Viewed logically it seemed a fair enough bargain to him, with no danger of hurt for either of them. In addition to Fenby House, which he didn't need, it looked as though he had also inherited a bride, which he most assuredly did need.

He ignored the niggling little voice that suggested the Earl of Rutherford might be biting off rather more than he could comfortably chew, and that Marc had better look out for himself.

Later that night Meg lay on her stomach in her battered tester bed, trying very hard to cry silently into the pillow. She did not wish to disturb Agnes, snoring comfortably on the other side of the bed, did not wish to acknowledge to anyone the depth of despair and hopelessness to which she had now plummeted. Desperately she buried her face in the lumpy old pillow with its worn and darned slip. Her slight shoulders shuddered with the effort to muffle her sobs.

In the morning she would have to go to the Vicar and ask for his help in finding a job, but if Mrs Garsby's self-righteous attitude was anything to go by she thought that she might as well enter the workhouse in York immediately. Granted his lordship had offered assistance, but that was before he knew who she was. Besides, she had refused his offer and could hardly turn around now, expecting it to remain open.

The future stretched out remorselessly before her, bleak and terrifying. Now even the prospect of earning a living looked grim. Fear rose before her in the darkness, black and threatening. She fought it down before it could take control. Above all, when she saw Lord Rutherford on the morrow, he must not see how frightened she was. No one must know what a coward Meg Fellowes really was.

Except Marc, she thought as she finally drifted towards sleep. He probably wouldn't pity or despise her. He was kind and practical, dumping her into his own bath and lending her his nightshirt. She was still wearing it and she snuggled down into it, pretending he was holding her. Marc would have had some solution for her problems...

Chapter Four

Despite her exhaustion Meg awakened quite early the following morning. Agnes Barlow was bustling quietly around the room and Meg watched her through half-closed eyes. There was no need to get up yet. It was pleasant to lie quietly, later in the morning she would have to give some thought to the future, but not now. At the back of her mind loomed the knowledge that she was facing disaster, but just now she was comfortable and safe and she meant to enjoy it.

Eventually Agnes slipped out of the room, evidently convinced that she had not disturbed Miss Meg. Which was fair enough, because Miss Meg drifted back into a deep and dreamless sleep very readily. When she surfaced again the light in her room told her that it was past time to get up. Her rumbling stomach reinforced the impression that it was well past time for breakfast. She looked around for her portmanteau, but it was nowhere in sight.

Frowning, she tried to recall what she had done with it, but all she could remember was that his lordship had stripped her gown off and bathed her. She blushed, not so much at his behaviour as at her own pleasure in it.

Perhaps Mrs Garsby had a point…was she a wanton? Was that how you were meant to feel? Or was there something wrong with her? She had never realised that her breasts were so sensitive, could feel as though they were on fire, sending tongues of flame throughout her body… She had better stop thinking about it…her body was starting to tingle again…

What must he have thought of her? He had done it as though it were the merest commonplace and she had made not the slightest effort to stop him! She would be well served if he did think her a bit of muslin.

And where the hell *was* her portmanteau? Glancing down at herself, she realised that she was wearing his nightshirt… Why in the world…oh heavens…of course! All her clothes had been soaked. All she had was this nightshirt, a dressing gown—belonging to his lordship—and a driving coat with about a dozen capes, also courtesy of his lordship.

Damn him! Not only did he have to strip her in that shameless way, but apparently he was also going to dress her! It seemed she was always having to be grateful to someone for their beastly charity! Furious and embarrassed, Meg scrambled out of bed and pulled on the dressing gown which was draped across a chair. The driving coat was there too, but she thought that trying not to trip over the absurdly large dressing gown would be difficult enough.

Clutching the skirt of the dressing gown around her, she made her way down stairs. No doubt her clothes were drying in the kitchen. She would go and eat her breakfast there as she had always done, while she waited for them to dry. Agnes might even have a job for her which would take her mind off what lay ahead for a brief space.

Tapping gently on Meg's door a few moments later, Marcus was surprised to receive no response. Perhaps she was still asleep. It was after ten and he had break-fasted over an hour ago but no doubt the poor girl had been exhausted. Hesitantly he opened the door and peered in.

The bed was empty, the covers flung back. She had gone down already, probably still in his nightshirt and dressing gown. Very well, he would go and find her. It was most improper, but he admitted ruefully that the situation had gone a long way beyond the proprieties.

As he went back down, he thought carefully about the best way to deal with Meg's pride and scruples. Obviously this was one female who would not submit to being ridden roughshod over as he had attempted yesterday. He suspected that had he dealt with her more gently, she might have told him her whole story. She seemed to swing unnervingly between confiding trust in him and a stiff reserve, sometimes calling him Marc, sometimes my lord or Lord Rutherford. Very well. He would have to try to encourage her to trust him, treat her gently, listen to her.

Now, where the hell was she likely to be? Probably the breakfast parlour. She must be hungry.

He drew a blank there. And in the library, the parlour and everywhere else that he looked in the next half-hour. Surely, she hadn't bolted again! Not in a nightshirt and dressing gown. She must have collapsed some-where! Frantic, he rushed back to the library and tugged the bellpull vigorously.

When Barlow arrived in response his lordship did not mince words. 'Barlow, where the devil is she?'

Barlow blinked at the panic in his lordship's face and

voice. 'Miss Meg? Why, she's in the kitchen with Agnes, me lord. Eatin' her breakfast.'

'In the kitchen?' Marcus said. 'Why not in here? With me! Where she belongs!' Relief flooded through him. He hadn't thought of that.

'She's…she's still in your lordship's nightrail,' explained Barlow, trying not to laugh. 'Likely she thought it better to wait for her clothes to dry… Me lord, no! Agnes won't even let me in there!'

He stared in consternation as the master left the room, a steely glint of determination in his eyes. Surely his lordship wasn't going to brave Agnes's kitchen? Even if he was the master, she'd have a fair bit to say about that! Very protective of Miss Meg was Agnes, especially after yesterday. Like a hen with one chick, so she was!

His lordship was indeed going to brave the kitchen. He entered very quietly, without even bothering to knock and so came upon a scene which shook him to the core.

Meg was sitting at the big table, an empty plate in front of her and a small earthen coffee pot. Her face was buried in her arms on the table top, her shoulders shuddering with suppressed sobs. Agnes Barlow was leaning over her, holding her, murmuring gently.

'There now, dearie, just you have a good cry. Vicar will know what you should do. Never you fear! 'Twill all come out in the end.'

Marcus stood as though rooted to the floor. Never in his life had he seen a woman cry like this. As though she were desperately trying not to. Most women he knew made play with wet eyelashes quite happily in unavailing attempts to move his sensibilities. He had

seen so many artful female tears that they generally had
not the slightest effect on him. Except to bore him.

Not this time. He felt something tear deep inside him
at the sight of his little Meg's utter despair. He was
certain that she would not have allowed him to see her
fear and misery at what faced her. No, she would have
hidden it. Just as she had no doubt glossed over the full
reasons for Mrs Garsby's behaviour. Just as she had
hidden her full tragedy from him yesterday morning.

Suddenly aware of his presence, Agnes Barlow
looked up and gave a startled gasp. Meg lifted her head
and the tear-drowned eyes stared up in dawning horror.
Making a valiant effort at self-control, she stifled her
sobs, catching her underlip between her teeth.

'Meg.' He kept his voice very gentle. 'I need to speak
to you privately, if you have finished your breakfast.'

'Now?' It came on a hopeless gulp. Marcus thought
he had never heard a more despairing acceptance of
fate.

'Miss Meg's clothes…' began Agnes, frowning dire-
fully.

The look on his lordship's face stopped her. 'Mrs
Barlow, you need not have the slightest fear for Miss
Meg's safety at my hands. In any way whatsoever.' His
eyes were gentle as they rested on Meg and he came to
her side.

Reluctantly Agnes stepped back, and he swung Meg
up into his arms with easy strength. She gasped and
clung to him in shock. What was he about? He had
guaranteed her safety so he couldn't mean to…yet there
was something so tender and possessive in the way he
was holding her. Shaken, she recalled the pleasure she
had felt in his touch the previous night. Had it been

apparent to him? Did he think that with her history and after what had happened that he might as well take her?

Shame and bitter disillusionment swept through her, with anger treading hotly on their heels.

'I can walk!' Breathless and indignant, Meg wriggled as he kicked the kitchen door shut behind them. And felt those iron muscles tighten around her again.

'I dare say you can,' agreed Marcus mildly. 'But you aren't going to.'

Nothing more was said as he carried her back into the main part of the house to the library where he placed her in a chair beside the fire and tucked a rug around her. He met the nervous glance she stole up at him. Every line of her body proclaimed her mistrust. She put up a shaking hand to push her hair back.

It didn't fool him in the least. He saw instantly the surreptitious attempt to wipe her eyes and his heart clenched in his chest. Proud as the devil, he thought admiringly. Without a word he produced a handkerchief and dried her cheeks with it before tucking it into her hand.

He straightened up and asked quietly, 'May I know what your plans are now, Meg?' Take this slowly, he told himself. Don't rush her now, any more than you would in bed! And wished he hadn't thought of that particular analogy.

Drawing a shaky breath, Meg answered. 'I…I shall walk into the village and see the Vicar. He may be able to find me another situation since Mrs Garsby has…is already satisfied…' He wondered if she did that often, concentrating on the practical issues, hiding the paralysing fear behind her polite façade.

He demolished that façade effortlessly. 'Since Mrs

Garsby has accused you of being my mistress and kicked you out to walk home? Is that what you mean?'

She looked up, startled into the truth. 'Who told you…how can you possibly…? I mean, no!'

'Meg.' Despite the seriousness of the situation, a note of amusement came into his voice. 'I am not stupid. And I know my reputation and the ways of the world. No one had to tell me. It was obvious, you silly child.'

'Oh.' Plainly she hadn't thought of that. 'Well, I…I dare say it doesn't matter very much,' she lied valiantly. 'I'm sure someone will employ…'

She was interrupted firmly. 'No, Meg. They won't. Take it from me. You stand as much chance of gaining respectable employment now as you have of flying. And I am not going to permit you even to make the attempt.'

'But…I must…'

He continued relentlessly. 'Tell me, Meg. Why did you wish to be a nursery governess?'

She was silent a moment and he wondered if she were seeking another polite lie with which to protect herself.

At last she said softly, 'I thought…well…if I couldn't have children of my own…that at least I could be with children.'

'I see.' He kept his voice very light. This, he had no doubt, was the truth. 'Then you would prefer marriage and children?'

'Please, my lord…' Her voice shook with anguished intensity. 'Please don't mock me!'

He stared at her in shock. Mock her? She could think that he would mock her? Had no one ever listened to her desires before? He felt suddenly exultant that he was going to make her happy, enable her to realise her dream. But his voice was carefully controlled as he said,

'Then I think my solution to our problem will meet your approval.' He smiled down at her as she looked up in amazement.

'You…you have a solution?' Her voice was breathless.

'Mmm. You're going to marry me, Meg.'

The world turned upside down and then miraculously righted itself. Marry *Marc*? For it was Marc offering her marriage! For one mad, golden instant, joy surged through her and she nearly yielded to temptation. He would be kind to her, might even come to care for her a little, he would give her children…because he felt obliged to. At that inescapable fact, all her joy turned to dross.

She couldn't do it. Marguerite Fellowes was no fit bride for the Earl of Rutherford even if he wanted to marry her, which was patently not the case. And she could not think of one single reason why he should wish to do so. It wouldn't even be convenient. On the contrary, it would be a scandalous alliance for any gentleman, and for the Earl of Rutherford it was unthinkable. And for the kind friend who had tended her so carefully it was doubly unthinkable. She would not allow Marc to ruin himself for her.

'No.' It was said quietly but with finality.

'Will you at least listen to my reasons for offering you the protection of my name? After your refusal to accept any charity yesterday, I did not expect you to leap at my offer.'

The diffidence in his voice reassured her. He would not attempt to ride roughshod over her again. She nodded. It could do no harm. Her mind was made up. His reasons were perfectly clear. They did him honour. But she would not accept an offer made under duress. An offer made out of pity.

Or so she thought. As she listened to him she began to wonder.

'To start with, Meg, I have to marry,' he stated. 'It is my duty. The cousin who is my heir neither wants, nor is fitted, for the responsibility of the title. If he were, I would probably never have considered marriage.'

He went on. 'You are thinking that your background will be a problem. Forget it. The Earl of Rutherford can marry whom he damned well pleases!' A little strong, but his credit would certainly survive an alliance with Meg Fellowes.

'My only requirements are that my wife should be well born, reasonably attractive and should desire children. And that I can respect her. You meet all four requirements.' His words sounded cold and cynical. Hardly an encouraging proposal of marriage, but she forced herself to meet his eyes, expecting them to be hard and uncompromising.

She swallowed hard. 'N…no!' His voice and words might sound cold, but his eyes were still oddly gentle. He was offering marriage out of pity and obligation, not because he wanted to for any of his stated logical and practical reasons. She would not accept that sacrifice under any circumstances and especially not when she had nothing to offer in return.

He sighed. 'Meg, rid yourself of the idea that in marrying you I am performing the supreme sacrifice. I dare say it must look like it to you, but I assure you it is not the case.' He smiled at her widened eyes. 'Oh, yes. I know what you are thinking. And you are partially right. Marriage is the only way in which I can adequately protect you from the consequences of this business. And technically, yes, I do *have* to marry you. But believe me, I am offering you a fair bargain. In return for my name and protection, you will give me your discretion and children.'

'My discretion?' Meg was puzzled. She could not think what he was talking about. Did he mean that she must not get into scrapes all the time and must be a model of propriety? If that was what he meant, then she wouldn't have the slightest idea of how to go on. Who had there ever been to tell her? And as for his second stipulation…

'My lord—'

'Marc,' he corrected her softly.

'I *cannot* accept!' Her voice wobbled. 'You…you are offering certainties in return for something I do not know if I can…' She stopped, very embarrassed, but he had understood.

'You do not know if you can have children? Is that it?' Marcus smiled wryly. 'My dear, *that* would be a problem no matter who I married. I can assure you I have no desire to be a stepfather just to ensure my wife is fertile.'

'But…'

'Marry me, Meg.' His voice was low and persuasive.

She stared up at him. He meant it. He really did wish her to marry him. It would be a bargain between them. Suddenly she wondered what he had meant by discretion. She had to know before she answered.

'What did you mean by *discretion*?'

His amazement at the question showed in his dropped jaw and the faint flush on his cheekbones. What on earth had she said to startle him? Doggedly she faced him with the wide candid eyes of a child.

He drew a deep breath. 'I do not offer love, Meg.

That is not part of our bargain. I neither offer it nor want it. If, however, after you have provided me with an heir, you decide that you require love, then you are free to seek it. I ask only your discretion.' He looked at her soberly. 'I am no saint, Meg, and neither am I a hypocrite.'

'I…I see.' And she did see. He was giving her a *carte blanche* to embark on an affair once she had fulfilled her duty. He was telling her that she need not fear to meet the same fate as her mother. That he would consider himself free to pursue his amusements and was prepared to offer her the same freedom. He was indeed offering a straightforward bargain. Bitterly she thought that she must be almost the only woman alive to whom he could have offered such a contract openly.

Yet his eyes were still gentle. He had intimated that he respected her.

In a voice she hardly knew was hers, she asked, 'Why…why do you respect me?'

There was a pause and she looked up to find a considering look in his eyes. Then, holding her gaze with his, he said, 'I like your courage, your determination…I like your pride. You were so determined to manage for yourself, to accept no charity despite your destitution. Those are qualities I admire, that I would like the mother of my children to possess.'

It was a good answer, she thought. He had judged her on her actions as he had seen them. He was wrong, of course, it was not pride or any of those other things, just a loathing of being the despised, poor relation. But nevertheless he liked the way she had behaved, did not resent the fact that she had disobeyed him. He was just. And, she reminded herself, he has offered a bargain. A bargain made between equals. No matter what she might think of such a contract, it was still a contract in which she would be an equal partner. And, above all, he did not seem to expect her gratitude.

At last she heard herself say, 'I accept your offer of marriage, my lord.'

She shut her eyes, feeling very dizzy. Surely this wasn't happening. But it seemed that it was. She could feel his hands grip hers and draw her up to stand before him..

Trembling, she forced herself to look at him. He was very close, his tall frame towering over her. Meg was a tall girl, but she felt incredibly small and weak before him. He was looking down at her with a strange, intent glitter in his eyes.

'Shall we seal our bargain, Meg?' His voice was very soft, a velvet caress. He bent his head and touched his lips gently to hers in a featherlight kiss. She did not draw back, but stood unresisting as his mouth moved over hers tenderly. Fire seemed to ripple through her body as he released her hands, only to gather her in his arms and pull her into an engulfing embrace.

Meg was lost in a world of sensuous enchantment. His lips moving over hers evoked magic, darting fires of delight which urged her closer to his powerful body. Instinctively she nestled against him, joy exploding in her heart as she felt him pull her even closer, felt him deepen the intensity of the kiss. Here at last was someone who actually wanted her for whatever reason... someone who would care for her... She felt as though her heart would burst with happiness at the thought that here at last was someone she could care for...love...

She froze. He wasn't offering love...didn't even want it...love would not be part of their bargain. He had said quite clearly that if she wanted love, she was free to seek it...elsewhere. The question hammered in her brain— *What will happen to me if I fall in love with him?*

In the last ten years Meg had not dared to love. She had come to Fenby House prepared to love Samuel and Euphemia Langley, but they had made it plain that they had taken her out of duty and expected her to be grateful. They had no use for her childish affection and had never tried to comfort her confused grief over her parents.

Indeed, on the one occasion when she had given way to tears in Cousin Euphemia's presence, she had been told that her parents were a disgrace, her mother especially so, and that she must learn to control herself if she did not wish to grow up the same way. And when she had brought a posy of flowers for Euphemia on Mothering Sunday, they had been stigmatized as weeds and thrown on the fire. So she had retreated into a shell of seeming meekness...it was much safer than having your offered affection spurned. That hurt unbearably. Even with Agnes, who pitied her, she had tried to conceal her real thoughts and fears...until this morning.

Now Lord Rutherford, who by his own admission would have not the least use for her affection, threatened to force her out into contact with the world and its chill. It had been easy enough not to love Samuel and Euphemia. They had never shown her the least affection or kindness. Marc would be quite another matter. She shuddered at the thought.

Marcus released her at once, raising his head and sliding his hands down her arms to hold her hands again. He looked deep into her eyes and she dropped her gaze at once, veiling the sudden fear. 'Meg?' His voice was a little unsteady. 'Meg, am I frightening you?'

Meg stared up at him. He mustn't know what she feared! But she couldn't let him think that his embrace frightened her. It was the most wonderful thing that had ever happened to her. And if he thought she feared him, he would hold off from her. Of that she was certain. She found her voice. 'You? Frighten me? Oh, no!'

His concerned eyes searched hers. 'You're sure, Meg? I'm not frightening you...' he hesitated slightly '...physically?'

She shook her head, shaken by his concern, his consideration, his sensitivity. Her heart lurched in fear. If his lovemaking was difficult to withstand, how would she survive his tenderness?

He was pulling her back into his arms, resting his cheek on her hair and murmuring. Her already-besieged heart shuddered at the words he spoke. 'I swear to you, Meg, you will be safe with me. Always. Nothing will hurt you now.'

Except you, thought Meg in despair. She did not see how her heart's defences could possibly hold out against his unwitting assault on it. She didn't want to love anyone! And if she did fall in love with him, how would she bear knowing that he did not love her in return, did not wish her to love him? That he expected her to seek love elsewhere...as he would.

In bed that night Marcus worried about her response to his kiss. He had been very restrained with her, shackling his urge to deepen the kiss, fully taste and explore the sweetness of her mouth. Her body had trembled in his arms, whether in fear or pleasure he was not sure. Then she had pressed closer, her arms coming up to wind themselves around his neck. His arms had tightened as desire flared through him, and was ruthlessly held in check. Had he alarmed her in some way? He couldn't bear it if he had. He wanted her to feel safe with him, protected.

Something had scared her, he was sure of it. Yet her fingers had clung to his and her mouth was so soft, trembling from his kisses. He'd swear she'd wanted more. He thumped his pillow in frustration. He wanted her. But he didn't want her to submit to him out of duty.

What he did want was beginning to scare *him*.

So much so that he forced himself to think about his family's likely reaction to this unlikely match. Sheer, unmitigated outrage at first, he'd be willing to bet. Especially his Aunt Regina, Lady Grafton. He didn't doubt that he could manage Di; but Aunt Regina was another matter entirely. She'd be quite capable of scaring Meg into crying off and seeking refuge in the workhouse.

He swore. Di was going to have his hide for this, but there was only one safe option—tell her too late for a family deputation to descend upon him. Which meant he'd have to forgo having Jack as his groomsman. It would be the outside of enough to write and ask Jack to come and not tell Di. She was going to be hurt anyway; there was no need to make it worse for her.

Chapter Five

Four weeks later Marcus St John Evelyn Langley, Eighth Earl of Rutherford stood before the Vicar of the parish, listening to the Reverend Andrew Parker marry him to Miss Marguerite Fellowes. The bride, after her four weeks' recuperation in the care of Agnes Barlow under the Vicarage roof, looked to be well on the road to recovery. She had lost the dark shadows under her eyes, her brown hair was alive with golden lights and a flush of delicate colour glowed in her cheeks.

Marcus, after securing Meg's agreement to marry him, had ridden into the village to find the Vicar and arrange to have the banns called as fast as possible. He considered applying to the Bishop of York for a special licence, but on consideration thought that, since Meg needed time to recover from her illness and get used to the idea of becoming a countess anyway, he might just as well have the banns called. Besides, he could think of no better way of flinging back Mrs Garsby's insults in her teeth. To hear them called three Sundays in a row would tip her a settler she would not forget in a hurry. And a special licence would give credence to any tale that a hasty marriage was essential.

The Reverend Andrew Parker, a mild scholarly widower in his late fifties, had been extremely upset at the story Marcus laid before him and had immediately offered to house Meg until the wedding if Agnes Barlow would act as her chaperon.

'I should have taken her in at once if my wife were still alive,' he explained apologetically. He was conscious of a most unchristian desire to give Mrs Garsby one in the eye and was positively looking forward to calling the banns the following Sunday. A sermon too... Surely he could find a suitable text or two that would give Mrs Garsby pause...that old testament story of Susannah and the Elders might serve his turn...and what about 'Let he who is without sin cast the first stone...' No, probably not. Madam Garsby was so convinced of her own moral superiority that it would have no effect whatsoever; besides, he didn't want to suggest that Meg and Lord Rutherford were guilty as charged. The good Samaritan would do very nicely instead.

Once Meg was safely established at the Vicarage, Marcus flung himself into action to provide everything he thought his bride ought to have. A two-day visit to York enabled him to discover a surprisingly skilled modiste. By dint of laying down a positively shocking sum of money and promising to support Madame Heloise in every possible way in her projected move to the capital, he had succeeded in persuading her to make the journey out to Fenby in two post chaises to fit Meg for her wedding gown and trousseau. The second chaise was piled high with bolts of cloth and several awed assistants. Madame Heloise, after dismissing her first conviction that his lordship was escaped from Bedlam, had decided that lunatic or not, he was possessed of enough of the ready to make any effort expended on behalf of his bride well worth her while.

Indeed, after making Meg's acquaintance and finding out through the inevitable village channels the true circumstances of her betrothal, Madame Heloise was much inclined to regard his lordship as being straight from the pages of one of Mrs Radcliffe's romances and one whom she was more than happy to oblige.

Mademoiselle Meg, she quickly realised, was a young lady who, with a little confidence and inspired dressing, would blossom into a beauty. And not just in the common way. Her tall, slender grace, waving dark hair and blue-grey eyes with their expression of wistful abstraction would admirably become the prevailing classical modes. The raised waists and straight skirts would set off her lissom charms to perfection.

Besides, Madame Heloise liked Mademoiselle Meg. Liked her so much that in their second session, as she made some minor adjustments to the silken ivory sheath in which Meg was to be married, she dropped her French accent and told Meg, through a mouthful of pins, to, 'stop the Madame Heloise rubbish…' and just call her 'plain Louisa' since that was what her parents had christened her anyway!

Meg had stared at her in stunned amazement and then burst into a delighted peal of laughter, in which Louisa Thwaites had joined wholeheartedly. She had explained with a grin that every shopkeeper in York knew she was no more French than a bannock, but it would never do for her exalted clients to guess as much! By which admission Meg, who was rapidly gaining the aforementioned confidence, adjudged she was one of a favoured few.

Those four weeks wrought a miraculous change in

Meg. For ten years she had not known what it was to be consulted as to her wishes, deferred to and considered in every possible way. Now she was left in no possible doubt that even if her betrothed did not love her, he wished her to be happy and fully intended to look after her.

He even spent quite a lot of time with her while she stayed at the vicarage. He tooled her about the countryside in his curricle, remained to dine with her and never gave the slightest hint that she was not precisely what he had intended his bride to be. The only thing that bothered her was that he had never kissed her again after she had accepted his offer of marriage. The memory kept her awake at nights as she wondered if she had done something wrong, if his lordship had not liked kissing her. Then she reminded herself that he did not offer love and perhaps preferred to kiss her only when absolutely required to. She would do better not to dwell on the magical touch of his lips…

Instead she concentrated on his politeness, his charm of manner and his unfailing kindness to her. He seemed to take pains in remembering her likes and dislikes. She remembered clearly the first afternoon he had come to visit her and had suggested she might ring for a pot of tea…

'How do you like it, Meg?' he had asked, preparing to pour her a cup and calmly ignoring the convention dictating that she should pour for him.

Flushing deeply, she had admitted that Cousin Samuel had forbidden her to drink tea, on the grounds that it was far too expensive and he did not wish her to develop extravagant tastes.

Marcus had informed her that he would take it as a personal insult if his bride lost any time in acquiring as

many extravagant tastes as possible! He had then en-
larged her vocabulary with a pithy and unflattering series of remarks on the subject of their mutual relative
as he poured her a cup of tea, reducing her to helpless
giggles, and the very next time he had come to take her
driving he had brought her a gift.

Elegantly wrapped, he had dropped it on her knees
after lifting her up into his curricle to go for a drive.
She stared at it in disbelief...a present...a real present.

She opened it with hands that shook as he got up
beside her and set the horses in motion. It was a tea
caddy, full to the brim with fragrant tea. A dainty, leaf-
shaped silver caddy spoon sat on top of the tea and eight
silver teaspoons were revealed when Marcus showed
her the cunningly hidden drawer at the bottom. And she
had found herself unable to speak, with silent tears
pouring down her cheeks.

Since she had come to Fenby no one had ever given
her any sort of present at all, let alone one that showed
such attention to detail, that tried in an odd way to make
up for everything that had been lacking in her life. True,
Marcus was providing all those lovely clothes, but no
doubt they were just what he felt his countess ought to
have. This—this was somehow different. This was for
Meg—not the Countess-to-be.

Her silence had totally unnerved Marcus. Never in
his life had he bought such an unromantic present for
any woman, but it had felt so right when he thought of
it. At first he had just intended the caddy full of tea,
but the box had that little drawer for the spoons...so he
had dashed off to a silversmith...and then he had seen
the caddy spoon...and all the time his heart aching to
think that she had been treated as though she were one
of the servants. Worse. At least they had been paid.

He concentrated on his team, not daring to ask if she liked it, until an odd sound caught his attention: a sniff, an unmistakable sniff. He steadied his horses and looked down at her…there were tears on her cheeks and she was clutching the caddy to her as though it were the most precious thing in the world. A tea caddy for God's sake! Apparently he *had* got it right, absolutely right. He shook his head slightly in amazement. Obviously he had yet a few things to learn about women.

As for Meg, she was torn between fear at the unwitting assault his kindness made on her heart, and joy at having someone to treat her as though she mattered. It was just kindness she told herself, nothing else…he doesn't care about you. Why should he? He scarcely knows you. But the mere fact that he was kind, despite his air of coldness, despite not caring for her, only tore at her all the more.

So Meg went down the nave of the village church on the arm of Dr Ellerbeck to be given into the keeping of Marcus St John Evelyn Langley in a very strange mixture of trepidation and joy.

Marcus, looking at the results of Madame Heloise's labours, had no complaints. She looked lovely, radiant. He watched her proudly as she came to him down the aisle. His bride. He vowed silently that he would be a good husband, that he would make up to Meg for the barren years she had endured.

Often cynical at weddings, no trace of cyncism tainted his response as the Vicar declared them man and wife. She was his. The fierce surge of possessiveness stunned him. Forcing back a wave of desire, he turned to her, smiling tenderly as he bent his head to feather a gentle kiss over her soft lips. For a spine-tingling instant he felt them tremble under his, parting slightly.

Again, desire seared through him and he drew back at once to offer her his arm and escort her to the vestry to sign the register. His body blazed with his awareness of her and this was definitely not the place to succumb to his inclinations. He was still haunted by the suspicion that he had frightened Meg in some way. Despite her denial, he was sure that he had upset her. And he was not entirely sure that he would be able to control his passions another time. She was so soft and sweet that he was actually looking forward to his wedding night and he did not want his bride to be in a frenzy of nerves beforehand just because he couldn't control himself. He certainly didn't want to give her a foretaste of the intimacies of the marriage bed in church.

Meg signed the enormous old register with a trembling hand. Even that brief kiss in front of the small congregation had wholly overset her intention to maintain the sort of detachment his lordship desired. She had not been able to stop herself leaning into his kiss, had actually started to kiss him back…and he had immediately withdrawn. Taking a deep breath, she turned to her husband, holding out the quill.

He took it with a slight smile and his fingers brushed hers gently as he said quietly, 'The Countess of Rutherford need fear no one. Especially not her husband.'

The velvety darkness of his voice held a world of reassurance and her eyes flew to his in consternation. Was that it? Did he still think she feared him? That she feared what he would do to her in the marriage bed? Agnes had told her last night, very gruffly, what his lordship would expect, would do. It sounded most uncomfortable, but Agnes seemed to think that he would not mind kissing her while he was doing it. In that case Meg was inclined to think she might be able to manage…that it might be rather nice to feel his body against hers… She just hoped that he wouldn't be bored and disgusted by her total lack of knowledge.

She gave him the pen and said very shyly, 'The Earl of Rutherford is very kind and he is the last person the Countess would ever fear.' She looked up into his suddenly arrested eyes. They seemed to bore into her with a burning question. She flushed, but held his gaze with her own. He must not think she feared him!

Marcus felt a strange surge of triumph mingled with tenderness as her eyes answered his unspoken question. Whatever it was that had scared her, it was not him! He signed his name with a flourish and stood back to allow the Barlows to sign.

After the Barlows had signed in witness to the marriage, Marcus escorted Meg back through the nave slowly, pleased to note that the little church had quite a respectable number of witnesses to his marriage. The Barlows, of course, but quite a number of his tenants had turned out in their Sunday best, several of them clutching bunches of primroses or violets and wind flowers. These were bestowed on Meg as they left the church, pressed into her trembling, gloved hands with smiles and muttered wishes for her happiness.

Meg felt thoroughly dazed as she changed in her bedchamber at the vicarage. And not just from the unexpected flowers. His lordship—no, she must try and think of him as Marc…he wished it—Marc was confusing her completely and there was no time to think. She had to change so that they could leave for town immediately. She had no idea why Marc was so determined to go at once, but she was only too happy to shake the dust of Fenby from her feet. It had held little but misery for her. So she changed into a carriage dress of deep blue with a matching bonnet as quickly as possible.

Agnes Barlow bustled about her, twitching her sleeves into position, handing her the York tan gloves and shaking out the white lace collar to frame her face.

'Now you look after yourself, Miss Meg...my lady...or rather let his lordship look after you!' The faded eyes were full of tears. 'There now, I'm crying! An' there's nothing to cry about...' Her tears flowed all the faster at being hugged by the new countess and soundly kissed on her withered old cheek.

'Goodbye, Agnes.' Meg too had tears in her eyes and her voice wobbled. 'I'll...I'll write and his lordship says he will need to come back later in the year, so perhaps I can come with him and see you...'

'Go on with you!' said Agnes gruffly, trying not to sound pleased. 'My Lady Rutherford to be traipsin' all the way to Yorkshire! Just to see an old woman like me!' She smiled through her tears. 'Not but what I dare say you might come to keep his lordship company!'

Ten minutes later Meg was settled alone in a post chaise, gazing out the window at the scenery flashing by. Marc was driving his own curricle. She felt a little sorry that he did not wish to be sitting beside her, but she couldn't blame him. It was a lovely day, too good to spend in a chaise. She could hear the sky larks soaring in ecstatic song over the moors and could smell the vanilla scented gorse. Perhaps when they stopped she could ask...perhaps he wouldn't mind if...

By the time they reached the first halt she had quite made up her mind that she would ask. After all, he could only say no.

He came to the door of the chaise to ask politely if she required anything as hostlers rushed out to unharness the sweating team and pole up the new one. His many-caped driving coat hung elegantly from his broad shoulders and she found herself wondering if it could possibly be true that she, Meg Fellowes, was actually married to this man.

She swallowed hard. Her voice seemed to have seized up but she finally managed to say, 'Yes, my...I mean... Marc.' She hesitated. Perhaps he preferred his privacy...she usually did after all.

He cocked his head on one side. 'Something outrageous, my dear?' His eyes twinkled kindly. 'Ask away!'

'May I...may I drive with you for a little?'

His face registered startled disbelief and he hesitated slightly before responding. 'If you are lonely I will travel in the chaise with you then,' he said stiffly as though it were the last thing he wanted to do. 'You will hardly wish to sit in an open carriage for any length of time in this breeze—'

'Yes, I would!' She interrupted him without thinking and then blushed. 'I...I mean, it is such a nice day... why waste it cooped up in a chaise? At least...if you wouldn't mind...'

Her voice trailed off uncertainly. Marcus was looking positively stunned. Oh, dear...had she stepped over some invisible line...offended against some obscure social code? She was conscious of a feeling of immense disappointment that he didn't even want her company just for a stage. She supposed he had found those drives over the last few weeks rather dull...

'It doesn't matter my lord, M...Marcus...'

She stopped. He was opening the door and holding out his arms with a faint smile.

'Come, Meg. I will enjoy some company. In fact, Burnet may take your place in the chaise and we can be quite private.' A beaming smile lit her eyes as she jumped to her feet and prepared to get down. He forestalled her, setting his hands to her slender waist and swinging her down effortlessly.

It was not the first time Meg had experienced the easy strength in his powerful frame but it *was* the first time since Agnes had explained just what her marital duties would entail and she suddenly felt shy and breathless at the pressure of his hands. Agnes had assured her that his lordship would be considerate, gentle, would understand it was her first time…try not to hurt her too much, but still… She was not frightened of him…but his strength awed her…and he was so much bigger than she was. She was stunned to feel the peculiar shivery sensation that ran through her whole body at the thought of her husband undressing her…kissing her again and— how had Agnes put it?—oh, yes…possessing her body.

Unaware of the tangle of innocent confusion rioting through his bride's thoughts, Marcus walked her over to the curricle and lifted her up into it. The exquisite softness of her body under his hands sent his imagination into a complete spin. Memories of her body nestled up against his while she was sick transformed themselves into visions of her body nestled up against him tonight…her body yielding and arching in response to his lovemaking…and she would respond…he would make quite sure of that.

He looked up into her eyes as he lifted her to the seat and his hands tightened unconsciously on her waist. That soft blue-grey gaze was wide and startled. He could feel her body trembling…

Again those delicious tremors ran through Meg's

body. Her breasts seemed to tingle and she was conscious of a feeling of inexpressible yearning which engulfed her as his hands encircled her waist. She thought dazedly that it was as though her body actually wanted him to…to possess her…despite what Agnes had said about it hurting, at least at first… And his eyes! His eyes were so compelling—it was as though he could see what she was thinking.

Then Marcus was up beside her in one easy, athletic movement and Burnet was jumping down and heading off to the chaise. His large body beside her on the seat was even more overwhelming and she gave herself a mental shake. Better not to think of it. Just enjoy the day and leave the night to the future. For now she would pretend that she was just Meg Fellowes, out for a drive with her friend Marc. Not the Countess of Rutherford being driven by her husband to the posting inn where they would spend their wedding night.

'How long do you think it will take to reach Grantham?' she asked. She rather hoped it would take most of the afternoon. It was such a perfect day. The sun was actually shining and the scents of the wildflowers in the ditches were rising in perfumed clouds. Birdsong rippled from the hedgerows and the air was full of darting birds.

Marcus glanced down at her, amused to see that she was taking such interest in the scenery. It seemed commonplace enough to him at first, but after a moment he found himself seeing it as though for the first time. The fragrances and delicate hues of flowers were suddenly apparent to him, the arching bowl of blue sky above them and the pale spring sunshine gave him the illusion of youth, of what it must be like to approach everything fresh…like that frothy lace collar framing her face. Her slender neck rose out of it swanlike…

Dammit all! What was she doing to him? He was five and thirty and a cynical, world-weary rake! Not a dewy-eyed youth about to spout poetry! There was nothing he had experienced which hadn't, on further sampling, turned out to be a dead bore. If he expected anything more of his marriage he was in for a crashing disappointment. Meg was very sweet, but she was only a woman after all and as such he would do well to keep a decent distance between them. He would enjoy her in bed…make sure she was happy and satisfied, but that would be the extent of their intimacy.

But still the thought persisted. *You could have so much more.* And he could lose it all too. Just as his father had. Every emotion congealed at the mere thought of facing that sort of pain.

It was with all this tumbling through his mind that he answered her question rather more coolly than he had intended.

'After five, I should think,' he said, concentrating on steadying his team, which had shied slightly at a hare who dashed across the road under their aristocratic noses. 'We were rather late starting.'

Meg felt crushed. Doubtless she had kept him waiting while she changed! Then a sensation of irritation seized her. It was all very well for him. He hadn't had to change his raiment! And she couldn't believe that he would have expected her to travel in her wedding gown. He couldn't be that stupid! Besides, she had taken very little time to change. She was willing to bet it had taken him longer to tie his cravat! And she was no longer meek little Meg Fellowes, poor relation! She was Marguerite, Countess of Rutherford, and she would not allow herself to be squashed like a...a...a beetle! Especially not by the Earl of Rutherford!

'Oh,' she said sweetly. 'If you had told me you were in such a hurry I would have changed in the chaise.' She gazed straight ahead between the ears of the offside leader, waiting for the inevitable riposte with an expression of complete innocence on her face.

Eventually, as the silence lengthened, she ventured to cast a glance up at her husband. He was frowning slightly but returned the look with a faint lift of one brow, before giving all his attention to his horses.

'Your trick, Meg,' he said evenly. 'I did not mean to criticise.' Little hornet! Who would have thought the quiet, downtrodden Meg had a sting like that on the end of her tongue? Plainly there was more to his bride than met the eye. For the first time he wondered just what Meg really thought of him and their forced marriage. And would she ever tell him? She had said that she would never consent to be someone's despised poor relation again. She had preferred to seek employment as a governess rather than submit to that.

Obviously the quiet façade hid an unknown Meg that he had glimpsed once or twice when her defences were down. Proud—he knew that. Courageous, certainly— although she would probably laugh at the idea. But what were her dreams? What had she wanted of life before she had learnt to hide everything behind the polite mask? And whatever it was—did she still want it? Uneasily he realised that even if he wanted to understand Meg, she might never let him close enough to do so. She was just as capable of presenting an impenetrable reserve as he was himself.

Satisfied that she had made her point, Meg sat back against the seat and settled down to enjoy the drive. At least she was out in the fresh air and on her way to London. She spared a contentedly unkind thought for the shock it was going to give her cousin Delian and his horrid wife Henrietta to find their despised cousin suddenly so far above them on the social ladder. She knew that Marcus had written to his sister and charged her to have the marriage advertised in the papers tomorrow. Meg hoped that Lady Diana had not been too shocked. There had been no reply from London. Marcus said he had told Di not to bother. By the time she had written they would be on their way and the letter would miss them.

By the time they reached Grantham Meg was extremely tired and ravenously hungry. It was well past five and she definitely wanted her dinner. It was with considerable relief that she realised that the red brick building ahead of them was the George where they had rooms reserved for the night. As Marcus guided his team through the archway into the yard she heaved a mental sigh of relief.

She was exhausted and stiff with sitting for so long and could only marvel as Marcus swung down from the curricle with unimpaired grace. Had she attempted anything of the sort, she was tolerably certain that she would have collapsed in a heap on the cobbles. It was only sheer pigheadedness that had kept her from leaning against Marcus's broad shoulder for the last couple of hours.

He came around to her and looked up with a smile. 'Tired, my dear? I bespoke dinner for six so you will have time to freshen up. It is only half past five.'

She stared down at him in consternation. Half an hour? She would starve if she had to wait so long! Her

stomach, heartily in agreement, gave an audible and un-
ladylike rumble just as Marcus placed his hands on her
waist to lift her down. Judging by the lift of his brows
and the severely repressed twitch at the corner of his
mouth he had heard and probably felt the rebellious
organ's response. The intimacy unnerved her…she tried
not to think just how much more intimately he would
probably know her in a very few hours.

Marcus set her down very gently, keeping his hands
firmly on her waist until he was assured she was quite
steady on her feet. Despite her silence on the subject he
was fairly certain that Meg was utterly exhausted.
Hungry too, he thought with an inward smile.

Tucking her arm in his, he strolled across the yard
towards the inn door, wondering if she were so tired
that it would be better not to insist on his matrimonial
rights and allow her an uninterrupted night's sleep. He
had booked two bedchambers to give her some privacy,
so it would not be such a strain on his control as if he
had to share a bed with her. Still pondering the question,
he bowed to allow her to precede him into the inn. His
mind on his dinner and his intentions for the night
ahead, he heard a rumble of wheels and a rattle of
hooves on the cobbles, but did not observe the natty
gentleman who had just tooled a phaeton and pair into
the yard.

Sir Blaise Winterbourne stared after Lord Rutherford
in patent disbelief. Good God! How did the fellow do
it? He had even found an attractive filly to mount in the
wilds of Yorkshire. Must be a lively little piece too for
his lordship to bother bringing her back to town and
rigging her out in the first style of elegance like that.
My, my, my! A pity Althea Hartleigh had been so virtuous…well, circumspect…in ignoring the lures he had

cast out to her, but by the look of things this little game pullet might be even more worthwhile... She looked rather younger than Rutherford's usual fancies...no doubt she would refresh his somewhat jaded palate nicely...especially if he could have his way with her right under Rutherford's nose. That would add a certain spice to the occasion.

Humming to himself, Sir Blaise sauntered into the inn after giving his orders to the ostler who took charge of his horses. It would be as well if Rutherford did not realise that his little bit of game had been sighted. No need to put the fellow on his guard.

With not the least idea that he needed to be on his guard, Marcus dined with his bride in the private parlour he had bespoken and continued to ponder the question of how to spend his wedding night. He had no doubt of his own inclinations...he wanted to take Meg to bed and make love to her...probably for most of the night. But she sat there before him, gallantly pretending that she wasn't exhausted and trying not to look scared.

When they had finished he stood up and went around the table to her. He intended merely to assist her to her feet, but she smiled up at him with such devastating sweetness that he found himself pulling her into his arms with no warning at all.

For a moment he felt her stiffen in his embrace and then she melted against him, her soft curves moulding to the hard arrogance of his body. With a groan he lowered his mouth to hers in a searing kiss. He was gentle with her, but his passion was undeniable. He wanted her in his bed, wanted to feel her body yielding under him just as her mouth was doing now. Her lips had parted in response to the subtle command of his probing tongue and he took instant advantage, tasting and exploring her sweetness in sensuous assault. And she was responding with an innocent delight that fanned his desire to a blaze. Her tongue was curling around his in shy, untutored abandon. Small, uncertain hands crept up over his shoulders to thread themselves in his thick, tawny locks and he shuddered in pleasure.

And then confusion hit him. This was not what he had intended for his marriage. Enjoy her, yes. But this was not mere enjoyment. This was sheer intoxication. It wasn't just her body he wanted, it was her!

Time! He needed time to get himself under control. Besides, he thought in frantic justification, better not to be too eager her first time and run the risk of really hurting her.

Abruptly he released her. 'I think, Meg, that you must be very tired. You should go to bed.' His voice was distant, cold. It shocked him, but he couldn't help it. He had to think. 'I need to stretch my legs so I shall go for a walk about the town. Goodnight. I shall see you in the morning.' Without awaiting any reply he was gone, leaving a very confused bride behind him.

Meg retired to her bedchamber, uncertain whether she was relieved at his lordship's forbearance or not. Did he really think her tired, or was he just being polite? His face had given her no clue as to his real reasons for not sharing her bed. He had seemed so chilly and remote. Perhaps he just wasn't interested…found her unattractive…regarded it as an inevitable duty and one which he was in no hurry to perform. She swallowed nervously at the thought. How could she possibly share these…intimacies with him if he viewed her with distaste? It would be humiliating!

She poured water into the bowl on the nightstand and cleansed herself thoroughly, trying not to think about the way he had kissed her…the way he had possessed and plundered her mouth… Had her response disgusted him? Should she not have kissed him back? She was stunned to feel an aching, empty sensation between her thighs as she washed there. Shocked, she gritted her teeth and dried herself as quickly as possible before pulling a nightgown over her head and scrambling into bed. The soft feather mattress welcomed her weary body and she admitted to herself, with a sigh, that whatever his reasons for deciding to go for a walk, she should at least be grateful to her husband for an unexpected night's sleep.

Blowing out the candle, she settled down and snuggled under the blankets, enjoying the cosy glow from the fire. She had never had a fire in her bedchamber before…except, of course, when she had been sick and Marc had looked after her… Sleepily she allowed herself to think about Marc. He had been so kind to her…it was a pity that he kept on turning into Marcus, Lord Rutherford. Of course Marc would not have dreamed of forcing himself on her if she was tired…but then he wouldn't have to. Tired or not, Meg would have surrendered herself to his loving without the slightest hesitation…as indeed she had thought she was doing until his lordship put her from him so abruptly. Still puzzling over this, she drifted off to sleep.

She was awakened some time later by the sound of someone moving around in her room. At first she was confused—the fire had nearly died and the room was in near darkness. In her half-waking state, she thought it must be Agnes, but then a very masculine grunt, followed by the sound of first one boot, and then another, hitting the floor, woke her up completely.

She froze. All at once she knew the true meaning of the term *bride nerves*. Marcus must have changed his mind and he had come to…to…possess her body. Half-excited and half-terrified, she lay in the great bed, shaking with nervous anticipation as she listened to the faint sounds of him undressing. Even though her scared brain was trying to persuade her to panic, her body had other ideas. She could feel tingling warmth spreading through her limbs, that extraordinary feeling of weakness that was at once frightening and exciting.

A moment later she felt him get into the bed beside her. What should she do? Let him know she was awake? But if she spoke then he would know she was scared. Was he even going to speak to her before…? She could feel the hard length of his body against her and turned towards him instinctively, trustingly, her arms open, body soft and trembling, her mouth ready for his tender kisses…a world of warm, intimate darkness.

Then the world went mad. She felt a hand reach out for her, grasping, and then she was taken in a rough grip and his mouth was on hers…brutal, greedy. Frantically Meg forced herself to recall her wedding vows and lie still. She had sworn to obey him…it was no part of a bride's duty to struggle against her husband's rightful claim to her body…but it was so horrible! His gentle kisses earlier had given her no inkling of what his behaviour would be like in bed! She had expected that he would be a gentle, tender lover…at the very least considerate. Not this brute beast with his hot, lustful mouth that reeked of brandy, slobbering all over her face. His lips were cruel where once they had been tantalising…she could taste blood. The friendly dark had become a dungeon full of pain and fear.

And what was he doing now? His hands were grabbing at her breasts through the cotton nightgown, actually hurting her. She must lie still…she was his wife…it…it was his right to take her. Terrified, she schooled her body to obedience, even as she felt his hands at the neck of her nightgown jerk apart, ripping it open to the navel. Even worse than her physical terror was the feeling of betrayal, the thought that she had trusted this man, had thought he cared for her at least enough to deal gently with her virginity. His hands were now seizing her soft breasts, crushing them cruelly as he savagely forced his tongue into her mouth.

She gagged, and panicked completely as she felt his weight shift to pin her to the bed. She couldn't! She just couldn't! He could have the marriage annulled! She simply could not submit to his desires! She tried desperately to throw him off and heard a light, mocking laugh as her mouth was released momentarily. And then he took it again, even more brutally as he thrust one leg between her thighs, leaving her with no doubt that he meant to have her even if he had to force her. She couldn't believe it…that Marcus was to all intents and purposes raping her…enjoying her terror…it couldn't be happening.

But it was. She was fighting a losing battle. His weight held her down, helpless, and his powerful right hand had encircled both her wrists above her head while his left was raising the hem of her nightgown. She could feel it sliding down between her thighs, felt his fingers reaching, probing in hard, merciless lust…could feel a heavy ring scrape against her soft flesh…and then she realised… As clearly as though it were before her, she could see Marc's heavy signet on his right hand—his left wore no ring!

Her scream of protest was cut off by that hand which

was suddenly clamped over her mouth and a light, unfamiliar voice said, 'You would be most unwise to do that, my dear. I can assure you that he will not believe you were unwilling. Lie still and I will be on my way before he comes up.'

It was not Marc! It was a stranger! She fought with the strength of desperation to escape that iron grip on her mouth and finally bit savagely. With a curse, he hit her face a stunning blow but her mouth was free and she dragged in a breath and screamed as loudly as she could, struggling fiercely to get out from underneath him.

It was no use. He gave up trying to silence her and seemed to be concentrating his efforts on taking his pleasure as quickly and roughly as possible.

She twisted her legs together tightly and heard him mutter, 'God help me. Anyone would think you had your virtue to defend!' She could feel a hand at her throat, gripping mercilessly, she couldn't breathe…oh, God… Despairing, she could feel him forcing himself between her legs…something hard and blunt… pushing… She screamed again as the grip on her throat relaxed slightly…

And then there was a crash as the door burst open to the accompaniment of a roar of primitive, masculine rage and a blaze of light.

Marcus had taken a rather longer walk than he intended in his efforts to regain his usual sangfroid. And he felt just slightly foolish at his idiotic panic. So much did he want to hurl his stupid decision to the four winds and go back and make love to his bride that he walked right around the town a second time to cool off, before returning to the George. She was probably asleep already and it would be the height of cruelty to awaken her.

Upon his return he made his way upstairs with an oil lamp pressed on him by mine host and past Meg's door. Ruefully he thought that she must be asleep by now, it would be outrageous to go in and wake her up. Perhaps if he rose early in the morning he might go in and wait for her to awaken…

Comforting himself with this thought, he set his hand to the latch of his own door…and froze as a terrified scream rang out.

He didn't pause for thought. He knew beyond all possible doubt that it was Meg…something was wrong… she must be having a nightmare… He was already running back to her door. It was locked, but he didn't bother to knock, just hurled his shoulder at it and burst in as another agonised scream seared through him.

At first he could not believe his eyes and then with a roar of fury he surged across the room to drag Blaise Winterbourne off Meg. Winterbourne was too quick for him.

He rolled off the bed on the opposite side to the door and said mockingly, 'I did warn her not to be too enthusiastic in her excitement! Never mind. Another time, perhaps. Do let me know when you have finished with her, my dear Rutherford. A little unschooled, I must say, but I'm sure she will be worth the effort.'

Meg, half-fainting, managed to pull up the bedclothes with shaking hands. She was safe but she felt sickened, soiled by his body, his touch. What must Marcus be thinking? Would he believe what had happened? Or would he think she was truly her mother's daughter? His voice when it came was like a shard of ice, sending fresh shudders through her overwrought senses.

'Get out of my wife's chamber, Winterbourne.' Searing rage held him in its grip, but through it a cold voice counselled discretion. The last thing he wanted was the landlord up. If this story got out, there would be the very devil to pay! Very few would believe Meg's innocence. He had to protect her! She was huddled under the bedclothes, shaking visibly, her face white and dazed, her lip cut and there was a red mark on her cheekbone that looked as if it would bruise later. His little Meg…if that bastard had actually—

'Your wife!' For a moment Winterbourne was disconcerted, but he recovered his urbanity in a flash. 'Dear me! How very *maladroit* I have been. I thought her one of your little indulgences, my dear Rutherford. Do not trouble to see me out, I know my way.'

Never taking his eyes off Marcus, he pulled on his shirt and breeches, picked up his boots and edged around the bed towards the door, saying, 'Naturally I shall not breathe a word of this…unless of course you wish me to name my seconds, my lord?'

For a mad instant Marcus was tempted, but a terrified murmur from Meg recalled him to his senses and saner counsel prevailed. If he challenged Winterbourne the story was bound to leak out and Meg would suffer, even more than she had already.

Coldly he replied, 'Winterbourne, I would not care to soil my riding whip with a cur like you! Get out! But rest assured, if I hear so much as a whisper about this, I will overcome my reluctance and thrash you to within an inch of your life!'

Chapter Six

As soon as the door shut behind Winterbourne, Marcus turned to Meg. His heart contracted in his chest as he looked at her wide, terrified eyes, and saw the racking shudders that were convulsing her slender body. Her breath was coming in sobs which bordered on hysteria.

What the hell should he do? He wanted to hold her, comfort her, but when he moved towards her she flinched and cried out incoherently, cowering away from him. He couldn't blame her. After what had happened it would be a miracle if she ever trusted a man again. He was not even sure if he had been in time…had Winterbourne actually deflowered her? The thought that Meg had been raped made him feel physically ill. His little Meg…so lost and vulnerable behind her polite mask…he had sworn to protect her and he couldn't even comfort her when he had failed so abysmally!

She was speaking. 'Marc…I'm sorry…I didn't mean…I let him…'

He froze in disbelief, his eyes suddenly boring into her, an unbelievable pain lancing through his body. She had *let* him!

'I thought it was you!' She could not go on and turned to bury her face in the pillow, sobbing bitterly at the thought that she had even accidentally betrayed Marc who was now looking at her in such disgust. Then she felt a gentle touch on her shoulder, a hand warm and comforting, patting her.

A deep voice, husky with emotion, saying, 'Meg, it's all right...you're safe now. Come...let me hold you...' Those gentle hands were turning her, lifting her to lie cradled in his arms against the solid, protective bulwark of his chest. He was stroking her hair, whispering words of comfort, of reassurance. Slowly she began to relax under his touch, although her tears continued to flow unabated.

Marcus just held her, his cheek resting on her dishevelled hair, his hands stroking and soothing as he murmured softly. He could never afterwards remember just what he had said to her, but at last her terrible weeping stopped and she lay silent in his arms except for an occasional hiccough. They were quiet for a while and then Meg spoke again in a voice which cracked pitifully.

'I thought it was you...that you had changed your mind...wanted me after all...'

She had thought he didn't want her? Oh, God, no! She was still speaking and he forced himself to concentrate.

'So I...I welcomed him... He didn't say anything...just grabbed me and started...started—' She broke off, shuddering convulsively. His grip on her tightened and she seemed to gain strength. 'He...he started to kiss me...and...touch my breasts...I thought it was you... I couldn't believe it but...I thought I had to submit so I tried to just lie there...but he was so rough I panicked in the end. I tried to fight him…and then I realised…realised what I had done…that it wasn't you…'

She was crying softly again and Marcus stroked her tenderly. 'It's over, Meg. He'll never touch you again. It's over, I swear it.'

Then, to his amazement, she whispered, 'I'm sorry, Marc…I betrayed you…'

He was stunned. *She* had betrayed *him*? When he had left her alone? Not even thinking to tell her to lock her door!

'You didn't, Meg!' His voice was urgent, desperate to reassure her. 'How was it a betrayal to have been attacked?' He shied from the word *rape*. But then he thought, No, I have to know. I can't help her if I don't. How can I help her get over this if *I* fear the truth?

Hesitantly he asked, 'Meg, did he actually…?'

She shook her head, 'N…no, at least I don't think so. You came in just as…' Her voice failed at the memory of that dreadful, helpless moment when she had felt Winterbourne's body forcing itself against her in violent lust.

Marcus's blood practically congealed in his veins as he realised that in another second or two he would have been too late to save her. His voice cracked as he whispered, 'Thank God! Oh thank God! Meg…I'm sorry…I should never have left you alone. It was selfish…just because I wanted you so much…and I didn't trust myself not to…' He stopped. It would hardly reassure Meg to know he had been burning with desire for her, had wanted to change his mind and come to her room.

And what was he to do now? Should he stay to look after her or would she prefer him to leave her alone? She needed a woman to help her but there was no one he could call. If they had been in London Di would have helped, but here…he couldn't leave her alone all night.

Meg lay quietly, conscious of the comforting strength of his body. She felt safe in his arms, as though nothing could touch her there…except him. The thought came to her unbidden and she tried to force it away. It was obscene to fear what Marc would do to her…but the fear persisted; not that he would force himself on her, but that even if he dealt with her gently, she would panic in the dark, forget it was him…if he wanted her after this. Perhaps he would not want to touch her. She felt dirty, befouled as though a slime clung to her, filthy and degraded.

Marc was speaking softly. 'Listen, sweetheart, I will go to my room and change for the night, then come back to look after you, if that is what you want. I don't want you to be alone, but…' He hesitated.

'Yes, please.' She tried to keep her voice low, hiding the relief that flooded into her. He would stay! She had not dared to ask it of him. She felt that she would contaminate anything she touched.

He released her and stood up, looking down at her worriedly. She sounded so…so utterly lifeless, broken. The torn nightgown hung open, revealing her soft, creamy breasts. Dark bruises were beginning to appear and he swore softly as he realised just how brutal Winterbourne had been with her. The bruise on her cheek was stark against her chalk-white face and her cut lip was swollen. A knife seemed to slice through his heart at the thought of what had so nearly happened. Even if the bastard hadn't known she was a virgin, to force himself violently on an unknown and unwilling girl! It sickened Marc to his very soul. Even he hadn't quite realised how vile Winterbourne could be…

Swearing under his breath, he went to make up the fire and then rifled through Meg's trunk, finding another nightgown. He took the nightgown to her, saying, 'Change while I am gone. Bolt the door behind me. The lock is smashed. I'll knock when I return.'

She nodded, beyond words. Maybe it would help to change. She got up and stood shakily for a moment before following Marc to the door. He touched her bruised cheek gently and went out.

She bolted the door and stared at it, lost, bewildered; the urge to open it and beg him to come back was almost overwhelming…she was being silly—he would be back in a few minutes. In the meantime she must change.

The nightgown he had found for her was on the bed. She put it on and looked with loathing at the ripped one she had removed. It lay on the floor, its torn innocence accusing, a whited sepulchre, rotten, full of corruption. Burn it! She bundled it up and pushed it into the fire Marcus had rekindled. The flames flared up the chimney and for a moment she wished that she could be cleansed, annealed in their purifying blaze. How else could she ever be clean again?

She was still staring into the fire when Marcus came back. His knock recalled her to her senses and she almost ran to let him in. The sight of his tall figure was immensely comforting in the familiar red silk dressing gown. His arms were full of blankets and she looked at them in confusion.

'What are they for?'

'For me,' he said quietly. 'I thought you would probably prefer me to sleep in the chair…that you wouldn't want me in—'

'No!' Her voice was frantic. She could hear it and tried to control herself, but the words came tumbling out. 'Please…please…just hold me…please, Marc—' She forced herself to stop. Impossible to tell him how she felt…that if he didn't hold her that she would never feel safe… Then, looking up into his bleak face, she realised that he understood.

'If that is what you wish, Meg.' His voice was low. He felt humbled and elated all at once that she would trust him like that. Very slowly he went to her and lifted her into his arms as easily as he would have lifted a child. There was nothing amorous in his touch, just solid, protective comfort. He carried her to the bed and settled her in it before climbing in.

'Do you want the lamp, Meg?' She might feel safer that way, he thought. Then if she wakes, she can see it's me.

She shook her head. 'I don't think I'd sleep, but…' In the dark, though…

'A candle,' said Marcus. He got up again and lit one, setting it on the nightstand. Then he came back to bed and blew out the lamp. The little flame danced and glimmered, a glowing island in the encircling dark.

Marcus lay down and reached for Meg, drawing her into his embrace, settling her safely into the curve of his shoulder. He felt her body, tense at first, slowly relax against him until at last her breathing steadied and deepened into the haven of sleep. He lay wakeful for a long time, half-expecting to have to fight his own body's urges, but although he was profoundly aware of her soft curves nestled beside him, and although it would have taken very little to stir him to passion, he could hold himself easily in check by concentrating on the trust she had showed in him.

Meg awakened in a cold sweat, confused and terrified from a dream in which Marc kept turning into Winterbourne and a smothering, greedy blackness enveloped her, body and soul. There was a heavy weight across her waist, pinning her down. Marc's arm, strong and reassuring. The fire was very low but the candle flame still danced bravely. Clean, bright…she envied it its effortless purity. She wanted to wash, totally immerse herself in water to cleanse away the stains left on her, especially the stain of fear. There was water on the nightstand…if she were very quiet…

Careful not to wake him, she lifted Marc's arm and got out of bed. Perhaps if she washed she might feel clean. Stripping off her nightgown, she stood shivering in the chilly air. A flannel lay on the stand. She dipped it in the bowl and began to wash herself in the icy water, wincing as the cold bit through her. She washed and washed, scrubbing at her body until it felt raw and stinging—her breasts, her thighs…but still she felt mired.

Marcus had woken as soon as she moved his arm but he lay quietly, unwilling to intrude, trying to understand. The faint light gleamed on her white curves as he watched her, creating shadowy mysteries in the intimate hollows of her body, mysteries that he longed to penetrate, possess… He could hear her teeth chattering, but still she was scrubbing obsessively. And suddenly, with a blinding flash of understanding, he knew why she was doing it. He shut his eyes, appalled.

Never in his life had he forced himself on a woman. Ever since he and Jack had caught Blaise Winterbourne at a house party, forcing his attentions upon a terrified chambermaid, he had thought it to be the most despicable of acts, scorning those who boasted of the defenceless maidservants they had coerced.

Naturally he and Jack had stopped Winterbourne, but even so, he had never quite realised how devastating it would be for a woman—how sullied she would feel afterwards—until now, as he lay watching his bride frantically trying to cleanse the memory from her bruised and shivering flesh, a victim of Winterbourne's twisted, ongoing vengeance.

At last she stopped with a despairing murmur. 'I'll never be clean again...never!'

Marcus flinched at the dull pain in her voice, watching as she dried herself and pulled the nightgown back on. It slid down over her breasts, puckered with cold, her slender waist and those flaring hips, the long line of her thighs, all graceful, tempting curves. He shut his eyes to block out the vision but it danced before him mercilessly in all its seductive beauty, inviting him to touch, caress, burn kisses over the silken skin...show her how tender and intimate the act could be...erase, or at least counter, the dreadful memory of her near rape. It was too soon, he told himself. Perhaps if she will let me tell Di, or if I can persuade her to tell Di...

He could hear the soft pad of her feet as she came back to the bed and he lay there, gritting his teeth for control. It would be safer for her if he went and slept on the chair, but he knew if he did that she would read it as a rejection of her, a confirmation of her vileness. And he could not tell her the real reason and frighten her still further. She trusted him, had no one else to turn to. Though it killed him, he would not betray that trust.

Meg got back into the bed, shivering violently. She longed to cuddle up against Marc's warmth, feel his arm around her, holding her fear at bay, but hesitated to wake him. So she lay huddled under the blankets, trying to ward off sleep in case she should dream again. She forced herself to think about Marc's kisses, how different they had been, how tender and…exciting. She had been a little scared, but only of her own response, the wild, aching need that had pierced through her. She had not been scared of him, and when she had thought he had come to her bed to possess her, her heart had soared in an ecstasy of joy… She found that tears were sliding down her cheeks again and buried her face in the pillow to muffle her sobs.

She felt a gentle hand grip her shoulder, heard a deep voice say, 'Come here, little one.' She turned at once, wriggling into his arms and clinging to him, pressing herself against him, conscious only of the solid heat of his body, the reassuring strength of his arms. Somehow the fact that he was willing to hold her like this made her feel cleaner.

The sensation of her trembling body seared into his unruly flesh. He suppressed a groan with extreme difficulty. She must not know he wanted her…wanted her with a desire that shocked even him in its raw, primitive longing. He forced himself to stroke her hair gently, holding her against him protectively while his body screamed silently at the torture it was subjected to. It had been a physical relief when she had not nestled back up to him at first, but he could not, just for the sake of his own comfort and sanity, leave her to cry herself to sleep.

He could feel her tears soaking through his nightshirt as she wept, and said quietly, 'Tell me, Meg. It will make you feel better.'

'I…I can't.'

'Tell me, Meg.' His voice compelled in its gentle compassion.

Her voice shaking, she told him, in pitiful broken phrases that seemed to tear her apart. He shut his eyes to hold back the hot, pricking sensation. It was even worse than he had thought. She had not only thought it was him, she had been willing, pleased, had welcomed him...or so she thought...and then...she had thought it was him brutalising her. Cold horror seeped into him as he realised how terrified she must have been, thinking that she would have to endure similar acts of savage lechery regularly.

Finally she lay quietly in his arms. He held her tenderly, still burning with desire, but he managed to speak normally. 'Go to sleep, Meg. I'll hold you.'

She shuddered as he spoke and he at once released her, drew back, mentally cursing, thinking she had realised his arousal. But she clung to him in frantic terror. 'No, don't let me go!' It came tumbling out as though she could no longer contain the fear. 'I don't want to sleep. In case I dream again...'

'Dream?' She had said nothing about a dream. He should have realised. He had had nightmares after the siege of Badajoz. 'Come, Meg. Tell me everything. Trust me.'

Convulsive shudders racked her. 'No...it...it is obscene,' she whispered.

'Then it is better told and got rid of,' he said softly, his long, experienced fingers tangling in the curls at the nape of her neck, massaging the tension he could feel there. 'Told and exorcised...not hidden within where it will fester.'

So she told him.

He was silent for a moment and then he said carefully, 'One day, Meg, when you are ready, we will do something about that.'

'What? What can possibly help?' Her voice sounded hopeless, dead.

He drew a deep breath. Even saying it was enough to threaten his precarious self-control. 'By making love, Meg. When you are ready to trust me with your body, you will come and tell me. And I swear to you that I will take your gift gently.' After a minute he said haltingly, 'I want you very much, Meg, but I will not take you until you ask me to.' He could not bear that she might think he did not want her.

His fingers were still stroking her soft creamy nape, gentle and compelling, unwittingly casting a tender, seductive spell. She closed her eyes, imagining those fingers at her breast, pressing her thighs apart. And instead of black, choking horror, she felt again that wild, sweet ache…that yearning, beckoning emptiness. She already trusted him, there was nothing else to wait for. If he truly wanted to make love to her, those fiery sensations he evoked might become a blaze that could cleanse and purify her again.

Summoning all her courage, she pressed a small, shy kiss on his chin and faltered, 'Marc…would you…if you are not too tired?'

It took him a moment to realise what she was saying, for her meaning to sink in. He lay there in disbelief. He had thought it might take weeks, months perhaps, before she would trust him. He couldn't take advantage of her like this. No matter what his body thought of the idea.

'Meg…no,' he said with difficulty. 'It is too soon for you…'

She pulled away from him, numbed by his gentle

rejection. He was just being kind, he did not really want her. Perhaps he even felt as she did, that she was somehow unclean, that he would be soiled by touching her.

'I'm sorry.' Her voice was a mere thread which threatened to snap under the strain of her hurt. And then she felt his hands on her again, bringing her back into his embrace.

His voice, hoarse and shaking. 'Meg, are you sure? Quite sure?'

She was sure and turned to him, desperately raising her mouth for his kiss. She could feel his trembling hands cup her face as he feathered his lips over hers in a caress so tender, so hesitant that it brought tears to her eyes. His arms were around her, pulling her to lie against his hard, aroused body.

He had been careful earlier to lie so that she did not feel his flagrant desire. Now he held her to it, rocking his loins against her gently, whispering again, 'Are you sure?'

'Yes.' Her answer was breathed on a sigh of pleasure as he trailed light kisses over the ivory column of her throat. There was no fear at his blatant demonstration of need, only joy that he still wanted her. She felt one large hand slide down over her shoulder to tease her breast through the cotton of her nightgown, felt those darting fires under her skin as he rubbed a thumb across the nipple. It sprang to painful life, a taut, burning little bud which forced a whimper of delight from her.

His mouth was on hers again, still gentle but imperceptibly more intense, his lips warm and firm as they sipped and sampled her inexperienced sweetness. Shyly she kissed him back, opening her mouth under his instinctively, in response to the subtle pressure. She could feel his tongue flickering lightly over her lips and arched against him in unspoken longing.

With a tearing groan Marcus succumbed to temptation and slid his tongue into the soft, vulnerable recesses of her mouth. Ready to break the kiss at the first sign of fear, he explored gently and thoroughly, sweeping across the roof of her mouth in slow, sensuous strokes. Then with a surge of joy which stabbed through him like a sword, he felt her tongue, hesitant and uncertain, entwine with his in shy passion.

Endlessly patient and skilful, Marcus kissed her until she was moaning with pleasure, drowning in the sea of sensation aroused by his mouth and hands. She stroked his shoulders, astounded at the shudders of delight that racked his hard, powerful body. She wanted to feel his bare skin under her hands, wanted to feel his hands on her breasts.

His mouth was at her ear, tickling with his warm breath and then she heard him say, 'Wait, sweetheart.' He pulled away from her and got off the bed. She lay there, watching his large, dim outline as he crossed to the nightstand. A moment later there was a flare of light as he lit the lamp from the flickering candle.

He turned to look at her and said very deeply, 'I want to see you, Meg. And I want you to see me. There will be no darkness in our loving.' And with slow deliberation he drew off his nightshirt to stand naked before her, watching her reaction for the slightest hint of fear.

She stared for a moment with wide eyes and parted lips. He was so beautiful! So very powerful. So very male. Her gaze roamed over his broad shoulders and wide, muscular chest with its thick mat of hair, lower to his narrow hips…and… Her breath came in shallow gasps as she forced herself to look at his potent, unfettered virility.

For a split second she felt fear, physical, gut-wrenching fear as the darkness beyond the pool of light threatened to close in and overwhelm her. She fought it down and looked into Marc's face. Desire, concern and acceptance were all there. If she said no, it would go no further. He would shackle his own desire and respect her decision. That was why he had lit the lamp, so that he could know beyond doubt what she really wanted.

She wanted him. Despite her fear, she wanted him. And she knew that if she backed away now it would become harder and harder to face her fear. Somewhere deep down she knew that the only way forward was straight on, through her fear and out the other side. If he would leave the light on...if she could see it was him...

He was picking up his nightshirt, preparing to put it back on when she spoke. 'Can we have the lamp on while...while we...?'

The garment slipped through his nerveless fingers. He would have sworn that she was about to refuse, that the sight of his aroused body had terrified her. His burning grey eyes held her gaze, searching her face. She *was* afraid...he could see it in the wide eyes and trembling mouth. And something else was there, warring with the fear—desire...and a determination to face out her fear. Of course she wanted the light on. Then she would know it was him...but still he was uncertain.

As he hesitated she held out her hand to him imploringly and said, for the last time, 'I am sure, Marc, please...'

Her voice trembled and he suddenly knew that if he

refused she might never be certain of his reasons, ~~might~~ always think that he hadn't wanted her despite the evidence of her eyes. His mind made up, he dropped the nightshirt and approached the bed. Kneeling on it beside her, he drew the bedclothes back and lifted her against him, his fingers at the buttons of her nightgown, undoing them one by one until it hung open almost to her waist.

He sat back and gazed at her partially revealed breasts, creamy, velvety flesh that his fingers ached to cup. Delectable rosy peaks, which seemed to cry out for the ministration of his tongue, peeped out shyly. With incredible restraint he set his hands to her shoulders and, looking deeply into her eyes, he slid the nightgown off, pushing it down to lie around her hips. Then he drew her very slowly into his arms.

Meg thought she would die of the sensation of being held half-naked in his arms. His hands roamed over her gently, possessively, rubbing and stroking as he explored her shape and texture. She could feel the rough hair on his chest rasping against her nipples and shuddered with delight as they burned with joyful pain. And all the time his mouth never left hers, kissing her deeply as his warm strength seduced her completely. Her eyes closed in ecstasy as he fondled her.

At last she felt him gather the nightgown into his hands and with a gentle movement slip it over her head. Then she felt his hand sliding into her hair, tangling in the soft curls as he tipped her head back to expose her throat and rain kisses on it. His other hand was at her breast, teasing and tantalising artfully, evoking little gasps of pleasure from her. Slowly his lips moved lower, and lower, into the white valley between her breasts and then with a groan of triumph he closed his mouth hotly over one tightly furled, rosy little bud.

All that had gone before was as nothing to the jolt of fire that exploded through her now as she felt his tongue rasp over her nipple in a caress that robbed her of nearly all power to think. She gasped, writhing against him in ecstasy, arching her body in frantic pleading. The only thought that hammered through her veins was how much she wanted him.

She shivered in excitement as he urged her to lie back on the pillows, following her to lie half on top of her, one powerfully muscled thigh slipping to rest with suggestive intimacy between her legs. She could feel his arousal, rock hard, pressed against her. Opening her eyes, she gazed straight into his, burning with desire.

Holding her eyes trapped with his smouldering gaze, he stroked her stomach, his fingers teasing, tickling. And then lower, to drift lightly over the triangle of soft curls. She quivered, and her eyes widened as he deliberately placed his hand over her swelling mound in a gesture of intimate possession. She lay quite still and slowly, gently, he slid his long fingers between her legs to caress her tenderly.

His mouth took hers deeply, as his fingers explored the soft, yielding folds of flesh that melted in welcoming warmth. His tongue plundered in relentless, dizzying passion as he lay beside her and loved her with consummate, devastating skill for what seemed like an eternity. She was going to die, it was so beautiful...explode with the tension that was building inside her. Someone was sobbing...crying out in longing. Dimly she was aware that it was herself and that Marc had moved, was speaking to her.

'Open your eyes.' His voice was cracking with the

effort of restraint. If he was going to take her, it had to be now. Her response was so shattering, so complete. It scalded through his veins in racking desire... But he wanted her to know it was him and he had to give her one last chance to stop him...

She obeyed and stared straight up into his flaming eyes. He was lying between her legs, she could feel him hot and hard against her quivering, virgin body. His face was hard-edged with the pain of his longing, but she heard him say hoarsely, 'Meg, little one, you know what I want...are you sure? It will hurt...no matter how careful I am...there is no help for it the first time.'

Meg's eyes filled with tears. Even now he would stop. Even now he would let her change her mind, despite his own need. In that moment, as she fully realised his tender compassion, she yielded him her heart, completely and irrevocably. She loved him and she had only one thing to give him that he wanted...

Keeping her eyes upon his face she managed to say in a choked whisper, 'I am yours, Marc...please... please take me.'

And he did. With exquisite slowness he tenderly positioned himself, parting the soft flesh with gentle fingers, and then, as she clung to him in her inevitable fear, slid into her melting heat until he found the frail barrier of her innocence. Back and forth he moved, until her tension eased, until her body softened and arched against him in need. He breached her with one powerful thrust, sinking deeply and inexorably into her body. He groaned as he fought for control, as she shuddered under him at the hurt he was inflicting. He looked into her face. Her eyes were shut and her lower lip was clenched in her teeth in an effort to hold back the soft whimper of pain. It stabbed into him...gleaming and terrible.

He remained very still for a moment and when she relaxed a little he moved gently inside her with a sigh of pleasure. She gasped and her eyes flew open. He smiled down at her tenderly and said, 'Now you are mine,' as he moved again, as if unable to control his response to her yielding softness.

She knew exactly what he meant. He held her in thrall, his gentle motions were spellbinding. She clung to him as he lowered his mouth to hers and took it in a deeply erotic kiss, plundering and pillaging in complete possession as his loins rocked back and forth in the same compelling rhythm which swept her into a whirlpool of stunning sensation as the tension mounted until at last she cried out in ecstasy as wave after wave of passion broke over her and she was conscious of nothing but his body claiming hers forever.

He couldn't sleep. Meg lay safely clasped in his arms, a peaceful smile on her face as she slept, warm and secure. She had wept in his arms after their loving, shattered by the loveliness of what they had experienced. And he had kissed the tears away, unspeakably moved by her final, unconditional surrender. In resigning her maidenhead to him, she had given him an even lovelier gift; her complete trust.

Dimly he was aware that this was not what he had expected of marriage. He had thought to take an experienced woman to wife, not an innocent who had to be cherished and protected. Even when he had decided to take Meg, he had thought it would be a relatively simple matter. Bed her with the consideration due to her virginity, teach her to enjoy her marital duties and get on with his hedonistic life while granting her every possible indulgence.

He had not expected to take her in a burning of passion such as he had never experienced. A passion that left him dazed and confused with the knowledge that he wanted her more than he had ever wanted any woman. That possessing her had only increased his desire tenfold. Certainly he had not wanted to feel this shattering urge to protect and defend his wife. He had certainly not wanted to find himself caring about her any more than any other woman he had enjoyed in the course of a long and misspent career. Jack Hamilton's words came back hauntingly: *You'll think I've run mad…find a girl you can care for…* And he had laughed, told Jack he had slipped his moorings. Had thought the notion of risking the same grief his father had suffered to be rank insanity. And yet, here he was with Meg in his arms, rapidly finding her way into his barricaded and cynical heart. His blood ran cold as he recalled the chilly bargain he had struck with her. In return for his name and protection, he had asked for children and her discretion. Nothing more. And she had accepted him on those terms. He had not the slightest right to ask for anything else. He was by no means even sure that he wanted more, never had he felt so completely out of control in his life and the sensation was not at all an agreeable one, like a ship adrift in a storm. No, the best thing Lord Rutherford could do would be to return to London and try to get on with his life while allowing Meg to discover hers.

Chapter Seven

It took them another two days' travelling to reach London. By himself Marcus would have covered it easily in a day's driving, but the chaise was far slower. Besides which Meg slept well into the morning after their wedding night, not stirring even when Marcus left her bed to go down to breakfast. She was still sleeping when he came back after arranging a basket of food with the landlord.

It was another glorious day and he thought that a picnic somewhere for lunch would be pleasant. He was tolerably certain that Meg would feel happier if she did not have to deal with the world at large just yet. It was with relief that he learned Winterbourne had left very early. He was not entirely sure that he would have had the self-control to leave the cur with a whole skin and he certainly did not wish Meg to encounter him.

They set forward just after eleven with Meg perched up beside him in the curricle. She had been very quiet since arising and seemed very shy with him. Hardly surprising, he thought with tender amusement. She was not a chatterbox at the best of times, and with Burnet up behind them there was little opportunity for any private conversation.

Meg having breakfasted late, they did not halt for their picnic until well after two, driving down a lane between high hedges and spreading a rug under a beech tree. Burnet, who had hitherto maintained a proper distance, proved to be a very agreeable companion. He had been with Marcus for years and took the opportunity to make a speech and wish the bride happy, toasting her heroically with lemonade.

'Here's a health to a bonny bride, my lady! An' wishin' you very happy!' he finished cheerfully, raising his glass to her.

Meg blushed and stammered her thanks shyly. She had thought that Marc's servants might look down their noses at her, but the genuine goodwill in Burnet's face told her she had at least one friend.

Marcus clapped lazily and said with mock severity, 'I thank you, Burnet, for your approval. But do tell me! Do I not rank as worthy of your wishes for future happiness?'

Burnet grinned at him unrepentantly. 'As to that, sir, if you ain't happy now, you never will be! I'm happy to congratulate you howsumdever on gettin' a damned sight more than you deserve! Beggin' her ladyship's pardon!'

Marcus chuckled and said, 'Well, I'm glad you only speak your mind with such beautiful frankness out of hearing of the rest of my staff! Thank you, Burnet.'

He turned, to Meg who was giggling. His heart skyrocketed in his breast to see the laughter in her eyes again. She had been so quiet and reserved during their drive that he had been quite worried. 'This is the sort of insubordination I have to put up with, Lady

Rutherford! I am counting upon you to reform my unregenerate staff out of all recognition!'

After lunch Meg found that she was very sleepy and it did not take much persuasion to convince her to travel in the chaise. In fact, Marcus insisted.

'You may curl up on the seat and have a nap. We have another three hours before reaching our night's lodging,' he said firmly.

'But—'

He fixed her with a glare of mock severity and said, 'I have a distinct memory of you vowing to obey me yesterday morning! I'm trying to do my bit in cherishing you!' Then, very tenderly, 'Come, Meg. You will feel very much more the thing if you sleep in the chaise.'

His care for her was disconcerting and she raised her eyes shyly to his face. 'You know I am not really such a poor creature as you think, but if it will please you...'

'It won't,' he said frankly. 'I like having your company, but I will forgo it this afternoon if it means I may enjoy it tonight.' His eyes quizzed her wickedly and he touched her suddenly flaming cheek lightly, lingering at the corner of her mouth in sensuous reminiscence. Meg swallowed hard as the caress sent shivers down her spine. Perhaps it would be an idea to sit in the chaise. Even if she didn't sleep she needed to think, and sitting in the curricle with Marc's powerful body beside her seemed to disrupt her thought processes completely.

Having won his point, Marcus escorted her to the chaise and handed her up into it. She turned to smile at him, that shy, considering smile which turned his stomach upside down and made him want to kiss her senseless. He reached up and slid his fingers into the soft curls at her nape, stroking lightly and drawing her face down to him in a brief kiss.

'Until tonight, little one,' he whispered, his husky tones full of tantalising promise.

Meg sat back in the chaise, trying to collect her whirling thoughts and even more chaotic emotions. She had known from the start the danger of marriage to Marcus. Despite his occasional coldness, he had a charm and kindness that made it impossible not to respond to him. But she had not expected to succumb to it so swiftly, so completely.

It was not just his lovemaking. It was his tenderness with her, his compassionate understanding. Had he not taken her last night, she would have still loved him. The problem she now faced was that their physical intimacy would make it much harder for her to hide how she felt. And he did not want her love, had no intention of loving her. He had made that quite clear. They were not to make demands upon each other's sensibilities. And she had already made enough demands upon him. From now on she would have to try and stand alone.

Indeed, she was a great deal better off than she had been. She had a kind husband, a position in the world and a home. God willing she would have children on whom to spend her love. A tremor ran through her as she thought of how she would be given those children. She should be counting her blessings, not feeling depressed because one thing would be forever denied her! She had known the danger and had accepted it. It was just that in her inexperience she had not realised how much it would hurt.

And he must never know. Somehow she had to keep her guard up at all times to hide her secret. Perhaps leading a life of fashion would make it possible to conceal her love. She had heard much of how fashionable couples lived largely separate lives: attending their own functions, entertaining their own friends, taking lovers. She shuddered at the last. Never would she be able to bring herself to accept another. And it would hurt immeasurably to know that Marcus had a mistress.

A tear trickled down her cheek. She had agreed to it and she would have to pretend not to mind, not even to see. She would have to live the life he expected her to live. Perhaps when the children came she could be in the country for much of the year and not know what he was doing. Somehow the thought was not at all comforting.

Tired out and lulled by the rocking of the chaise, she lay down on the seat as Marcus had suggested and pulled the travelling rug over her. Perhaps she ought to sleep now. The last thing she wanted was for Marcus to decide she was too tired to share his bed.

That night, as she lay exhausted in his embrace, she wondered if she would need to have a rest every afternoon. It had not hurt at all this time. He had entered her with such gentle patience, urging her to stop him if she felt any pain. But all she had felt was wild excitement as his powerful body invaded hers and possessed it so tenderly, an excitement which had swelled and finally exploded in response to his loving. And this time he had encouraged her to join in, showing her how to please him, his delight in her pleasure and growing confidence reassuring her that in Marc she had the best of husbands.

Her body glowed with the aftermath of passion and, as she drifted towards sleep, she could feel his large, exquisitely knowing hands soothing and stroking her.

One muscular leg was thrust between her thighs in possessive intimacy. His deep voice murmured soft endearments as she pressed sleepy kisses against his shoulder, thinking that even if he didn't love her, at least he seemed to care about her. Half a loaf was better than none, after all. Wasn't it?

Chapter Eight

The following afternoon the Countess of Rutherford preserved a friendly smile, as one stiffly polite servant after another was presented to her in the great hall of Rutherford House, an imposing mansion in Grosvenor Square. By the time the maidservants had been presented in a group she was wilting mentally under the glare of the staff's unspoken disapproval.

As she recalled her husband's laughing suggestion that she should reform his staff, she shuddered inwardly. It was plain enough that they held their master in the greatest awe and affection while respectfully opining that, in marrying a provincial nobody with a family history like hers, the master had taken leave of his senses. She stole a scared look up at Marcus, who looked quite unperturbed. His aristocratic countenance gave no hint that he was aware of the unmistakable outrage among his staff.

Once the ordeal was over Marcus escorted her to her bedchamber and said, 'Here you are. This was my mother's room. Why don't you have a rest before changing for dinner? I am going to go around to Mount

Street to let my sister know that we are in town. I will ask her to call on you in the morning if you wish.'

'You don't wish me to come now?' Meg asked hesitantly.

He shook his head. 'No, it is for Di to call on you.' She flushed slightly and he added reassuringly, 'Meg, I am not ashamed of you. But I think under the circumstances it might be as well if I saw Di first. Come...' he held out his arms '...give me a kiss and I will be off.'

Meg went to him, trying to hide her eagerness. Their lips met and clung briefly and then Marcus was gone, leaving Meg feeling utterly lost and quite unlike sleeping. She was so stunned by the elegance of her surroundings that her tiredness had vanished to be replaced with an overwhelming urge to explore.

She looked around her with wide eyes. Never in all her life had she seen such a sumptuous bedchamber. The wall hangings were of a delicate violet silk with a printed black border and buff silk pelmet. A very graceful chimney piece in white marble held a number of beautiful and obviously valuable examples of oriental porcelain as well as an ornate clock, with an elaborate gilt mirror surmounting all.

The bed was such a contrast to the old-fashioned and clumsy four poster she had been used to that Meg could hardly believe this fairytale confection was to be used by a mortal woman. Black with gilt mounts, it had a domed canopy, the deeply fringed, white-muslin drapes spangled with gold stars and seemingly suspended from a gilt Cupid.

Meg blinked. Was it possible one was actually meant to *sleep* in this creation? She could not, for the life of her, imagine unsophisticated Meg Fellowes doing anything of the sort! With a blush she realised that she was having no difficulty at all imagining the other sorts of things the new Countess of Rutherford might be called upon to do in this bed.

Hurriedly she fixed her attention on the rest of the furnishings. A very charming inlaid fold-over tea table stood behind a gilt sofa, and matching chairs upholstered in the same hue as the wall hangings stood grouped before the fireplace. A dainty dressing table and stool completed the furnishings. Several candelabra were scattered about, presently empty. No doubt the servants would bring the candles in later. Meg did not for one moment, in the face of all this luxury, entertain the least doubt that they would be wax, rather than the tallow to which she had hitherto been accustomed.

A respectful tap at the door distracted her from a delightful daydream in which her late and unlamented guardian totted up the bill for all this feminine froth and suffered a very gratifying seizure in the process.

'Come in,' called Meg, trying not to giggle.

A maidservant entered and said, 'If you please, m' lady, your luggage is being brought up and I am here to unpack for you.'

'Oh, how very kind, thank you so much,' said Meg with a friendly smile which was received with patent surprise by the maid. Oh, dear, thought Meg. Should I not thank her? But how rude not to, even if she is a servant. I always thanked Agnes.

The mention of unpacking made her look around for somewhere to put the unpacked gowns. A puzzled frown creased her brow as no closets or armoires met her eyes.

Before she could stop herself she asked, 'But

where…?' And then blushed with mortification as the maid silently pointed to another door.

'Oh, th…thank you,' said Lady Rutherford, feeling more and more like ignorant, countrified Meg Fellowes. A dressing room! How many more gaffes was she destined to make? Would they be talked over and sneered at in the servants' hall?

It was at this point that the previously suspicious maid realised that her new mistress was not a scheming hussy at all but, on the contrary, a young lady in a very unfamiliar and daunting situation. Without wishing to compare herself with her betters, Lucy Brown was put forcibly in mind of her first meal in the servants' hall when she had accidentally sat in the seat reserved for the head housemaid and had found herself sent to Coventry for the entire repast in consequence of this appalling solecism.

'Never you mind, m' lady,' said Lucy cheerfully. 'I dare say things is different in Yorkshire.'

'Just…just a little,' said Meg with relief at this sudden change. 'Are there any more little surprises for me?'

'Bathroom's through that other door,' offered Lucy. 'And his lordship's room beyond it.'

Meg stared at her. She shared a *bathroom* with her husband? A *bathroom*? The very idea was completely and utterly scandalous. And terribly intriguing. Had not Marcus said that this had been his mother's room? Meg was beginning to get some very interesting insights into her deceased mother-in-law.

Unable to resist, she went over to the door indicated and opened it.

And could not repress a startled squeak of shock.

A vision of subtle eggshell blue, laced with tastefully gilded mouldings, greeted her stunned gaze, hexagonal in shape with another door directly opposite hers, leading, she presumed, to her husband's bedchamber. Benches covered in more fringed white muslin stood in four niches. One side of the hexagon was taken up with a large window draped with some gauzy white material, which softened rather than blocked the light. A large alcove opposite the window was entirely taken up with an extremely elegant, canopied sofa-bed, hung with ivory silk and upholstered in silk damask the same shade as the walls. It seemed an odd item of furniture to have in a bathroom, but the bath itself was far too interesting to waste time worrying about details like that.

It was a very large, circular bath, sunk into the centre of the cream-tiled floor. In fact, it was so large that Meg had no difficulty believing that it would hold two quite easily. She cast another lingering look at that sofa-bed…and hastily returned her attention to the bath. Six small bronze lions' heads were set around it at intervals, their mouths wide open. Goodness! Did the water come out of them? How very ingenious! A lever at the side of the chamber caught her eye. She bent down to try it and sure enough water came pouring out. Meg took a deep breath as she considered the possibilities of such a bath…and the sofa-bed…

Blushing furiously at the scene her rioting imagination had conjured up, Meg turned to the decoration of the niches. Classical scenes adorned them, which seemed innocent enough until she looked more closely. The pointed oval-and-cameo decoration of the pilasters comprised dancing nymphs and satyrs, while the large central panels held scenes which even the innocent Meg recognised as well-known classical seductions.

In scarlet-cheeked fascination she examined them one

by one: Danaë and the shower of gold, Leda and the Swan, Persephone being swept up into Hades's dread chariot and, finally, Europa and the Bull. Had this room really been decorated for Marcus's mama? And did Marcus expect her to use it? Did he use it? The possibilities made her feel distinctly wobbly at the knees.

A discreet cough behind her recalled her scattered wits. She turned to see her maid with an unnaturally straight face in the doorway.

'Shall I unpack, my lady? Your luggage has been brought up.'

'What? Oh. Oh, yes. Thank you…?' She ended on a faintly questioning note.

'Lucy,' supplied the maid.

'Lucy,' repeated Meg to impress the name on her memory. 'Yes. Unpacking. A very good idea.' She marched straight back through to her dressing room, leaving that scandalous bathroom behind her. Unfortunately the equally scandalous images it had conjured up refused to remain behind, following her into the bedroom where they intruded on her thoughts with unflagging enthusiasm while she assisted Lucy to put her clothes away. Her precious tea caddy was unearthed from one trunk and Meg placed it proudly on the tea table, where she could see it from the bed. Her hands caressed it lovingly. Her first present.

By the time they were finished it was well after five. Dinner, Lucy informed her, had been ordered for half-past seven. If my lady wanted a nap she had best have it now, since she would need to dress for dinner and leave enough time to put her hair up.

Lucy explained this very tactfully, adding, 'I will come back in an hour to wake you and help you, m' lady. Mrs Crouch, the housekeeper, said as I'm to wait on you until you get a proper dresser, like all the fine ladies have.'

'Thank you,' said Meg, acquiescing in the first part of this suggestion. She was not so sure about a proper dresser. She had better ask Marcus, but personally she would far prefer the simple, kindly Lucy to wait on her, rather than a grand dresser who would probably compare her unfavourably with previous employers. Meg was reasonably sure that, despite her unexpected elevation, she could remember how to look after herself.

Yawning, she permitted Lucy to help her off with her carriage dress and snuggled down in her fantastical bed, which added extreme comfort to its aesthetic charms, in her petticoat and chemise. Silk sheets and pillow slips! Goodness! Meg wriggled against them in voluptuous pleasure as Lucy drew the gorgeously draped ivory-brocade curtains. Within minutes she was fast asleep and dreaming.

In the meantime her husband had called upon his sister and was listening patiently to a blistering condemnation of his intelligence, morals and manners.

She received Marcus in her drawing room and, once her unconvincingly disinterested butler had closed the door, glared at Marcus and asked furiously, 'What the *devil* did you mean by sending me that letter, telling me to insert the announcement of your marriage to Miss Marguerite Fellowes in yesterday's papers? Do you have any idea of the scandal broth you have whipped up? Do you have any idea of the number of people who have taken such sympathetic pleasure in condoling with me on the tragic *mésalliance* my only brother has made?

'You *idiot*, Marc! Do you realise what people are saying? That Robert and Caroline Fellowes's daughter entrapped you! How did you of all men fall for such a trick? Aunt Regina has retired to Bath in hysterics!'

'Well, thank God for that!' interjected the afflicted lady's undutiful nephew heartlessly. 'One furious female relation is more than enough to deal with at once!'

She swept on, very properly ignoring this facetious remark. 'And if you had any *notion* of the embarrassment I felt in not understanding the *commiserations* I received! It was not until Jack Hamilton enlightened me that I realised who the girl was! And not even to be invited!' She paused for breath and a perfectly genuine tear trickled down her cheek. The last thing she had wanted for Marcus was marriage to some scheming little hussy!

'Tell me, Di,' said Marcus with a faint twinkle that made her itch to slap him, 'how long did it take you to calm down this much?'

She fixed him with a sizzling glare and said dangerously, 'I'm acting, Marc. I haven't calmed down! *You* may choose to think it funny! *I* do not!'

'Very well, Di,' said Marcus ruefully. 'You have made your point. Now, would it be too much to ask you to let me explain? Meg did not entrap me in any way whatsoever. In fact, she did her level best not to accept anything from me, let alone my name! And I'm sorry about the late notice, but the last thing I wanted was Aunt Regina to appear and scare Meg into crying off.'

Di looked up at him sharply. He did not bear any signs of a man forced into an unwanted marriage. On the contrary, he looked quite cheerful and relaxed as he stood twinkling at her. And she could definitely see his point about the redoubtable Lady Grafton, since she had, on hearing the news, shrieked for her travelling chaise, saying that she would send the little hussy about her business in double-quick time. Only the realisation that the wedding would have taken place before she could reach Yorkshire had stopped her. By that stage she had been packed, so, to save face with her agog staff, she had directed her coachman to Bath.

'Very well, tell me the worst,' she said resignedly.

By the time Marcus had told her about how he had discovered Meg, she was beginning to see daylight. Marc and his overdeveloped sense of duty! Meg's flight made her blink. Was the girl mad? The tale of Mrs Garsby's inhumanity shocked her greatly and by then Marc's decision to marry had her full, if reluctant, approval.

'I see,' she said thoughtfully. 'And she accepted.'

Marcus outlined the terms of his marriage much as he had done to Meg and his sister winced inwardly. Good God! What a recipe for disaster! No matter what he might think now, Marc was not the man to acquiesce quietly if his wife took a lover. Just look at all the mistresses he had broken with after they had taken a tumble with Sir Blaise Winterbourne. Although that might simply be because he despised the oily baronet for some reason to which she had never been privy. Nevertheless, Di could not see Marc in the role of complaisant husband.

And what of the child he had married? From the sounds of it she had accepted out of desperation, having nowhere else to turn. What was her attitude towards the marriage? Did she care for Marc at all? Understand what she had let herself in for?

Di's assumption that Marc had been trapped was abandoned. Marc would know if he had been tricked. No fool her cynical, rakish brother. He might have accepted the inevitable, but it would have been with his eyes fully open and he would not have been able to hide it from her. Certainly he would not be here, championing a scheming adventuress.

Looking up at Marcus with a softened face Di said, 'Then I shall call upon your bride tomorrow morning, little brother. Be happy, my dear.'

He returned her smile and said oddly, 'Do you know, I almost think I will be.' He saluted her cheek and took his leave of her.

Di stared at the closed door, her mind full of speculation. Marc, of all men, to wear that dazed, uncertain expression on that hitherto-bored mask he presented to the world at large! Was he finally going to realise that it was not necessarily a death sentence to care for someone?

She went upstairs in a thoughtful mood to dress for dinner. Clasping her sapphires around her neck, she suddenly wondered if Marc was even aware of how different he seemed. She had never heard him speak of anyone with such feeling, never known him to express such anger. Yet he seemed to think he had acted on the promptings of duty and logic. Had he even hoaxed himself with his aloof façade?

Marcus walked home thoughtfully. Di had really taken it very well. He only hoped his formidable Aunt Regina could be won over as easily. He hoped to God she meant to stay in Bath until she had calmed down. Now he would go home and change for dinner. It was after six and he did not care to sit down with his bride for their first formal dinner together looking anything less than immaculate. He hoped that Meg had taken his advice and rested. She had looked tired, poor girl. With a twitch of his lips he wondered just what his innocent bride had thought of her bedchamber. And their bathroom.

His steps slowed as he remembered the outrageous woman who had designed that bedchamber and had the bathroom installed. His heart lurched painfully and he strode on quickly, as if to leave the hurt behind.

The tapping on her door awoke Meg after what seemed like five minutes' sleep in her cosy, silken nest. She yawned and stretched, then tweaked the curtains aside to look at the clock. Half-past six! Already!

'Come in,' she called.

Lucy bustled in with a large jug of water and said, 'I brought some warm water for you to wash with, m'lady. Unless you'd like a bath drawn? I've had the water heater lit so…'

Meg thought about that. It was tempting, but if dinner was in an hour she would have to rush and she had an uncharacteristically hedonistic desire to positively wallow in the steamy luxury of that bath. No, she would have a bath before retiring for the night. Then she could take her time.

She shook her head. 'I shall take a bath before going to bed.'

'Yes, m'lady. Now, which dress will your ladyship wear?'

Which dress indeed? Never before had Meg concerned herself in the slightest about her clothes since they were all equally dowdy. Except, of course, in wishing they were not so dowdy. Now she had a wardrobe in the first style of elegance and she had no idea what to wear. For the last two nights she and Marcus had not bothered to change for dinner since they were travelling. Now she would sit down to dinner for the first time in her new home and she wanted Marcus to be proud of her.

She went through to the dressing room and looked at the three gowns which Madame Heloise had designated for evening wear. There was really no question. A gown of shimmering blue silk with an embroidered bodice, to be worn over an underdress of ivory satin, simply begged to be chosen. The colour very closely approximated the wall hangings of her bedchamber.

'This one,' said Meg firmly.

Lucy took the gown reverently, saying, 'Oh, it's *lovely*! It will make your eyes look so blue, m'lady!' She carried it into the bedchamber, laid it on the bed and turned to her mistress.

Lady Rutherford took a deep breath and steeled herself to being waited on hand and foot.

Floating down the stairs fifty minutes later, she thought to herself that she could get used to it very easily. It was not that she had permitted Lucy to attend her like a Roman bath slave, but that it was very pleasant to have someone to make suggestions, pass things to her that she didn't even know were there…like that violet-scented soap Lucy had found. And it was lovely to have someone tell her how nice she looked! Not that she really believed it. The gown was lovely and having her hair swept up into a knot on top of her head with the soft curls falling from it was certainly very pretty, but surely she was still plain Meg Fellowes.

When she reached the hall she hesitated, unsure of where she was meant to be. Before she could panic, however, the stately individual she remembered to be the butler, Delafield, appeared from some fastness and bowed low to her.

'His lordship's compliments, my lady, and he would like you to await him in the library.'

My lady. Meg almost looked around to see if he were speaking to someone else. It didn't seem possible that he could mean her.

'The library?' she faltered.

He inclined his head. 'If your ladyship would follow me.'

He led her to a huge mahogany door which he opened to usher her in, saying, 'His lordship will be down directly. May I pour a glass of ratafia for your ladyship?'

A deep voice came from halfway up the stairs. 'No, you may not, you old villain! You may leave me to pour my lady a glass of Madeira. Ratafia, indeed! I didn't think we had any of the filthy stuff!'

The look of stern disapproval, warring ineffectually with pride, on the old man's face told Meg that Marcus, though he might be a grown man and a belted earl to boot, was still an overgrown schoolboy to Delafield.

The butler's outraged response confirmed it. 'Ratafia, my lord, is a suitable drink for a lady.'

'You go and tell that to my mother's shade,' recommended Marcus disrespectfully.

Delafield's lips twitched but he bowed and said in quelling accents, 'As your lordship pleases.'

Marcus grinned as he reached the bottom of the stairs, and said, 'Give us fifteen minutes, Delafield. I have a present for her ladyship.'

He followed Meg into the room and looked her over admiringly. The gown was cut in the classical high-waisted style, outlining the soft curve of her breasts. Alternately clinging and drifting, the filmy skirts revealed and concealed the lovely, long legs in a way that made his breath tangle in his throat. The narrow cut made them look even longer. The squared neck line with its *rouleau* was quite discreet, but it was shaped to follow the delicate curve of her breasts, coming down very subtly to a point between them, so the veriest suspicion of voluptuous cleavage was displayed. Tiny puffed sleeves left the graciously rounded, creamy arms bare. And her hairstyle accentuated the graceful line of her ivory throat.

That was quite enough, thought Marcus dizzily. Anything more and he'd be gibbering like a moonstruck halfling! As it was, all he could think of was how those arms had wrapped themselves about him, how he had pressed kisses on that lovely throat, feeling her soft moans vibrate under his lips. He had had some odd idea that the innocently sensuous siren who had shared his bed for the last two nights would be somehow invisible to the rest of the world. That no one else would see what he had seen in Meg. In the face of this celestial vision, shimmering before him in blue silk, he rapidly revised his opinion.

Dowdy little Meg had blossomed into a swan. Admittedly she had looked far more presentable in her elegant carriage dress the last three days and quite lovely in her wedding dress, but this! Any man who couldn't see what he saw was blind. Abruptly he turned away to a console table to pour her a glass of wine.

Meg watched him nervously. Something was wrong. He was staring at her as though he had been struck dumb. Was the gown ill fitting? Ugly? Was she wearing it back to front? Or was it her hair? That was it! She wished she had not let Lucy persuade her into this mode. She felt so dreadfully exposed…but wait, he was saying something.

He turned back to her and handed her the Madeira.

'Your health, my lady. You…you look quite…lovely my dear.' He had to clear his throat twice to complete the sentence. What an inadequate remark, he thought ruefully. It was the understatement of the century. And the sudden glowing look in her eyes was doing impossible and dreadful things to his heart and stomach. The two organs seemed to have got themselves inextricably confused. He had never in his life felt so wildly, gloriously out of control.

Desperately he reached for his usual sangfroid and said, with a tolerable assumption of calm, 'Yes, that gown suits you.' He told himself he was relieved to see the glow of joy fade very slightly. He did not want to feel like this! It was dangerous for both of them. They had made a bargain about how they should chart their course through marriage. He must not tip the delicate balance, not if he wanted his marriage to fulfil his expectations.

'Th…thank you, my lord,' said Meg in a low voice.

Marcus frowned slightly. He had not meant to be *that* forbidding; still, perhaps it was as well. The difficulty of maintaining the sort of relationship he had intended would be doubled if she were to look at him like that too often. Better if he saved his compliments and tenderness for the bedchamber. There at least he could be himself with her. She was too sweet and yielding in his arms, had trusted him too unreservedly, for anything else to be possible.

Belatedly he remembered that he had a present for her. 'I have a gift for you my lady,' he said politely, reinforcing her sudden formality. He walked over to the small Pembroke table which stood behind the sofa and opened the drawer, taking out a long, flat, wooden box. He turned to her and beckoned.

Shyly she went to him, wondering what he had for her. Not another tea caddy, obviously.

Then she gasped as he opened the box and drew out a long rope of shimmering pearls. She stood transfixed as he clasped them around her throat. Surely he could not mean such an expensive gift for her! It was unthinkable!

It was even more unthinkable when a moment later, after viewing with satisfaction the effect of the pearls against the blue silk, he reached into the box again and produced a pair of earrings which he screwed into her ears with surprising assurance. Another dip into the box and he was clasping a bracelet about her wrist.

'My…my lord, you cannot give me these…I…' Meg was overwhelmed. She stared at the glimmering pearls on her breasts and at her wrist.

'Why not?' he asked in surprise. 'They are always given to the brides in my family. Have been for three generations. You are the fourth countess to wear them.'

'Oh.' Meg looked up at him apologetically. 'I beg your pardon. I…I didn't understand.' She had thought he was giving them to her for her very own, and the thought was terrifying. But he was bowing to tradition, wished his bride to present a creditable appearance, no doubt. They were to adorn his bride; not a present for Meg. She stifled the longing for something of her own, not jewellery, just…something…something from Marc, rather than the Earl of Rutherford, as the tea caddy had been.

He was frowning again. Why the hell should she mind being given jewellery? She hadn't been wearing any, except her wedding ring, of course, and he'd wager if she had any it would not be the sort of jewellery that Lady Rutherford should wear. Mere trumpery, no doubt! And in his experience no woman ever minded being given jewellery. Most of 'em had any number of hoaxing ways to cajole a new jewel out of a man.

He acquitted his bride of hoaxing ways, but he did wish she looked a little more enthusiastic at the priceless articles with which he had just adorned her. Could she not see how well they looked on her? On reflection he realised that she probably couldn't.

'Come with me,' he said firmly and, gripping her shoulders, practically frogmarched her towards a console table over which hung an elderly looking-glass with a battered gilt frame.

'Now, look at yourself.'

Marcus discovered that, unlike the basilisk, Meg's wide-eyed stare did not lose a jot of its heart-stopping power in the glass. Rather it seemed to double because he was seeing her startled reaction to herself. And then he could see the disbelief on her face, the look of puzzled confusion.

'That's not me…is it?' She glanced up to meet his eyes in the mirror. He could barely hear her next words, so softly were they uttered. 'That's Lady Rutherford.'

He stared down at her sharply. 'I beg your pardon, Meg?'

An odd little tremor ran through her. 'Nothing. I…nothing.' She sounded oddly dazed, as though the mirror had shown her a stranger. 'Thank you, Marcus.' Hesitantly her hand lifted to touch the necklace briefly. 'They are beautiful.'

For the first time, as he gazed at the reflected vision of his bride adorned in the family jewels, Marcus understood why pearls were considered so suitable for a young girl or bride. Their chaste beauty was the perfect foil for Meg's unselfconscious loveliness. He had seen these jewels countless times before, since his mother had loved the set, but never had they looked more right than they did at this moment.

Forgetting his resolve to keep tenderness strictly for the bedchamber, he gave her shoulders a gentle squeeze and pressed a kiss below her ear. 'You look beautiful, my sweet. And you make the pearls look beautiful.' He felt the tumultuous pulse in her neck and released her with difficulty.

'Drink up, Meg,' he said, moving away from her. 'Dinner will be served shortly.' For God's sake! Could he not keep his hands off her for five minutes? Tonight at least he should leave her to sleep undisturbed. She could have no fears in his…their…house. He was within call if she needed to find him in the night. Theirs was to be a marriage of convenience. As such it was ridiculous to expect her to share his bed every night.

Meg sipped her Madeira and found to her surprise that she liked it. She smiled at Marcus over the glass and said, 'It's lovely, thank you. And thank you for the pearls. I have never worn jewellery at all, so…' She stopped, embarrassed. It would never do for him to think she was begging for more.

He shrugged. 'There is quite a collection of family jewellery. I selected the pearls because I thought they were bound to go with whatever you chose to wear tonight. The rest all needs cleaning, it hasn't been worn in years.'

Not since his mother had died, in fact. He flinched inwardly as he thought of the lovely, laughing creature who had gone from his life so unexpectedly… He tried not to think of her too often, but seeing Meg decked in those pearls, thinking of her sleeping in that silken apartment, bathing in that outrageous bathroom…

suddenly his mother's piquant, laughing face was before
him and would not be banished. What would she have
thought of her daughter-in-law? Another question struck
at him brutally: What would she have thought of her
son?

Not for several minutes did Marcus become aware
that Meg had set down her empty glass and stepped
away from him to the fireplace, where she was examining the painting of Alston Court, his principal country
residence, that hung above it. He flushed slightly. How
very rude of him to just ignore her like that so that she
felt obliged to occupy herself! And if she had finished
her wine, he must have been in a brown study for some
time.

Before he could apologise the door opened and
Delafield announced, 'Dinner is served, my lord and
lady.'

Dinner, as Meg found, was a very formal and nerve-
racking affair. Marcus described it as a neat, plain dinner, but Meg could think of no two adjectives more
completely inappropriate for a meal that consisted of
two courses of at least half a dozen dishes each. She
found it quite bizarre to be seated at the same table as
her husband with twenty feet of highly polished mahogany between them and to have a footman at her
elbow every time she showed the least interest in one
of the dishes before her.

This, however, was what Marcus expected of her, so
she assumed an air of enjoyment and bravely lifted her
voice in order to be heard when she replied to her husband's polite conversation. She wondered what he
would say if she suggested removing some of the leaves
from the table when they dined alone. Perhaps it might

be better to wait until she was more familiar with the household before embarking upon such radical reform.

Had she but known it, Marcus was not enjoying it in the least. It had always been his custom when dining alone, or with one or two close friends, to have dinner set out on a table in the library where they could serve themselves. He had been quite taken aback when he had realised that his staff had quite different ideas now he had taken a wife. Plainly they were set on doing the thing properly with the maximum of pomp.

It was on the tip of his tongue to inform Delafield that he had no intention of changing his habits just because he had married, when it occurred to him that a seemingly endless expanse of polished mahogany was one way to keep a polite distance from his wife. If they dined intimately tête à tête in the library, it would be very much harder to hold her at arm's length.

So he held his tongue and resigned himself to the tedium of dining formally every night. He supposed ruefully that he could not expect to maintain all his bachelor habits now that he was married. Which reminded him that he had yet to make a decision about Althea Hartleigh.

Thoughtfully he accepted a helping of syllabub as he pondered this ticklish question. Should he maintain the connection or…? A slight movement at the far end of the table caught his eye. Delafield was refilling Meg's glass. She turned to him with a slight smile and soft word of thanks. The pearls at her throat shone softly in the candlelight… He had nearly asked Althea to marry him…how would she have looked in those pearls? With a shock he realised that he could not imagine her in them. He would not have even thought of giving them to her.

Conscious of his gaze, Meg looked up from her syllabub. He was frowning slightly and she lifted her chin proudly. She would not flinch before his glare. If she was doing something wrong then he should not have half a mile of dining table between them, preventing him from tactfully pointing it out to her!

Defiantly she finished her sweet and her wine and watched as the footmen began to remove the dishes from the table. She knew exactly what she had to do and rose from her seat gracefully.

'I shall leave you to the enjoyment of your wine, my lord.'

Her voice rang out clearly, taking Marcus by surprise. He hurried to his feet and went to open the door for her. She looked absolutely lovely, but so reserved, remote.

'Goodnight, my lady,' he said quietly. 'I shall leave you to your rest tonight.' It was said very softly, for her ears only. Her eyes flew to his face. For one split second he thought he saw hurt there, but it was gone instantly.

Her voice, cool and unconcerned, 'You are always considerate, my lord.'

She was gone and Marcus went back to his chair to confront an array of decanters. He stared at them unseeingly. Considerate? *Considerate?* He didn't feel remotely considerate. What he felt like was following her upstairs and showing her just how *in*considerate he could be! He heaved a sigh of resignation. He wanted a cool, uninvolved relationship with his wife. He could hardly complain when she obliged. If she had taken the hint so readily, it would save him having to explain it to her. Somehow he thought the task might have proved difficult.

After leaving the dining room, Meg pondered her options. It was far too early for bed, even if his lordship had dismissed her for the night. She had only just eaten and she didn't feel in the least bit sleepy after her nap. She would go and find a book in the library, retire to her bedchamber and read for a while, then she would have a long, luxurious soak in that bath. She might even read in it. There were all sorts of possibilities that didn't involve her infuriating husband. And why the devil should he get to sit in solitary state over his wine? Why could she not have a glass with him and chat? All these rules and formalities gave her a headache!

She had no difficulty finding a book in the library. There were several shelves devoted to novels and she selected quite a few before turning her attention to the poetry. Here she browsed happily, finding old friends and meeting new ones. Almost the only alleviating feature of her residence at Fenby House had been its library, which she had been permitted to visit weekly to select reading matter. Novels, however, had not previously come in her way and she could hardly wait to get back upstairs and open one.

Marcus spent a solitary and lengthy evening by the fire in the library, attempting to read. Never had his cosy, welcoming library seemed so utterly bereft of comfort, so empty. He wandered along the bookshelves, seeking something more entertaining than Carey's translation of the *Inferno*, noting Meg's depredations as he did so. What had she taken? Mostly poetry, but a few of his mother's novels as well. He smiled. No doubt she would enjoy Hatchard's and Hookham's. He must take her to both… He caught himself up sharply. Meg would be quite capable of finding her own way around…he was not going to sit in her pocket.

He glanced frequently at his watch and eventually, realising that he had not turned a page for the past ten minutes and that it was half-past ten, decided to retire. After all, he had been driving all day. An early night would not hurt him. He thrust away the thought that, despite retiring early for the last two nights, he was a trifle short on sleep.

In his bedchamber he found his nightshirt laid out ready, the bed turned down, everything as it should be. Yet he hesitated. The bed was enormous. A huge, old-fashioned four poster. The Earls of Rutherford had slept in it and bedded their brides in it for generations. No matter what else might be brought up to date and modernised in the London house, the Earl's bed remained, a monument to generations of feudal privilege. Unfortunately it was empty and it looked damned chilly and uninviting. Which was ridiculous, since he knew perfectly well that his valet would have passed a warming pan through it as soon as he knew his master was on his way to bed.

Marcus swore fluently. The only thing that was going to warm that bed to his satisfaction in the foreseeable future was Meg. And the thought infuriated him. He did not wish to be held in thrall by his wife's charms. Surely he could control his desire for at least one night! He had shared her bed for the last *two* nights, for heaven's sake. What more did he want? And she had seemed happy enough with his intimation that he did not wish to avail himself of his…rights—he found the word *rights* rather unpleasant…as though he could take her when and as he pleased without any regard to her wishes. No doubt Winterbourne had thought he had the *right* to force himself on an unknown girl.

He should at least check that she was comfortable

and happy in her room, and know that he was within call. No doubt she was sound asleep by now, but if she wasn't, he could just tell her that…that he was near by, would come if she needed anything.

He pulled on his dressing gown and padded on bare, silent feet to the bathroom door, finding it slightly ajar. He pushed it open and stopped dead, his eyes almost popping out of his head in shock.

It was not dark as he had expected. A brass oil lamp set on a stand cast a golden glow over the chamber, creating mysterious shadows within the sofa-bed and glinting on the gilded mouldings. But that was not all. It shone with a tender radiance on something much softer, something infinitely alluring and utterly desirable…

His bride was lazing in the bath with her back to him, her hair tucked up on top of her head with a tortoiseshell comb, one ivory arm outstretched as she languidly soaped it. Her head was resting on the edge of the bath as she half-sat, half-floated in the water. Her breasts gleamed as the lamplight slid over her wet skin, which shimmered between pink-tinged ivory and gold. Steam drifted upward from the surface of the water, catching the light as it twisted and wreathed in the draught from the door.

Marcus found that he was scarcely breathing and he would not have been at all surprised to find steam escaping from his ears. Never in his entire life had he been confronted by anything so incredibly, so deliciously erotic. He watched in something approaching agony as Meg, all unknowing, soaped her breasts, her stomach and then lifted one slender leg out of the water and casually soaped that.

His mouth was absolutely dry, his tongue practically

cleaving to the roof as his body registered what he was seeing. All his noble and unconvincing waffle about leaving her to sleep peacefully was incinerated in the volcano of desire that erupted inside him.

He licked his lips and, striving to sound matter of fact, said, 'May I join you, Meg?'

She spun around with a shocked exclamation, sending water swirling across the floor. Her dark eyes were wide and the blush on her cheeks did not stop there, he noted with wicked satisfaction.

'J…join me? In the bath, do you mean?' Her voice was a breathless squeak.

'Mmm,' said Marcus with a lazy smile. 'I understand that was what my mother had in mind when she persuaded my father to have it installed…' His smile held her captive as he shrugged off his dressing gown and tossed it on to one of the benches.

Meg could not tear her eyes away as he slowly removed his nightshirt. Even though he had shared her bed for two nights, she still caught her breath at the sight of his magnificent, naked body. It seemed so impossible that such strength could be allied to such gentleness, such tender skill. And his desire was so obvious, so flagrantly and potently obvious! She trembled as he lowered himself into the water beside her. Somehow this was far more frightening than the intimacy of bed. There at least she knew roughly what to expect now!

He was reaching for the soap and sponge. She watched him nervously. Was he just going to wash himself? She relaxed slightly and then gasped as he reached for her, a seductive twinkle in his eyes.

'But I…I washed already…' she faltered as she felt him begin to soap her arm. Surely he wasn't going to…he couldn't be!

'Did you?' he asked politely. 'Are you sure you washed…everywhere?' The sponge slid over her breasts, his fingers teased over the rosy peaks as his free arm slipped around her to draw her closer, silencing her half-hearted murmur of protest with a gentle kiss. Meg shut her eyes and gave herself up to the exquisite sensations he aroused as he washed her with intimate thoroughness. First her breasts, with slow, circling strokes, grazing over the suddenly taut nipples with agonising delicacy, then her shoulders and arms and back across her breasts to the gentle swell of her stomach, sensuous, sweeping motions that left her gasping and dizzy.

She felt him ease her across his lap and lay unresisting in the curve of his arm as he reached down and began to soap her legs. So lightly, so possessively, in some strange way she felt that he was cleansing the last faint traces of Winterbourne's vile touch from her body. Her eyes were closed, her lips slightly parted and she could only marvel at the riot of sensation he was evoking in her body. Her mind had long since ceased to function.

Marcus gazed down at his wife's blissful face resting against his shoulder, the dark, curling lashes lay softly on her cheek and damp curls clung to her brow. He kissed them away. God, she was so lovely! The lamplight gleamed on her soap-slicked body, gilding it rosegold. He rinsed the soap off and, with a groan of pleasure, lowered his lips to her waiting mouth.

His senses seemed to explode as he tasted her sweetness, felt the soft lips part in willing surrender. He deepened the kiss as he tangled his fingers in the wet curls at the base of her stomach, teasing, probing her melting warmth in possessive intimacy. Her body arched in shuddering response, leaving him in no doubt of her desire.

Controlling his immediate, instinctive response with difficulty, Marcus continued to tantalise and caress until she writhed in his embrace, turning in his arms to cling to him, her body pressed against his in flagrant need. Her small hands moved over his heavily muscled shoulders and back in shy exploration, tangled in his hair as she gave way to the inferno he had ignited within her.

At last he could stand no more. His body, white hot with desire, was screaming for release, to feel her lissom body under his, arching, pleading for his possession. He broke the kiss and stood up, drawing her with him, the water pouring off them as he assisted her from the bath and scooped her up in his arms.

Her mind completely drugged by his mouth and hands, Meg barely registered that her suspicions about the sofa bed had been quite correct as she was laid tenderly on the silken covers. She reached for him with a smile as he lowered himself to her. He hovered over her for a moment and pulled the comb from her curls, releasing them to tumble in chaotic abandon over the bed. And then his mouth was on hers again, fierce and demanding as he pressed her thighs apart and joined them with a single thrust of his powerful body.

His harsh gasps entwined with her soft cries in the tender counterpoint of passion, finally reaching an overwhelming crescendo as they soared together in the ecstasy of their joy.

When Marcus could at last bring himself to draw away from his wife's body, he wrapped her tenderly in a towel and carried her through to his own chamber where his bed awaited them. He had no intention of having to come looking for his bride in the middle of the night. That would be far too revealing.

Chapter Nine

Returning to her own room at an advanced hour of the morning, Meg blushed to find her maid there already. With an inward groan she remembered that she had asked Lucy to come up at nine. In future, she would arrange to ring. To her relief the maid did not appear to notice anything amiss and made no comment about the fact that her mistress was enveloped in nothing but a very masculine, red-silk dressing gown that threatened to trip her up at every step.

'Good morning, m'lady. What are you going to wear this morning?'

Trying to act as though nothing out of the ordinary had occurred, Meg gave a reasonable part of her attention to this important consideration. After all, she was to meet her sister-in-law for the first time and it would not do to look a fright. But as she dressed in a morning gown of soft fawn muslin, her confused thoughts persistently turned to her husband, to his tender, passionate lovemaking which contrasted so oddly with the polite formality he had assumed as soon as she had left his bed half an hour ago.

He had draped his dressing gown around her, informing her politely that he had business to attend to for the rest of the day and would see her at dinner. Almost as an afterthought, as she had been leaving, he had warned her that his sister, Lady Diana Carlton, would pay her a morning visit, doubtless to plan her presentation to society at large. Meg had simply nodded, clutching his dressing gown around her with trembling fingers.

How in the world, she wondered, could a man be so cold and formal when twenty minutes earlier he had been making love to her with a slow, sensuous passion that had brought tears of joy to her eyes? It seemed that in bed he was Marc, infinitely loving and tender. Out of it he was my lord, the Earl of Rutherford, with eyes like shards of ice.

Perhaps, she thought, as Lucy dressed her hair, this is what it means to have a marriage of convenience. Not for the first time she wished she were a little more experienced, knew what was expected of her. If Marcus wished to be very formal at all times except in bed, then she could hardly ask him. It seemed that the protective mask which had sheltered Meg Fellowes from the world for the last ten years was still needed.

Lucy obligingly conducted her mistress to the drawing room after breakfast, which she seemed to think was the right place for Lady Rutherford to receive her expected caller. As the very imposing mahogany door closed behind Meg with a soft *thunk*, she gazed around the apartment in wide-eyed awe. She had thought the library very elegantly appointed after the shabby and comfortless state of Fenby House. Now she realised that, in comparison to the neo-classical opulence and grandeur of this salon, the library was a mere private sitting room, relatively cosy and informal.

Wondering what she was supposed to do while she awaited morning callers, Meg occupied herself by exploring the room. An enormous and very soft carpet cushioned her sandalled feet as she moved about examining things. Gilt chairs, luxuriously upholstered in crimson silk brocade, stood against the wall. None of them looked terribly inviting, but the sofa set at right angles to the fire looked as though it would be reasonably comfortable. An Argand lamp stood on the sofa table behind it, and there were numerous other lamps scattered about on occasional tables.

A rectangular pedestal table with claw feet stood near the window, its crimson drapery matching the upholstery of the chairs and the tasteful swathes of fabric adorning the windows. An empty candle stand stood in one corner.

It was a very polite room, Meg thought as she examined a painting. You could not imagine anyone raising their voice, or feeling upset or indeed feeling anything in here except a respectful admiration for the wealth and taste that had created it. She did not dislike the room, but it was not a room for living in. It was, she realised suddenly, a room in which it would be easy to wear the polite mask of Lady Rutherford, which would have to disguise and protect Meg Fellowes and her foolish heart.

She looked around again. Seen in this new light the room appeared much less daunting. Its splendour was only a stage for her masquerade, a protective colouring like that fawn she had stumbled on once, its dappled coat rendering it practically invisible until she had nearly stepped on it. In this room and others like it she would be safe. No one would try to see behind the mask in these surroundings. No one would even realise that there was anyone there.

Just as she was laughing at herself for these fanciful thoughts, the door opened and a confident, feminine voice said, 'Don't be so idiotish, Delafield! You are not going to announce me to my sister as though I were Royalty! If his lordship has had the unmitigated gall to go out and leave the poor girl to receive me alone, then I'm sure we will manage!'

Meg braced herself for the ordeal and turned to greet her visitor with a polite smile firmly pinned in place.

Her visitor stopped dead inside the door, saying, 'Good heavens! Marc didn't tell me how lovely you are! How very typical!'

Whatever else Meg had expected, she certainly hadn't expected that! She was horrified to feel a wave of crimson wash over her face. How stupidly gauche this elegant creature would think her! And how like Marc she looked!

A friendly chuckle rippled from Lady Diana as she swept forward to enfold Meg in a scented embrace. 'Oh, dear! I am sorry! I didn't mean to put you to the blush literally. Now do come and sit down and we shall ring for Delafield to come back and bring us some wine and cakes! Poor lamb, it will give him something to do!'

Meg allowed herself to be drawn to the sofa and said weakly, 'Won't you sit down, my lady?'

Her sister-in-law shook her head. 'My lady won't. Di will.' She smiled at Meg. 'Don't be formal with me, my dear. Marcus has told me all about it, you know. And while it is not what I would have chosen for him, frankly I am so relieved that he has in the end married a girl of character, rather than the alliance he had in mind, that I vow I could kiss you!' She continued with disarming candour. 'Don't feel that you have committed a social crime in marrying him, my dear! From what he has told me, you will do very well. With Rutherford to protect you, your family scandal does not matter in the least. We have quite enough of our own to cancel yours out.'

'It…it is not a love match, you know,' said Meg shyly. She didn't want this kind new sister-in-law to be under any misconception about the marriage.

'I should be surprised if it were,' said Di gently. 'Marc prefers to hold aloof from caring too much, you know. But he will look after you well, of that you may be sure! Now tell me, where is the wretch?'

She frowned slightly at Meg's explanation and said, 'Men! They're all hopeless, even Marc!'

Then she determinedly led the conversation into happier topics, telling Meg that once the staff got over the shock they would be fine, and if they weren't then they had only to resign. Marcus would never tolerate any slight to his wife, so she had only to carry on as normal.

Hesitantly Meg explained that she was quite unused to any sort of staff. Di listened in disbelief and then gave it as her considered opinion that Samuel Langley had been all about in his head.

'For you may depend upon it, my love, it must have greatly reduced his own comfort and that is something most men will go to any lengths to preserve!'

'Even Marc?' asked Meg with the rare smile that lit up her whole face.

'Especially Marc,' affirmed Di, noting the smile and proceeding to impart a great deal of excellent advice on how to deal with her new status.

'Above all, my dear, don't pretend to be other than what you are!' she said wisely. 'The servants here are all devoted to Marc. Once they see that he is happy with you then they will be your staunchest allies. Why, they even adored our mother and *she* was a French-woman! Papa always said jokingly that it was a mark of the respect in which they held *him* that they accepted her, but I think it had as much to do with herself in the end. And I am sure they will accept you!'

'Oh, I didn't know your mother was French,' said Meg, resolutely ignoring the suggestion that Marc would be happy with her. He had made it quite obvious that while he was happy to enjoy her company and charms in bed, he would pursue his own course independently.

Di chuckled mischievously. 'What did you think of your bedchamber and bathroom? You don't think any self-respecting *Englishwoman* would have installed that shameless bathroom! Maman followed *all* the French fashions and took great delight in scandalising society with them!'

Meg blushed again as she recalled my lord's reaction to finding her in the bath. Had she been shameless in using it? Should she not, in future?

Before she could stop herself she asked, 'Should I…?'

'Yes,' said Di firmly. 'As often as you like! London has long since recovered from the scandal of Lady Rutherford's shocking bathroom.' It would do Marc good, she thought, to find Meg in there. Shake him up a bit. God knows he needed it!

Having set Meg's mind at rest, she outlined her plans for Meg's social life. She would hold a select assembly next week to launch her. Rather late notice, but people would come, never doubt it. Marc had a box at the opera, Lady Rutherford must be seen there. Marc would make up a party. Almack's, of course: she had already secured a promise of vouchers from Sally Jersey, who had a soft spot for Marc. He would escort her there, the first time at least. After that she could choose to attend under the escort of any number of unexceptionable, single men.

It all sounded quite dazzling to Meg. The only aspect which concerned her was Di's unquestioning assumption that Marc would be willing to have so many demands made on his time. She did not doubt he would do it, but she did not think he would like it and she had no wish to tease him.

Very hesitantly she explained to Di that she did not think Marc would wish to do all this.

'Why in heaven's name not?' asked Di.

'We…we promised not to interfere with each other,' said Meg, awkwardly. 'He only married me for an heir and because he…he had to.' She met Di's searching gaze proudly. 'So we are agreed to lead our own lives, not to tease each other.'

'Marc,' said Lady Diana Carlton, ominously, 'will do his duty to *my* satisfaction and that is all there is to it. Don't you worry, Meg. I'll deal with my little brother!' She snorted indignantly.

After promising to return to take Meg up for a drive in the Park at the fashionable hour of five, Lady Di took her leave, perfectly satisfied with her brother's wife. The child was quite lovely, she thought approvingly. Rather shy, but that would do her no harm—quite the opposite. She was not at all farouche; on the contrary, she had a certain dignity.

It would do very well. Unless Marc were more inhuman than she would credit, he would at least have to become fond of the child. And that would be a great deal better for him than the marriage he had been con-templating, which was exactly the sort of thing he had been so cynical about for years. Di didn't pretend to understand the logic behind her brother's conviction that he would only be married for his money and there-fore might as well go into it with his eyes open.

All she knew was that, in marrying Meg Fellowes, he taken on quite a different sort of relationship. She wondered if he were entirely aware of just what he had done. Meg was not the sort of girl to embark lightly on anything, let alone marriage. Di had known perfectly well that Marc had been prepared to offer his wife a *carte blanche* to take lovers as long as she were dis-creet. And Meg had married him on those terms. Did he expect her to take him up on it? And how would he react if he thought she was doing so?

Di was willing to wager that her cynical brother would be quite surprised by his own jealousy if his bride so much as glanced aside at another man. She would wait with interest to see what Jack Hamilton made of the situation. Perhaps he would join them in the park this afternoon. She must send a note around to his lodgings.

Dressed in a modish, Turkey-red walking dress, Lady Rutherford was handed up into Lady Diana Carlton's glossy barouche that afternoon with an air of confidence that she was far from feeling. The thought of braving London society terrified her but it would never do for anyone to know that. Not even Di, who was being so kind. And it would certainly never do for Marc to think she could not bear her part in his world.

Besides, she was damned if she'd sit around the house all day doing nothing, hoping against hope that his lordship would come home early and be a little less chilly. No, she would go out and enjoy herself and find out from Di exactly how she was meant to entertain herself in London. And if Marc did happen to come home before dinner then it would do him good to hear that his bride was out making her own way in the world.

Accordingly, when Marcus came home fifteen minutes after her departure, with a small box nestling in his waistcoat pocket and a feeling that he had been rather cowardly niggling in his conscience, he was greeted with the intelligence that Lady Rutherford had just gone for an airing in the park.

Marcus paled slightly. Meg? Alone in the park? At this hour? Dear God! He should have warned her! If anyone realised who she was…that he had not bothered to escort her on her first appearance! Without waiting to be told that his bride had gone in the unexceptionable company of Lady Di, he turned on his heel and strode out the door, fully intent on showing his world that Lord Rutherford was more than happy with his bride.

Rather to her surprise, Meg did not have to exert herself to enjoy the outing. People were actually very kind. It seemed Lady Di knew everyone, and the high-stepping bays which drew the carriage became quite fidgety at being halted so often in response to greetings and demands to be presented to Rutherford's bride.

Lady Jersey and her friend and fellow patroness of Almack's, Lady Sefton, both promised vouchers independently of each other. If Lady Gwdyr was cold and haughty that was nothing at all to tease oneself about, Lady Di assured Meg. She was always thus! Even when she had merely been Mrs Drummond Burrell! And so it went until Meg's head was in a whirl and she could scarcely remember the names of all the grand people who had been presented to her.

Lady Di, it appeared, was looking for someone in particular. She muttered to herself, 'Now where is the wretch? Not like him to fail…ah!' With an exclamation of satisfaction she indicated a tall, dark-haired gentleman on a dapple-grey horse approaching the carriage. Meg's heart plummeted straight into her kid boots. For one joyous moment she had thought Diana had seen Marc approaching. Sternly she told herself not to be such a sentimental little pea goose.

'Jack Hamilton,' said Lady Di. 'He is one of the Leicestershire Hamiltons, their head actually, and Marc's closest friend. We have known him for ever.'

The tall man brought his horse up beside the carriage and said easily, 'Hullo, Di. Thanks for your note. I'm honoured. Not but what I have observed that most of the world has been before me.'

Lady Di chuckled. 'Sad, isn't it? Here's poor Meg, fresh from Yorkshire and the ordeal of marrying Marc; and all people can do is come and stare at her as though she were a rare beast at the Royal Exchange!' She turned to Meg and said, 'You must allow me to present Jack Hamilton, my dear.'

'I am happy to make Mr Hamilton's acquaintance,' said Meg with a shy smile. She held her hand up to him and he leant down from his horse to clasp it warmly.

'Lady Rutherford, the pleasure is mine, I assure you,' he said with obvious sincerity.

Lady Di opened her mouth to deprecate this formality between two who were bound to become good friends, but shut it again as she caught a warning look from Jack. Instead she turned to Lady Wragby, who was riding on the other side of the barouche, and left Jack and Meg to further their acquaintance.

Jack was in no hurry to rush his friend's bride into familiarity. He had seen the unmistakable reserve in her eyes. She was not a girl to be rushed into anything, this one. Had Marc had the brains to see that? She was not at all what he had expected. Di's hurried note to say that it was all for the best and Marc's appalling *mésalliance* a godsend, had not prepared him for this. He was not quite sure what he had expected, but it had not been this vision of shy, dignified loveliness.

Accordingly he confined his conversation to topics of general interest, and, finding that she had an ardent desire to visit Hatchard's as soon as possible, promptly offered to escort her there as soon as she liked. 'Tomorrow, if you care for it, Lady Rutherford. Just name the day.'

She blinked up at him. 'But won't you find it rather dull? I can very easily go with my maid, you know.'

Hamilton gave her to understand that he had never been dealt such a setdown. Her maid preferred as escort!

'I didn't mean that!' said Meg indignantly. 'You know I didn't!'

Jack laughed. 'I assure you, I am too well known at Hatchard's myself for my going in there to occasion the least remark. And who knows? If I take them a new and wealthy customer, they may even give me a handsome reduction!'

'What's that?' asked Lady Diana, turning to them after promising Lady Wragby a card for her forthcoming assembly and accepting in turn a vicarious invitation for Meg to attend a ball. 'Hatchard's? Are you going to take her there, Jack? How thoroughly typical of you. I vow if you ever fall in love, it will be with a girl who can help you catalogue that overstocked library of yours! Oh!' She broke off with an exclamation of annoyance. 'Would you look at that? How odiously provoking!'

Marcus had looked in vain for Meg at first. The park was crowded and people kept on coming up to him with words of congratulations and sly comments about keeping his intentions very *sub rosa*. He fended off his well-wishers with practised ease, but they delayed him and it was hard to keep an eye on all the strolling ladies while still being polite.

It was not until he met Maria Sefton, who told him that she had just had the honour of being presented to his bride by Lady Diana, that he realised his mistake. What the devil was he about, charging into Hyde Park for all the world like Perseus rescuing Andromeda, when the wretched chit was apparently sitting up in Di's barouche being presented to the world? He'd been imagining her bogged in all sorts of social quagmires requiring his protection, and it was no such thing.

With a polite murmur of an urgent appointment, Lord Rutherford bade Lady Sefton farewell and turned for home. Far too late.

A delicate hand was laid on his sleeve and an arch voice said, 'Is this the future you mentioned, my lord?' Wincing inwardly, he turned to confront Althea Hartleigh's peridot-green eyes, which held his in mocking challenge.

'Good afternoon, Althea,' he said politely.

'Is it?' she responded. 'I understood, my lord, that we were to discuss the future when you returned to town. No doubt we can still do so?' There was the very faintest of questions in her light voice.

Marcus's lips firmed in a hard line. Not at Lady Hartleigh's shameless advance to a newly married man, but at the shocking realisation that he had not the least inclination to avail himself of her offer. Plainly she was willing to swallow his marriage with a good grace, equally plainly she assumed that he wished to continue their connection as though nothing had changed. A week ago he would have said she was perfectly right.

Little though he might relish the thought, things had changed, himself not least of them. It was not merely that he felt it would be insulting to Meg and, in view of their circumstances, unwise to pursue the liaison; it was simply that he no longer had the slightest interest in Lady Hartleigh's experienced expertise. Meg's innocent passion had seared itself into his senses, making the thought of taking his pleasure with another woman seem ridiculous.

'No, Althea,' he said quietly. 'I am afraid that is not possible now.'

He attempted to lift her hand from his sleeve, but the green eyes blazed and she gripped hard suddenly, hissing, 'How dare you dismiss me like a common whore!' Then, seeming to regain control in a flash, she glanced past him, and said blandly, 'Why, I do believe you are right, Marcus. It *is* a delightful afternoon. Is not that Lady Diana? How very pleasant! I wonder who her charming companion can be?'

With a feeling of impending doom, Marcus turned slowly to encounter his sister's furious glare, Jack Hamilton's disbelieving gaze and, by far the worst of all, his wife's look of shocked hurt, which vanished instantly in calm, indifferent acceptance.

And this pattern card of wifely correctitude said in

the lightest of voices, 'Good gracious. It is my lord! How very singular!'

Jack Hamilton's head snapped around in amazement. The little devil! He wouldn't have thought she had it in her. But there she sat with cool composure, just as though Marc had not exposed her to ridicule and contemptuous pity. Perhaps she didn't understand, he thought. But a glance at her hands, clenched tightly in her lap, assured him that Lady Rutherford understood only too well. He found himself wishing heartily that he could be privy to Marc's thoughts right now.

They were indeed worth being privy to. His wife's reaction to his supposed misdemeanour aroused all sorts of conflicting emotions in Marcus's breast. Anger that she thought him so base that he would intentionally compromise their situation further was mingled with pain that he had hurt her. For he had. For that split second he had seen the truth in her eyes. And then she had withdrawn behind a mask of well-bred indifference. She had turned a blind eye, just as he had wanted his wife to do. What he hadn't counted on was seeing it happen. Seeing transparent, trusting Meg whisk herself out of sight, leaving behind a lovely, elegant stranger, who sat in his sister's carriage making polite conversation to Jack Hamilton.

Damn it all! She was smiling up at Jack as though she hadn't a care in the world. And he, the unprincipled rake, was smiling back in a way that made Marcus long to tear his throat out!

Lady Di instructed her coachman to pull up.

With a silent commendation for Meg's attitude, she opened fire. 'Good afternoon, Marcus. You see I persuaded dear Meg to take a little carriage exercise with me. Lady Hartleigh, how delightful to see you! I believe you have not been presented to my brother's bride yet. Meg, dear, permit me to present Lady Hartleigh.'

The two ladies exchanged the friendliest of acknowledgments while Di calmly watched her little brother practically grind his teeth in suppressed fury at the impropriety of presenting Althea to Meg in this way. Propriety, thought Di savagely, could be a two-edged sword!

She continued with her rifle fire. 'May we take you up, Lady Hartleigh? I'm sure it would be no trouble to deposit you where you belong!' A strange sound from Jack Hamilton made her say, 'Dear Jack, I do hope you are not feeling unwell. That sounded very like a cough.'

'Just some dust in my throat,' explained the afflicted Hamilton, still spluttering.

'Yes, do take Lady Hartleigh home, Di,' said Marcus, in what was obviously an attempt to take control of a situation that was fast deteriorating. 'You will be a trifle crowded with three, so I will escort my lady home.'

His hitherto biddable bride raised her dark brows at that. Get out of this nice comfortable barouche and walk home with *him* just so he could appease his conscience and silence the *on-dits*? When snow lay in hell, she would!

'How very kind of you, my lord,' she said sweetly. 'But I should not like to put you to so much trouble. And, indeed, if Lady Hartleigh does not mind a little crowding, I should like to further our acquaintance. I feel sure we have a great deal in common.'

Diana nearly broke her jaw keeping a straight face as Meg rolled up her husband, horse, foot and guns. Short of ordering her out of the carriage, he could do nothing but accept this masterly dismissal.

Biting back all the things he would have liked to say,

Marcus inclined his head, saying ironically, 'I am my lady's servant to command. I will see you at dinner, madam. Good afternoon, Di, Jack. *Au revoir*, Lady Hartleigh.'

He stalked off, wondering what on earth had possessed him to farewell Althea like that. Now she would think he intended to maintain their relationship! As would Meg, Diana and possibly even Jack. And he had no intention of doing anything of the sort! Not even to put his impertinent bride in her rightful place!

By the time Meg left him to the enjoyment of his wine that night Marcus was about ready to strangle her. It was not that she had said anything she should not have, or indeed given him the slightest reason to suppose she minded in the least if he had an affair. On the contrary, she had spoken cheerfully of how unexpectedly kind everyone had been, of whom Diana had presented to her, of the prospect of visiting Almack's and the opera. All in all she gave a convincing impression of a young bride intent upon cutting a dash in the world of the *ton*.

It was just that; an impression. By the time she left Marcus, Meg had a splitting headache and wished only for the privacy of her bedchamber. Accordingly she went straight upstairs, summoned Lucy to assist her and went to bed. She didn't even feel like reading. Her headache was making her slightly dizzy so she blew her lamp out and snuggled down in the silken sheets. For a few minutes she managed to pretend that everything was perfectly fine, that she had not a care in the world, that Marc was welcome to take his pleasures elsewhere. And then she dissolved into tears.

Despite having gone into her marriage with her eyes

wide open to what he intended, despite knowing the danger of caring for him, she realised that she had completely underestimated the pain involved in knowing he had another interest and the sense of betrayal in suspecting he had spent all, or part of, the day in Lady Hartleigh's no doubt experienced and expert embrace.

What chance did naïve, inexperienced Meg have against a sophisticated beauty like Althea Hartleigh? Oh, he had enjoyed her, had been kind enough to ensure her pleasure, but after seeing her rival, Meg could not believe that he would rate her charms above that green-eyed beauty. In fact, it did not even cross her mind that such might be the case.

Her shock, when she heard the door into the bathroom open and saw the light of her husband's candle, was intense. Surely he was not going to come to her bed now! Not after spending the day with… With her cheeks still wet with tears, Meg knew if he touched her now she was lost, would end up sobbing her heart out in his arms, revealing how deeply she had fallen in love. And he would resent it, would feel trapped by his pitying kindness. She didn't dare. His rejection she would not be able to bear. And pitying forbearance would be even worse.

'Meg? Are you asleep?' His voice was very soft, a velvet growl in the faint glow of his candle.

Lie still! Pretend to be asleep! She lay unmoving, hoping he might go away.

But the candle came closer, was set down on the night table and blown out as she felt her husband's large, naked body slide into bed beside her.

Unfortunately, since Marcus had not spent the day or even part of it in the enjoyment of Althea Hartleigh's charms, he did not go away. Since he had, in fact, spent a very large proportion of the day in pleasurable contemplation of his wife's enthralling passion, he was in no way minded to do so. If Meg were asleep, he would be content to snuggle her into his arms and hold her until she should chance to awaken, but he fully intended to spend the night with her, one way or another.

He wanted to reassure her somehow that he had not been so cruel as to betray her so early in their marriage. Short of telling her outright that he was innocent, the only way he could think of was to bed her and tell her that he wanted no one else.

So he gathered his supposedly sleeping wife into his arms with the utmost gentleness.

And felt her freeze and then jerk herself away from him to the other side of the bed.

Shocked, he lay still and then said reassuringly, 'Meg, sweetheart, it's me, Marc.' Perhaps, after her experience on their wedding night, he should not have just slid into bed with her in the dark.

'I know,' came the devastating response. 'I…I have the headache. Please, my lord, not tonight.'

For a moment he was stunned, and then he thought that despite her chatter she *had* looked rather pale at dinner.

'Then cuddle up and let me hold you,' he said gently. 'I promise I won't pester you.'

There was a moment's charged silence, during which Meg summoned up all the icy reserve of which she was capable. In the face of his tender consideration it was a daunting task.

Thankful that the dim light made her face unreadable, she said very politely, 'No. Thank you, my lord.'

Marcus felt as though a sword had passed straight through his guts. And then he lost his temper.

Swinging himself off the bed he said coldly, 'Then I will relieve you of my unwelcome presence, Madam Wife!' And in tones of brutal indifference, 'No doubt I can find amusement elsewhere!'

He waited a moment for Meg's response, but she was struggling with tears and remained silent so he turned on his heel and stalked out in a mixture of hurt and affronted male pride.

Hearing the door slam behind him, Meg buried her face in the pillow and cried herself to sleep, a proceeding which took over an hour and did absolutely nothing to help her headache.

Chapter Ten

A week later the Countess of Rutherford, exquisitely gowned in clinging, shimmering blue silk, stood between her sister-in-law and husband, being formally presented to society. Lady Diana's idea of a select assembly turned out to mean that she had not invited above two hundred or so people to have the honour of meeting Rutherford's bride.

Sir Toby commented on this with gentle satire and told Meg with a grin that he would quiz her on names later in the evening.

Meg was fairly certain that she would not remember a quarter of the names she had heard, although many of the people she had already met while driving with Diana. These she greeted with genuine relief as being lifelines in a sea of frothing, gossiping humanity. So confused was she by all the noise and new faces that she would have even greeted Lady Hartleigh with relief.

Lady Hartleigh was conspicuous by her absence, a fact which confirmed Meg's belief that there was some connection between her and Marcus. Why else should Di have been so annoyed at seeing them together? Perhaps he had even contemplated marriage with her.

Di had intimated that he had considered a marriage she disapproved of.

Trying to concentrate, she responded to Lady Castlereagh's gracious compliments on her looks with a shy 'thank you' which did her no disservice in that lady's eyes.

Lady Castlereagh had already been pleased to approve of Rutherford's choice and she confirmed it now, saying, 'I must wish you happy, Rutherford. I shall look forward to seeing the two of you at Almack's.' She passed on regally to inform her acquaintance that Rutherford's bride was just what she liked in a girl, dignified and with no simpering nonsense about her. Attractive too, trust Rutherford for that!

Despite his continuing hurt at his bride's rejection, Marcus swelled with unspoken pride in her composure. To anyone who did not know her she appeared perfectly happy with her surroundings, delighted to meet one curious stranger after another. Only Marcus suspected that she was finding the whole business somewhat of an ordeal and he could not have said why he had that impression. Certainly she did not shrink towards him, or cling to his arm. Her voice held no tremor and a friendly smile curved her soft mouth.

It was just that he had the oddest feeling that he was watching a play, in which a very talented actress held the stage. Which would have been all very well if she had ever relaxed and cast off her mask. But she didn't. In the last week he had seen very little of Meg. At first he had been too angry to trust himself near her and by the time he had cooled and approached her with overtures of friendship it had been too late.

She was caught up in a whirl of social engagements, fittings with Diana's dressmaker, visits to Hatchard's and Hookham's. And when he did see her she held him at arm's length with her chatter about her doings, how kind Diana was being and how much she was enjoying London. In short, he had lost Meg and acquired Lady Rutherford.

Even when he gave her a betrothal ring, which he had meant to do on that ill-fated day they had met in the park, she had maintained her barricade. Oh, she had thanked him prettily enough, put it on at once and turned her hand so the enormous diamond blazed. But he could not flatter himself that she was in the least moved by it. And he had not made the least attempt to enter her bed again or woo her into his. Never in his life had he been rejected by a woman and it had stung unbearably.

Had he but known that Meg had been hard pressed not to burst into tears when he gave the ring to her and went to sleep each night with her cheek cuddled against it, then he might have felt appeased. But he did not know these things; although he was observant enough to recognise the mask which Meg wore, he could not see past it to what lay underneath.

So Meg stood at his side, bitterly unhappy, and utterly determined that no one, least of all Marcus, should know it.

The throng of people flocking up the steps had died down and Di turned to Meg. 'Well, my love, I think it is time Marc took you to mingle with our guests.' Narrowly observing the slightest of shadows in the depths of Meg's dark eyes, 'And a glass of champagne too, I think! Oh, dear! Who is this arriving? I'm sure I didn't send out this many cards!' Then she fell silent as she saw who was coming through her front door.

Marcus beside her swore softly and said, 'What the hell did you invite them for, Di?'

'I didn't, you idiot,' she informed him with sisterly directness.

'Well, well, well,' said Sir Toby in detached interest. 'Your call, I'd say, Marc.'

Very puzzled, Meg gazed at the vaguely familiar couple ascending the stairs towards them.

She was sure she knew them, but couldn't remember having met them in the last few days with Di. Yet the red face of the corpulent gentleman puffing his way up to them was familiar, as was the hatchet-faced lady on his arm. Somewhere deep inside she began to shake. Who on earth could they be? She was aware that Marcus at her side was absolutely rigid with fury.

'My dear little cousin!' gushed the gentleman. 'I dare say Lady Diana did not realise we were in town! But really, we could not ignore you, dear Marguerite.' Then, as she continued to look at him blankly, 'I am your Cousin Delian, Marguerite!'

Her jaw dropped. Looking down at her, Marcus saw, for the first time in a week, a genuine reaction from his wife. Hurt, shock and disgust at this undisguised hypocrisy were all there for a fleeting moment. And something else which clawed at his heart. Briefly he had a glimpse of the frightened, grieving orphan, confused and alone. And then the mask slipped back into place.

But Marcus had seen enough. 'How charming, Sir Delian. But you did manage to ignore Marguerite for ten years very satisfactorily. You really needn't do such violence to your feelings now.' His silken tones cloaked a murderous rage at a man who could throw a ten-year-old child out of her home and not even settle money on her.

Sir Delian blustered ineffectually and his wife took over. 'How is this? Do you tell me that we are not welcome here, my lord? At our cousin's coming-out?'

'About as welcome as you made her ten years ago,' said Marcus with deadly emphasis. 'We, however, shall not be so ungracious as to turn you away. Unless Marguerite would prefer me to do so.' He turned to Meg. 'Well, my dear?'

She stared up at him. What was she supposed to say? Those icy grey eyes gave her no clue. The decision must be hers. It had been the dream of her life to one day repay Delian and Henrietta for casting her out and now she had her chance. She looked at them uncertainly. Sir Delian was obviously upset, his weak chins quivering as he passed a handkerchief over his florid countenance. Lady Fellowes looked as proud and disagreeable as ever.

Meg had a blinding flash of memory, recalling the day they had arrived at Thornaby, summoned her and pronounced sentence of exile from her home. Lady Fellowes had spelt out, in words the frightened ten-year-old had not understood for years, just why she was to be sent away. Sir Delian, she recalled, had protested a little but had been overruled. Now was her chance. She could refuse to acknowledge them and word would get out that she had done so. It would ruin them socially.

She couldn't do it. It was not in her nature to return evil for evil.

'No, my lord,' she said quietly. 'I will be pleased to acknowledge my only family.'

Sir Delian gasped, 'My dear child! I am so delighted! You must know we have been meaning forever to have you on a visit! Perhaps now that you are—' He fell silent before the searing scorn in the light grey eyes before him. They were like chips of ice, hard and implacable.

'Lady Rutherford has acknowledged you, Sir Delian,' interposed Marcus. 'It will be for her to determine what, if any, friendship should develop.'

With her head held high, Lady Fellowes towed her spluttering husband past them into the house.

'Really, Marc! Was that necessary?' expostulated Di.

Marcus looked down at Meg, a curious expression in his eyes. 'Yes, Di. It was.'

Meg returned his gaze, wide-eyed and defenceless. Just for a moment he was her Marc again, protective and caring.

Shyly she put her hand on his and said, 'Thank you, Marc.'

Her touch seemed to scorch through her kid glove, searing his fingers which longed to clasp hers. Instead he shrugged and said, 'I can't stand hypocrites. Shall we mingle?' And felt a strange pang of dissatisfaction as he saw Meg's barriers crash down, leaving him confronted with the polite and obliging bride he thought he wanted.

'Certainly, my lord.' What a fool she was to think he had responded to her need! He had merely found the Felloweses distasteful, for which she could not blame him in the least.

For the rest of the evening Meg circulated through the pressing throng and found herself feeling more and more at ease. People were kind and did not, thank God, expect her to remember all their names. Indeed, they were only too happy to present themselves to her notice.

'Dear Lady Rutherford. You won't remember, but Di presented me in the park…'

'We met in Hatchard's, Lady Rutherford...'

'You must have met so many people this evening, dear Lady Rutherford...'

And so it went on. Marcus, after an hour or so, had drifted away, satisfied that she was launched safely and could manage for herself. There was no danger of her being ignored or finding herself at a loss. So he brought her a glass of champagne and excused himself gracefully, leaving her deep in conversation with Lady Wragby on a sofa.

Meg rather liked Lady Wragby, who was fat and comfortable with absolutely no pretensions to fashion or beauty, but was possessed of an abundant good nature which ensured that she was everywhere welcome.

Lady Wragby was obligingly pointing out various persons of note and telling gently scandalous stories about them when an urbane voice from behind them said, 'How delightful. I have longed to renew my acquaintance with Lady Rutherford.'

As her veins congealed to solid ice, Meg turned to face the mocking eyes and thin lips of Sir Blaise Winterbourne. He had possessed himself of her hand and was raising it to his lips. Meg could barely repress a shudder as he kissed it. All at once she felt tainted, defiled, and sickeningly, shamefully afraid.

Regardless, she gave him back stare for stare and said, 'Have we met? Oh, of course! Mr Winterbourne. In Grantham, was it not?' She had the queerest feeling that Meg was standing a little distance away, quaking with fear, admiringly watching Lady Rutherford deal with an awkward situation.

Winterbourne laughed gently. 'I am flattered that you remember me, Lady Rutherford. But Rutherford made wretched work of presenting me! It will be more appropriate for you to call me Sir Blaise.'

He lingered beside the sofa for a while, chatting to Lady Wragby and idly quizzing Meg.

'Such an elegant gown, dear Lady Rutherford. But then you are always exquisitely garbed for the occasion, are you not?'

Meg deflected his barbed gallantries with increasing coolness until to her relief she observed Jack Hamilton approaching through the crowd. He had his head on one side and was regarding her with one cocked eyebrow.

As he drew closer Winterbourne excused himself and sauntered off. It would never do to give Hamilton of all people the least suspicion that he was sniffing around the Countess of Rutherford.

Hamilton bowed low over Meg's hand and greeted Lady Wragby with pleasure.

'How nice to find people I actually want to see. Didn't Di say something about a select assembly? Remind me not to come to a squeeze.'

Lady Wragby chuckled. 'Never mind. Should you like to come to a nice select card party next month? I'll only send out a hundred cards.'

Hamilton shuddered. 'Thank you for the warning. I believe I have a prior engagement that evening!'

'Why, you wretch!' protested Lady Wragby. 'I haven't even told you the date!'

In their relaxed and cheerful company Meg recovered slightly, laughing at their teasing and responding in kind. Yet, observing her, Jack thought she was rather pale. He could not say what it was that had told him she was upset, but he would have sworn that she was frightened by Winterbourne. Racking his brains, he could think of no reason for her to be so, unless of course Marc or Di had warned her that he made a habit of bedding Marc's mistresses and might think it amusing to seduce his Countess. He resolved to keep a brotherly eye on Meg. He thought she was the best thing to happen to Marc in years and he did not want anything to go wrong.

By the time Lady Fellowes sailed up to claim the privilege of cousinship, Meg was feeling thoroughly at ease again.

'My dear Marguerite,' she said, as she contrived to draw Meg away from Jack and Lady Wragby. 'I do trust there is no resentment on your part for your cousin's very understandable decision to protect his children from any breath of scandal. As a mother and dutiful wife I could only concur with his opinion.'

Holding herself proudly, Meg said steadily, 'My memory of the occasion is perfectly clear, *Cousin* Henrietta. I hold no resentment where it is not due.'

'Then we may be comfortable,' said Lady Fellowes with a sublime unawareness of the edge to Meg's response. 'Naturally, now you are so advantageously married, no one will give a thought to your past.'

'*My* past?' queried Meg. 'I was under the impression that it was my parents' past that was the problem.' She could not quite believe this bare-faced hypocrisy. 'I am still their daughter!'

'How you do take one up, dear Marguerite,' said Lady Fellowes with a tinkle of laughter. 'Now, you must know I am bringing out dear little Sophia this spring. She is presently recovering from this dreadful flu, so I have left her at home this evening. The most fragile constitution! But I am sure you will be pleased with her. Such a dear child. She is quite longing to meet her long-lost cousin.'

Since Meg's only memory of Sophia Fellowes was of a seven-year-old who had marched into her bedchamber and announced that it was hers now, as well as all the toys, and Mama wished to see Cousin Marguerite in the drawing room at once, she was not unnaturally startled at this announcement. But she did not wish to harbour a grudge so she said quietly, 'I am sure I will be pleased to make the acquaintance of my cousin.'

'It will be of the first importance to arrange a suitable match for her,' went on Lady Fellowes. 'I am sure Lord Rutherford has so many amiable friends—'

Meg interrupted at once. 'I beg your pardon, Cousin! I can see someone I wish to speak to most particularly. Pray excuse me.' With a charming smile she took her leave and looked around desperately for someone she knew.

A deep voice at her elbow said, 'At a loss, my dear?'

She stared up into her husband's enigmatic grey eyes.

He possessed himself of her hand and placed it securely on his arm. 'Never, my dear, make your escape before you have the route thoroughly planned. You may find yourself out of the pan and into the fire.'

'I don't know what you are talking about!' she snapped, furious that he should have been listening and seen through her ploy so easily.

'Did you not wish to escape from your hypocritical cousin?'

'Certainly not,' lied Meg, without the least hesitation. 'My cousin is perfectly amiable. I merely saw someone I wished to speak to!'

'Oh? Who is it?' asked Marcus. 'I will engage to escort you to your unknown friend.'

'That, sir, is none of your business!' Her eyes blazed at him. 'We have a bargain, do we not?'

'We do,' agreed Marcus. 'Are you bent on fulfilling your side of it?' Steel-hard eyes bored into her.

She met them bravely, shuddering inwardly at what he was suggesting. 'Again, sir, it is not your business if I am.'

Grey ice chilled her to the bone. 'I would point out, madam, that there is a little matter of an heir to be settled before you emulate your mother's career.' He bowed and left her.

Jack Hamilton, watching this exchange from an alcove, winced. He could not hear what was being said, but he didn't need to. He knew Marc well enough to know that he was hellbent on digging his own grave. And, to judge by the stricken look on Meg's face as he bowed and left her, he was doing a first-class job.

Casually he strolled out and greeted Meg. 'Come and have a glass of champagne, Lady Rutherford. You cannot possibly spend the evening chatting to your cousin and husband!'

He winced again as Meg turned to him and treated him to a brilliant smile. It was as though the hurt child had never existed.

'How kind of you, Mr Hamilton,' said Lady Rutherford. 'I'm dreadfully thirsty. Such a squeeze!'

It was dark…a myriad of greedy hands grasped at her breasts, her thighs…smearing a filthy slime over her…a hard, lustful mouth was forcing itself on hers… smothering her screams…choking her…

Meg awakened, sobbing and sweating in her terror. The fire was nearly out, but it cast enough light for her to avoid the furniture as she unthinkingly headed for the safety and reassurance of Marc's room. Despite the coldness between them, she did not think he would deny her the security of his arms.

She stumbled around the edge of the dark bathroom and found the door, groping for the latch. Unhesitatingly she headed for the bed, still shaking with fear as she scrambled in, reaching for Marc.

It took her a moment to realise that the enormous bed was empty, that Marc was not there. At first she could not think. Shock held her in its grip. And then the implications of his absence burst upon her like an exploding shell. He had gone out to seek consolation elsewhere as he had told her he would do. She lay there in his cold, empty bed and wept as though her heart would break until she slept again.

Coming up to bed half an hour later, slightly befuddled from all the brandy he had consumed in his library since he brought Meg home, Marcus stared in amazement at the sight of Meg in his bed. What the devil was she doing there? He cursed the brandy. Better go back downstairs. He was damned if he was going to get into bed with his wife in this disgraceful state! Be an insult to the poor girl.

Accordingly he wandered back downstairs and stretched out on the library sofa where he finally fell into an uncomfortable slumber.

Awakening from another nightmare in the early dawn, Meg found that she was still alone in her husband's bed and crept back to her own room. Bitter despair held her in its grip. She had driven Marc away and had no idea how to call him back without betraying her love for him. She eventually drifted into an uneasy sleep.

When she finally arose, not in the least refreshed,

Meg dressed herself in her prettiest morning gown and pinched her cheeks to force some colour into them. Lady Rutherford must not show the world a pale face if she were to protect Meg. Resolutely Meg left her chamber in the forlorn hope that breakfast would be of assistance in maintaining her façade.

By the end of her solitary breakfast she had made several decisions. Firstly, she must go to Marc and somehow let him know that she had not meant to refuse him her bed, that she had been feeling unwell, which had the merit of being at least partly true. Secondly, she had to tell him about Winterbourne. Ask him what she should do when she met him, and tell him about her nightmare. She felt cold at the thought of confiding so much to anyone but surely, surely to her own husband…

Accordingly she asked Delafield to inform her when his lordship was up and about and repaired to the drawing room to read. She had not been there more than an hour when the door opened and Marcus came in. He was his usual immaculate self, if a little pale, in buff breeches and a dark blue coat. His riding boots were polished to a shine which made Meg blink a little as she absorbed their splendour.

'Delafield mentioned that you wished to see me, madam.' He was feeling distinctly scratchy this morning. He had a stiff neck from the night on the sofa and a devilish head from all the brandy. If Meg were about to reproach him for his absence last night, he would have something to say about undutiful wives! He had absolutely no intention of confessing that he had spent the night on the library sofa since he had been far too under the weather to share a bed with her. Especially since the reason for his condition had been his frustration over her.

In the face of his formality, Meg completely lost sight of the course she had charted for herself and started in the middle. 'Y…yes. Did you know that Sir Blaise Winterbourne was there last night?' she asked, keeping her voice as steady as possible.

Marcus softened slightly, his tone gentler. 'I did know it. I should have warned you. He is everywhere received. Since I had not told Di anything, I could not strike his name from the guest list. It will be impossible to avoid him, I am afraid, but since he is not a friend of mine, you need not fear that I would expect you to receive him.'

Meg nodded. 'I see.'

She seemed collected enough, thought Marcus. He reverted to his former tone. 'Is that all you wished to speak to me about?'

She flinched inwardly. Could he just dismiss it like that? She felt cold and sick, as though the nightmare still rode her.

'No, my lord.' She drew a deep breath and again started in the wrong place. 'I…I came to find you last night—'

He interrupted at once. 'Might I remind you, or perhaps I should say, inform you, that it is a husband's right and privilege to indicate when he wishes to have congress with his wife.'

She stared up at him, stricken into silence and he went on coldly. 'You, of course, have the right of veto.' *Which you have exercised.* The words hung unspoken between them. His final comment set the seal on his fate. 'I would suggest, Lady Rutherford, that you adhere to this convention. You will thus be spared the humiliation of knowing that you are not the only desirable female in London. Our bargain, you may remember.'

Meg wondered if she were going to be sick. She had meant nothing to him, then. He cared as little for her as Cousin Euphemia had done, had dismissed her just as coldly. All his kindness and tenderness had been nothing more than a ploy to get her into his bed willingly. And even that had probably been to expedite the begetting of an heir. No doubt he found the more experienced Lady Hartleigh far more to his taste. Well, she was welcome to him! Lady Rutherford could stand alone!

'I beg your pardon, my lord,' said Lady Rutherford sweetly. 'You have made your position perfectly clear, for which I thank you. I shall endeavour to keep to my side of our bargain.' Bitterly hurt, she searched for the worst thing she could possibly think of to say to him. And found it with disastrous ease. 'You need not fear that I shall again refuse to do my duty. I am perfectly aware that my *right of veto* as you term it, is one that not many husbands would allow me. I would not like you to think that I am ungrateful, or taking advantage of your chivalrous nature.'

She rose gracefully and left the room with her head held high, praying that she would make it safely to her bedchamber before the scalding sensation behind her eyes became a torrent of tears. She had been a fool to think that it would be possible to confide in him, ask for his help. He had made his attitude quite plain. She was nothing to him, less than nothing, and it was as well to know it now, before her foolish heart imagined otherwise.

Marcus stood and watched her go, absolutely

stunned. Was that how she had seen it? Duty? Nothing more? Damn her! She was as cold-hearted and mercenary as any other woman and it was as well to know it now!

Chapter Eleven

Over the next month Meg hurled herself into the social gaiety of London. She attended Almack's, danced the night away at innumerable private balls, attended the opera, collected a court of devoted admirers and succeeded in persuading her husband that he had indeed made a marriage of convenience.

She made innumerable friends, mostly through Diana's introductions. She found that the people Di presented to her as her own personal friends were kindly, unpretentious and delighted to welcome her to their circles for her own sake.

The same could not be said of her Cousin Henrietta. Meg had no doubt that, had she married a man of lesser consequence, Henrietta would have refused to acknowledge her and would have ensured that Cousin Delian did the same. She actually found herself feeling sorry for Sir Delian. It was plain that he was ruled by his wife and that, left to his own devices, he would not have thought to turn his orphaned little cousin out of her home.

He had tried to explain and apologise to her one morning in the park when he had taken her driving. The morass of half-sentences, as he attempted to tell Meg he had never meant to leave her destitute, without revealing his wife's ascendancy, was utterly pathetic.

In the end she stopped him gently. 'Cousin, there is no need for all this. You acted as you thought best. No one can do otherwise.'

Sir Delian Fellowes swallowed hard. That was exactly the problem. He had *not* acted as he thought best. He never did if Henrietta disagreed. And now he felt guilty, ashamed of his cowardice. Especially since Meg seemed disposed to forgive what had been done to her and include them in her circle of friends despite the obvious disapproval of her husband.

He tugged at his neckcloth with one hand. 'You are very kind my dear. It…it is more than—'

'Oh, fustian!' said Meg cheerfully. 'I sent Cousin Henrietta a card inviting you and Sophia to join us for dinner and then go on to the opera next week. It is to be my first visit! Do say you will come! I am so looking forward to it. Lady Diana and Sir Toby are to come, as well as Mr Hamilton!'

'Jack Hamilton?' asked Sir Delian, suddenly intent.

'Why, yes.' Meg was a trifle surprised over his evident approbation.

'Henrietta will be most obliged,' said Sir Delian delightedly.

'Obliged?'

Sir Delian explained. 'You see, she has been trying for ever to introduce Sophia to his notice.'

'Oh,' said Meg hollowly. This was something she hadn't thought of. She had pondered over whom to invite. To keep the numbers even a single gentleman had been required. Jack Hamilton was the only one she could think of and she hoped devoutly that he would not think she was attempting to match him with Miss Sophia Fellowes. As far as Meg could see, Sophia was not so very much changed from the arrogant little girl she remembered.

'Yes, indeed,' continued Sir Delian. 'I think I may safely say that we shall all three be delighted to accept your kind invitation, my dear.'

'How...how lovely,' achieved Meg, thinking that the opera had better be good if she were to enjoy what promised to be an unexpectedly embarrassing evening. If Sophia made an obvious play to engage Jack's interest, Marcus would be utterly furious, she thought miserably. She was perfectly aware that he disliked her cousins, and scorned Sir Delian.

She was still worrying when Jack Hamilton approached the phaeton and hailed them.

'Good afternoon, Lady Rutherford. Sir Delian, your most obedient!' He smiled up at them lazily. 'I'm going to steal your fair companion, Sir Delian. Will you walk with me, Lady Rutherford?'

She glanced hesitantly at Sir Delian, not wanting him to think she wished to quit his company, but in truth she found it difficult to think of what to say in the face of his overwhelming guilt.

Sir Delian, however, was perfectly ready to oblige a man whom he definitely did not wish to antagonise. 'A theft indeed, Hamilton! But I shall forgive you and look forward to seeing you at my cousin's little opera party next week. Lady Fellowes and I shall be pleased to present our little Sophia to you.'

Meg suppressed a curse with difficulty as she caught Jack's glance, brimming with laughter.

He helped her down, saying, 'The pleasure will be all mine. Good afternoon.'

Meg met his eyes ruefully as Sir Delian gave his pair the office and said, 'Oh, Jack, I mean, Mr Hamilton, I am most dreadfully sorry!'

'Jack will do very nicely,' he said laughing. 'And as for the rest, don't give it a thought. 'Tis an inevitable part of being an eligible bachelor. Just ask Marc, he can tell you all about it.'

'I did *not* mean to expose you to that!' said Meg indignantly, ignoring the reference to her husband's erstwhile status as society's most sought-after *parti*.

'I never thought you did,' replied Jack with a chuckle. 'Tell me, how is Marc? I thought he was a little out of sorts when last I saw him.'

Meg hesitated. She hadn't actually seen Marcus for three days. Well, not to speak to, at all events. She had seen him at a ball the previous evening. He had greeted her politely and then gone on his way. He had next been seen dancing with Lady Hartleigh. A casual inquiry an hour or so later had elicited the information that he had taken his leave early. As had Lady Hartleigh.

Aware that Jack was watching her closely, she said unconcernedly, 'Oh, Marcus is well enough, I believe. He is always very busy.' Adroitly she changed the subject. 'I am so glad you are to come to the opera with us. I shall be able to ask you all sorts of questions.' Determinedly she kept the conversation focused on opera until Jack had escorted her home.

Jack was deep in thought as he left Meg. He'd noted her slim fingers clutching the dainty pink reticule and the slight firming of her lips, the gallant tilt of the chin as she lied to him. He'd had the impression that Marc was not spending much time in his countess's company. What he hadn't been sure of was how the countess felt about it. He had his answer. And there was not a damn thing he could do about it, except extend a hand of chivalrous friendship to her.

A slight smile curved his lips. That, of course, might be enough to bring Marc to his senses! If he thought his best friend was after his wife... Jack felt a twinge of unholy amusement at the prospect of Marc's outrage. The only difficulty would be how to mislead Marc without Meg, or indeed anyone else, getting the wrong idea—Meg especially. Marcus might have offered his bride a *carte blanche* to conduct discreet *affaires*, but Jack was morally certain she would never do so and would shrink from such a thing, and anyone who suggested it, in horror.

This little expedition to the opera should serve his turn very nicely. He spared a moment's compunction for the false hopes he was going to raise in Miss Fellowes's breast and in the more ample bosom of her mama. Oh, well! There must be some casualties in a war.

Just as Meg had feared, her first appearance at the opera was not an unalloyed pleasure. To begin with, it was plain that Marcus viewed the inclusion of the Fellowes with extreme disapprobation. It was not that he was rude to them or even inattentive. Quite the opposite. He was extremely polite. Nothing could have exceeded his civility to Sir Delian and Lady Fellowes, or to Miss Fellowes. But it was such a contrast to the easy, unceremonious manners he used towards his sister, Sir Toby and Jack Hamilton, that Meg wanted to throw something at him. Especially since he was equally polite to her!

To her immense surprise, it seemed that Jack

Hamilton was quite taken with Miss Fellowes. He certainly spent a great deal of time flirting with her in the most unexceptionable way. Meg began to feel rather nervous since it was plain that Marcus was viewing this with a rather jaundiced eye.

He took advantage of an appallingly long and dull anecdote related by Lady Fellowes to draw Meg aside and say, 'If you are attempting to fulfil your cousins' hopes by introducing Miss Fellowes to an eligible bachelor, might I request that you leave my close friends off your list of victims?'

For a moment anger blazed in those expressive eyes, but she dropped her lids swiftly to veil her fury. 'Oh? Do you not think Mr Hamilton can take care of himself? It appears to me that he is very well pleased with his company.' Her tone was light and unconcerned and her eyes, when she raised them to Marcus's face, betokened only innocent inquiry.

Marcus's temper slipped its leash somewhat. 'That's because he's too damned polite to appear anything else!'

Meg seemed to consider this for a moment. 'Really? What a pity it isn't catching. Do excuse me, my lord. I must attend to our guests.' She favoured Marcus with a glittering smile, calculated to make him want to wring her neck, and went to speak with her cousin Sophia. How dare he! To think that she would hatch vulgar, hateful schemes like that! He ought to know her better! Meg conveniently ignored the fact that she had been doing her level best to ensure that Marcus did not know her, that of late weeks he had seen only Lady Rutherford.

There was a snap in her step as she approached her

cousin and Jack Hamilton, her flushed cheeks and over-bright eyes a clear sign of temper.

Jack looked up at her approach with an encouraging smile that insensibly soothed her ruffled emotions. 'Ah, Meg. Come and add your voice to mine. I am trying to persuade Miss Fellowes to walk in the park with me one day. Perhaps you would care to join us as her chaperon?' His eyes quizzed Meg mischievously.

'A chaperon? Me?' Meg chuckled. 'What do I have to do?'

'Oh, just walk with us. Lose yourself at a prearranged signal. Feign deafness, blindness and generally act as though you aren't there!'

Miss Fellowes simpered in a sickening way, batting her lashes at Jack's outrageous parody of the duties of a chaperon. 'Dear Mr Hamilton, you are the most dreadful flirt!'

'Am I?' A tone of surprise crept into his voice. 'Good God! I thought I was doing quite well. It just shows how you can be mistaken! Meg, my sweet, I shall have to practise on you.'

This casual endearment smote on Marcus with stunning effect. He couldn't quite believe his ears. That Jack Hamilton of all men should be flirting with the Countess of Rutherford stunned him. He turned slightly to see how Meg had reacted and nearly choked on his Madeira. She had laid her hand on Jack's arm and was laughing up at him in the most natural, unaffected way. As though she were used to such over-familiar endearments!

The emotions that ripped through Marcus were utterly overwhelming. The urge to drag Meg away from Jack forcibly blazed in his heart. A remark from Lady

Fellowes, who was claiming his attention, recalled him to his surroundings.

'Dear Sophia is enjoying herself so much, Lord Rutherford. So kind of you to invite us. But then, we are family, are we not? You must give us the pleasure of entertaining you and dear little Meg very soon.'

Rutherford returned a civil, if automatic and uncommitted reply. Meg and Jack? Oh, surely not! Jack wouldn't do a thing like that! *Would he?* And Meg? He couldn't quite believe it. We had a bargain, he reminded himself. I told her she was free to seek love elsewhere, that I would not give it. That I didn't want hers.

So why the hell was he feeling as though he wanted to give Jack a leveller and wring Meg's elegant creamy throat? At the thought of touching Meg's throat a surge of pure desire roared through him. His fingers tingled at the memory of the soft skin, that deliciously skittering pulse that throbbed below her ear. With an internal curse he tore his mind away from the primitive and wholly discreditable visions it was conjuring up.

'Such a charming gentleman,' Lady Fellowes was saying. 'So much address. I vow he is quite a favourite of mine.'

Marcus smiled rigidly. Address? Jack? Too bloody much for his money! About the only thing he wanted to address to Jack right now was a cartel of war.

At this inopportune moment Delafield announced dinner and Marcus practically ground his teeth in rage as he watched his best friend take his bride into dinner. Which was all perfectly acceptable and above board, of course; if only Meg hadn't looked at him so glowingly, hadn't seemed so utterly content in his company.

It was probably just as well that the length of the table made it impossible for Lord Rutherford to hear

much of the laughing conversation which flourished between Mr Hamilton, Miss Fellowes and Lady
Rutherford. To judge by Lady Rutherford's laughing
eyes and sparkling smile, not to mention Miss
Fellowes's rather frequent recourse to her ivory brise
fan, it was excessively entertaining to both of them.

Unavailingly Marcus told himself that Jack would
never serve him such a turn. That he was flirting with
Meg to cover his attentions to Miss Fellowes. But why
on earth would he bother flirting with Miss Fellowes?
She was just the sort of arch, simpering, society virgin
that Jack detested. Which left the unwelcome possibility
that Miss Fellowes, not Meg, was the stalking horse.

By the time they left for the King's Theatre his temper was in a lamentable state. They went in two carriages and somehow Jack had managed to arrange it so
that he went in one with Meg, Di and Miss Fellowes,
while Marcus ended up with Sir Toby, Sir Delian and
Lady Fellowes. Upon their arrival in the Haymarket it
was perfectly plain to any observer that Lady
Rutherford was entirely happy with her escort.

Marcus drew a deep breath as he politely offered his
arm to escort Miss Fellowes to the box he rented. He
had made a bargain with Meg. If she chose to act according to the terms he had set, then he would have to
accept it. No matter how much it hurt. But Jack? Surely
it was just flirtation!

As they entered the box Meg gazed about in wonder.
The theatre was full. The boxes reserved for the wealthy
shimmered and glittered with silks, satins and jewels.
Below in the pit the less well-off milled about, awaiting
the rise of the curtain.

'Goodness,' exclaimed Lady Fellowes, peering across

the theatre. 'There is my cousin Winterbourne! Now who is he with? Oh, yes! That's Lady Hartleigh's box. Hmmph! It's a mystery to me how that woman contrives on her jointure. That box must have cost above five hundred pounds!'

Since he had paid for the box shortly before his visit to Yorkshire, Marcus could have told her exactly how much above five hundred pounds. He chose, however, to ignore the comment, looking sharply at Meg to see if she were panicked at the presence of Winterbourne.

Meg merely said innocently, 'Perhaps it was a present. After all, if she likes music it would be a very good present.' She must not, she told herself, make a cake of herself. Winterbourne could not possibly distress her from the other side of the theatre. And she supposed he had to have *some* relatives. But it was a dreadful shock to realise that he was connected to her family, however tenuously.

Jack was moved to comment, 'It would, of course. But I fancy Lady Hartleigh finds the entertainment of her peers quite as fascinating as the stage.'

Marcus glared at him. Jack, damn his eyes, knew precisely which of her *peers*, as he had so delicately put it, had made Lady Hartleigh a present of her most expensive box.

A choke from behind them caught their attention. Sir Toby, finding all eyes upon him as he spluttered, waved his hand excusingly. 'Just a crumb in my throat. Don't mind me. I shall be better directly.'

Eyeing the very elegant pair of opera glasses in his wife's hand, Marcus hoped devoutly that she would not think to turn them on some of the boxes opposite during the performance. Otherwise she would be bound to discover just why so many members of society, who could not so much as carry a note in a bucket, let alone a tune, chose to patronise the opera with its convenient private boxes full of discreet shadows.

'Now, what is it tonight?' asked Lady Fellowes brightly.

Meg turned an enquiring gaze upon her. Surely she had mentioned on the note that it was La Cenerentola? She reminded her politely.

'Oh, of course! Mozart! I dote on Mozart.' She beamed at Jack. 'Dear little Sophia is excessively musical, Mr Hamilton. She takes after me, you know.'

'Er...I believe Signor Rossini to have written this opera, my dear.' Sir Delian sounded a shade apologetic. He smiled deprecatingly at his wife as she glared at him.

'Dear me,' Marcus cut in smoothly. 'How very inconsiderate these foreigners are. They can't even manage to compose their own operas. It would never happen in England!'

'True,' said Lady Diana drily. 'Since we import all our operas and don't have any written by modern English composers. Ah, they're starting!'

'Di,' said Sir Toby apologetically to Meg, 'is most unfashionable in that she comes to the opera in order to enjoy the music.'

'Why, whatever else would anyone come for?' asked Meg innocently. Sir Toby's jaw dropped ludicrously. A glare from his brother-in-law warned him that he had said quite enough and he muttered something incoherent, which was common enough not to have aroused Meg's curiosity had not her cousin Sophia Fellowes looked so scornfully knowing. Realising that she had somehow made a fool of herself, she made a mental note not to ask any more questions unless it were possible to address them very quietly to Jack.

She sat expectantly in her seat as the orchestra swept into the overture. There had been so little opportunity to hear any music in Yorkshire. Uncle Samuel had never engaged any sort of governess for her so she had never learnt to sing or play the pianoforte. She heaved a sigh of pleasure as the music ebbed and flowed around her. By the end of the first act she was entranced. Despite not knowing a word of Italian she knew the tale of Cinderella well enough to follow the action, and the music, she found, told her exactly what the characters were feeling.

She had always thought that opera must be a silly sort of thing where people got up and sang in the most unlikely way. Now she discovered that on the contrary the music somehow took the story and added an extra level of emotion to it. That the music could somehow twist itself around her very soul. And she knew how poor little Cinderella felt, lost and vulnerable, dazed that anyone, let alone a prince, could possibly love her.

And sometimes, she thought sadly, Cinderella's luck is quite out. How would she have felt if her Prince had only married her because he had to, because society and his own sense of honour demanded it? That, far from returning her love, he regretted his chivalrous action in marrying a poor little nobody? Meg bit her lower lip hard. She had wanted so much to be a good wife to Marc, even if he didn't care for her. And now they could barely converse without trying to hurt one another. There was a hot pricking behind her eyes and quickly she raised her opera glasses in defence. The last thing she needed was to be caught crying in the middle of the King's Theatre.

Slowly she became aware of the oddest sensation of being watched. Puzzled, she lowered her opera glasses and stole a glance around the box. Sir Toby looked as though he were sound asleep...yes...that was definitely a snore! Diana was watching the stage and Marcus was trying to, albeit distracted by Cousin Henrietta's arch comments. Jack was leaning on the rail, his attention on the performance, seemingly unaware of the languishing glances being cast in his direction by Cousin Sophia, and Cousin Delian looked to be in a fair way to joining Sir Toby in the arms of Morpheus.

She must be imagining it. Then, as she swung her gaze back to the stage, a movement in the box opposite caught her eye. Startled, she looked more closely. And felt a rising wave of sickness.

Sir Blaise Winterbourne had his opera glasses trained directly on her. Suddenly Meg was appallingly aware of the low-cut gown she was wearing... Fear flooded her as the music receded, giving way to nightmare panic that surged up from the darkness to choke her, drag her down into the yawning pit... A simpering giggle from Sophia dragged her back from the brink of the abyss.

She still felt cold and sick, but at least she was in control of herself again, able to think and quell the terror. Casually she reached for the Norwich silk shawl on her lap and slipped it around her shoulders. At least she didn't feel naked to that lecherous gaze.

Jack turned to her. 'Cold?' he murmured.

'A...a little,' she returned, aware that her voice was shaking.

Meg had managed to regain control of herself before the interval, but she sat rather quietly during all the chatter. Marcus had ordered champagne to be served and she sipped hers dubiously, not entirely certain she liked it.

Jack leaned over and said softly, 'Now, whatever you do, don't pour it over the edge.'

'Pour it over the edge?' Meg tried not to giggle. 'Why on earth should I do that?'

He chuckled at her near slip. 'Well, that's what my sister tells me she did here once! Caused quite a commotion down below. Roars of protest about the decadent aristocracy, threats of insurgency. If you ask me, it was a miracle Barraclough was induced to offer for her after that.' He changed the subject. 'Are you enjoying yourself on your first visit to the opera?'

'Oh, yes!' Her enthusiasm was thoroughly unfashionable. 'But I don't know anything about music. I…I wish I did. My Cousins Sophia and Henrietta sound so knowledgeable.'

'But you must have learned to sing and to play the pianoforte.' He sounded amazed and she shook her head, blushing slightly.

'No. My guardian did not engage a governess for me.' She blushed. 'I…I have no accomplishments at all. I fear I'm not much of a bargain for my lord.'

It was said with a gallant attempt at humour, but Jack could hear the underlying pain in her voice. Several things clicked into focus for him at that point. Lady Rutherford was scared, scared that she would betray her ignorance and shame to Marc, scared that she would not be able to hold her own in the strange new world into which she had been pitchforked. None of which would matter very much if things were all right between her and Marc. But they weren't. And Meg's lack of confidence in herself would not help. He had the queerest notion that some other fear was making it all worse, undermining her natural courage and gallantry.

He cocked his head and said gently, 'Then we must do something about that.'

Her eyes flew to his in startled query.

He smiled back. 'First, engage a singing master. You have a lovely speaking voice. Learn to sing. As for the other accomplishments, talk to Di. You can learn to draw, paint in water colours, embroider, whatever you like. I'm sure if you wished you could go and join her daughters and their governess.'

'Jack,' she breathed. 'That's a wonderful idea! I feel such an ignoramus at times and I don't wish my lord to…to feel—' She broke off in embarrassment.

He nodded sympathetically. 'May I give you more advice, Meg? Or, rather, a clue about the admittedly base propensities of the male sex.'

She nodded.

'Most of us don't really give a damn about a woman being able to embroider prettily or draw or paint. Some don't even care if she's intelligent or not. Marc, I can safely assure you, will not be concerned if you have all the feminine accomplishments or none of them. On the other hand, I know he appreciates your intelligence. So, if you decide to acquire a few accomplishments, choose the ones that really appeal to you. You enjoy reading, so learn French and Italian. Learn to sing. For your own pleasure and satisfaction.'

Their soft exchange was interrupted at this point by Sophia Fellowes, who had watched Jack's attentions to Meg with ill-concealed annoyance.

She fluttered her lashes at Jack and said, 'Are you enjoying the performance, sir? I vow I have never seen so many modish gowns!'

Jack and Meg exchanged a speaking glance, full of

laughter, even as he responded politely to this revealing exclamation.

This, then, thought Meg, striving to control her incipient choke of laughter, was why people came to the opera whether they were musical or not. To see and to be seen. Very well. She would conform. And in the meantime she would allow the music to ravish her senses and comfort some of her loneliness. No one need know. To the world it would appear as though Lady Rutherford was obeying the dictates of fashion.

Still chuckling inwardly, she turned away from Jack and Sophia. And found her husband's cold grey eyes resting on her enigmatically. A faintly sardonic smile played at the corner of his beautifully cut mouth. Meg felt her throat close up and her mouth go dry as she imagined, remembered the skill of those firm lips and the long fingers, negligently holding the stem of his wine glass. Determined not to betray herself, she bit her underlip hard to stop its trembling and then gave him her most brilliant social smile. The grey eyes, that had once held tenderness, hardened slightly as he inclined his head in acknowledgement. And then turned away.

Marcus felt devastated. Adrift. He had seen Meg in action for over a month now and knew that she was playing a part for the benefit of society. Even for him. He thought he could have accepted that. But to see her lower her guard for Jack hurt unbearably. The way she had looked at him! Friendly, relaxed. Damn it! She was his! Or she had been, before he drove her away.

The music began again but Marcus heard little of it, lost as he was in his own worries. What the hell had he got himself into? He had never expected to suffer agonies of jealousy over the inevitable infidelities of his countess! Infidelity...the very word grated on him. It was the last word he would have associated with Meg, he realised. It just didn't fit. But he had set the terms of their marriage himself, and he would have to acquiesce...

A faint movement caught his eye. Sophia Fellowes leaning over to address some coy remark to Jack. Fury welled up in him. It was no more than Jack deserved if Meg did foist that simpering woman on to him, but he was damned if he'd let her get away with it! As soon as they got home he was going to have a long overdue chat with his wife.

'I should like to speak with you privately, madam,' said Marcus ominously as Meg started up the stairs towards her bedchamber with her candle.

She turned, concealing a yawn. The late nights were beginning to exhaust her and she had been feeling rather unwell recently. 'Could it not wait until morning, my lord? I am rather—'

'Now.' His voice was coldly inflexible.

Fury blazed in Meg's eyes. How dare he address her thus! 'Since you ask so charmingly, my lord, naturally I am delighted to comply.' The dulcet tones were strangely at odds with the simmering rage in her eyes. 'I shall await your pleasure in the drawing room.

She did not have long to wait. Marcus joined her almost immediately.

He stated his grievance with disastrous promptitude. 'I must demand, madam, that you do not subject my friends to such obvious matchmaking efforts. In particular, I object to Mr Hamilton being a victim of such schemes! Especially in connection with Sophia Fellowes.'

Meg thought it entirely likely that she might explode,

but she held on to the edges of her temper with difficulty. 'Pray, tell me, my lord, have you some specific objection to my cousin?'

'She is a mercenary little bitch!' said Marcus, not mincing words. 'On the catch for a husband and with not the slightest shred of feeling for anyone save herself! Besides which, I do not like her family!'

Meg felt as though he had stabbed her. Hurt mingled with rage. 'And what is left for her if she does not marry?' she stormed. 'A life of dependency! Poverty, perhaps! Do you think any woman wishes to marry for those reasons? Because she must?'

Belatedly Marcus realised that he had been tactless in the extreme. Furious with himself, he lashed out, 'She would be marrying for money alone! Do you think any man wishes to be married for his money and social position? If she cared in the least for Jack...'

Cared? Her own pain exploded inside her into coruscating fury. 'Care? Why should she care? What man looks for that in his marriage? I was under the distinct impression that *love* was to be sought outside marriage! That marrying for money, position and social security was all one could expect!'

Marcus's brows snapped together. 'Meg, I am well aware that your position and Miss Fellowes are vastly different. You had no one to care for you—'

'Damn you!' The words burst from her uncontrollably. 'I don't want your pity! Do you think I *wished* to play the beggar maid to your King Cophetua? I...I should never have accepted your offer!' She whirled and fairly ran from the room, slamming the door behind her.

Marcus slumped into a chair, his head in his hands. Hell! What on earth was he to do now that she was regretting their marriage?

Chapter Twelve

A week later, Marcus sat frowning as he watched his wife pick uninterestedly at her breakfast. She had eaten very little and seemed, in his opinion, to be existing on a diet of dry toast and tea. It was her business, of course, but he was conscious of a nagging, barely acknowledged worry that she was not looking her best. Faint shadows showed like bruises under her eyes and she looked so pale in the mornings, which was about the only time he saw her, here in the library having breakfast. She always came down, no matter how late she had been the night before. And he sat there absent-mindedly consuming sirloin while longing to consume her instead.

And there she sat, pushing her egg around her plate with a look on her face that suggested it exuded an unpleasant odour. What the hell did she come down for if she were just going to sit there playing with her food? Except, of course, for the tea and toast.

'Is there something wrong with the egg?' He had not meant his voice to sound so harsh and mentally kicked himself. Frustrated desire was doing absolutely nothing for his manners.

Sure enough her face froze into an expression of indifference. She would not willingly allow him to see anything of her feelings, he realised. Not even that she didn't like her egg.

'I am not terribly hungry,' she said, with a cool detachment she was far from feeling. In fact, she felt thoroughly nauseated, a normal state of affairs for her in the mornings just now. The smell of the egg was revolting and the sight of Marcus gobbling beef in that odiously insensitive way made it worse. About all she could face was tea and toast. And she had no intention of telling her husband. It was none of his business!

'Then why come down to breakfast?' inquired Marcus, before thinking how that might sound. His tact was suffering along with his manners, he thought with an inward groan.

Meg flushed. Why, indeed? The only reason she came down was to see him. They rarely dined together now, except in company. If they found themselves at the same social engagements, it was more by coincidence than design and on more than one occasion she had suspected that he had left a ball early after finding her there. No doubt he wished to avoid having to dance with her.

So she came down to breakfast each morning to see him, even if not to speak to him since he was invariably buried in the paper and returned the briefest of monosyllabic grunts to anything she said.

This query about her egg had engendered the longest conversation they had had in days. And she was certainly not going to tell him the truth. Not after he had made it quite plain that her presence was unwelcome.

She summoned up a brittle smile and said, 'I beg your

pardon, my lord. I didn't realise that I was expected to be fashionable at breakfast time.'

'What the devil do you mean by that?' A note of anger resonated in the deep voice. The little baggage was possessed of an uncanny knack of wrongfooting him!

Good! I've stung him out of that maddening self-control, thought Meg with undutiful relish. Aloud she said, 'Merely that I will in future breakfast in my room. I am not stupid, my lord. I can take a hint.' Despite her best efforts, a note of bitterness crept into her voice.

Marcus noted it at once. 'Meg, I did not intend—' He stopped. How long was it since he had called her Meg? Since he had spoken to her gently? He went on with difficulty. 'I only thought you looked pale and wondered if you were feeling quite well, getting enough sleep…'

Meg wavered for a moment. The urge to tell him everything was almost overwhelming, the nightmares about Winterbourne, the tiredness, feeling sick in the mornings. And most of all she longed to tell him she had not meant to refuse him her bed, that she missed him, did not wish to take advantage of their bargain, that she loved him, wanted only him. But the habit of years held her back. After being taught so brutally not to confide, not to let anyone know what she was thinking, she hesitated fatally.

Misinterpreting her silence, Marcus said stiffly, 'I have no desire to interfere with you. I merely wished to exercise my duty of care as your husband.' He forced back the words he longed to say. She obviously did not wish to be pestered.

Duty of care? Duty? Damn him! Why did he have to say that? I don't want to be a duty! It was all Meg could do not to burst into tears of frustrated despair. Fool that she had been to think that marriage could remove the hated stigma of being a poor relation, a charity case, that she would be able to live with Marc and not care how he regarded her.

Her voice commendably steady, she said, 'Then you have done so in asking after my health. Now, if you will excuse me, I have an engagement with my cousins.' She rose to her feet, trying to ignore the fact that he had risen as well to escort her to the door and open it.

Marcus moved to her side and was overwhelmingly aware of her slender body as he walked with her to the door. She haunted his dreams at night until he could barely control his desire to march into her bedchamber and get into her bed, overpowering her resistance with his body, silencing her protests with kisses. He wanted her so badly, it was physically painful, and the sight of her each morning alone at breakfast was almost more than he could bear.

Dammit all! She was his wife, wasn't she? With a muttered curse he grasped her shoulders and swung her around to face him. For a bare instant his scorching gaze seared into her startled eyes and then with another curse he dragged her into his arms and brought his mouth down on hers in unrestrained passion.

Meg was stunned. His mouth crushed hers mercilessly, holding her captive as surely as his arms. And she felt herself melt against him in unthinking surrender. Never had he treated her so before! He had always been so gentle, so considerate in bed. He had aroused her to passion without once allowing her to feel threatened by his own desires.

Now his mouth was ruthless, daring her to resist. She could feel his hands at her hips as he moulded her against him, forcing her to feel his arousal. His loins were grinding against her soft belly in flagrant, undisguised need. And his tongue, possessing her mouth in brutal, plundering intimacy, told her exactly what he wanted of her body. And she wanted it too! Her brain screamed feebly that she ought to be terrified but her treacherous body was useless, trembling, her knees shaking, her thighs dissolving into heated, melting desire.

And then she felt dizzy as the nausea she had been holding at bay threatened to overcome her. For one dreadful moment the room tilted and swirled into blackness as she went limp in his arms.

Marcus felt the change at once. She sagged against him helplessly as his arms tightened instinctively to support her. Horrified, he raised his head to see her eyes shut and her face appallingly, accusingly white. Shaken with remorse, he lifted her into his arms and carried her to the sofa where he laid her tenderly.

How could he have done that? Allowed his frustration and desire to ride him so that he abused her trust! Dear God, he was no better than Winterbourne to treat her so! Lashing himself with scorn, he stood waiting for her to recover for what seemed an eternity.

When at last her eyes opened, they stared up at him in unspoken hurt, shimmering with tears.

'Why—?'

He cut her short, unable to bear her accusations. 'I agree. Most distasteful. A regrettable interlude. You need not fear that it will happen again.'

'I...I needn't...' Meg's voice shook uncontrollably. He had found her distasteful. *That* was why he had stopped kissing her...no doubt why he had never attempted to share her bed again, why he had told her so brutally not to come to him.

'No.' His voice was icily uncompromising. He ought to hold her tenderly and comfort her, but after this he could not trust himself to touch her. For one insane moment he had thought she was responding to his passion with equal abandon. And now, as he looked down at her, all he wanted to do was to take her in his arms again and continue what he had started even if it meant he took her against her will. Swearing savagely, he turned on his heel and walked out of the room, slamming the door behind him.

When next he saw Meg it was at an evening party two days later. She greeted him coolly as though nothing had happened. So he shrugged to hide his pain and buried himself in most of the amusements he had enjoyed before his marriage. The only problem was that he didn't enjoy them any more.

One amusement he eschewed completely. Lady Hartleigh cast out her glimmering lures in vain. Not even to ease the frequently painful frustration he felt would Marcus avail himself of her charms. He wanted Meg and no other. But they had made a pact not to interfere with each other and, even if he told himself that she owed him children to fulfil her side of the bargain, he would not force himself on any woman, least of all her. So he greeted his wife politely when their paths crossed socially and held his tongue about the increasing air of fragility she wore.

'Ah, good morning, cousin.' Sir Delian greeted the elegant Countess of Rutherford cheerfully as he descended the steps of his Mount Street mansion. 'You will find Sophia and Lady Fellowes within. A stroll in the park, is it?'

'Yes,' said Meg, heartily wishing she had not agreed to it. True she did not feel as sick as she had done at breakfast, but she would have given much to be tucked up on a sofa with a book right now. Or practising her drawing. Her new master seemed to think that she actually had some talent and, judging by the way he had ruthlessly castigated and torn up her first efforts, she did not think he was indulging in flattery.

The butler escorted her to the drawing room and announced her in regal accents. The Countess of Rutherford. Meg shook herself mentally. Would she ever get used to it? Stop feeling like an impostor? She stepped into the elegantly appointed room. And stopped dead. An immaculately clad figure was rising to bow gracefully.

'Dear Lady Rutherford, such a pleasure to meet you in my cousin's house. I had no idea, when I first met you, how closely we are connected!'

Meg felt sick and giddy as Sir Blaise possessed himself of her hand and kissed it. It took all of her self-control not to snatch it back. She repressed a shudder at his touch. All at once the sense of degrading foulness came flooding back into her soul. And this time there was no Marc to turn to for comfort and protection.

'I understand you are well acquainted with my cousin, dear Meg,' interposed Lady Fellowes smoothly. 'Sir Blaise has offered himself as your escort this morning.'

'Such an honour,' said Sir Blaise. 'To escort two such charming young ladies.'

The ensuing conversation eddied around Meg, who was experiencing waves of nausea and blind panic.

Somehow she had to control herself, let no one see her terror. He could do nothing in the park. There was nothing to be afraid of. Except fear itself.

Sir Blaise insisted on having a lady on each arm as they strolled to the park. Every nerve in Meg's body was shudderingly aware of his touch, the loathsome proximity of his body. And she could not escape, leaving Sophia to be escorted alone. Not that she had the slightest fear for Sophia's safety, but Cousin Henrietta had made it quite plain that she regarded Meg as Sophia's chaperon. She would be furious if Meg left Sophia alone. Meg set her teeth and thanked God for Sophia's giggling, simpering presence. At least it saved *her* from being alone with Winterbourne.

They had not proceeded far into the park when even this dubious protection was withdrawn. Lord Atherbridge strutted up to them.

'I say, Winterbourne! Two lovely fillies! Demned greedy, dear boy! Demned greedy!'

'You wound me, Atherbridge.' Sir Blaise was all conciliation. 'What can I do to atone? Ah, I have it! I shall relinquish my dear little cousin to you. Dear Cousin Sophia, you will not mind exchanging me for poor Atherbridge?'

Since Lord Atherbridge was possessed of a handsome fortune and was blessedly single, Sophia had not the least objection. 'Oh, no, Cousin.' She smiled up at his lordship meltingly. 'It will be such an honour for me!'

Meg nearly gagged at this blatant toadeating. How could she? Never would she resort to flattering Marcus like that! And to do him credit, Marcus would be just as revolted as she was. They drew ahead, Sophia gossiping and giggling girlishly. Meg clenched her teeth. Her disgust went some way to dissipating the fog of fear enveloping her, but she was drawn back to reality all too easily by Sir Blaise.

Not having Sophia on his other arm left his hand free to press Meg's, captive on his arm. She shuddered noticeably and he smiled urbanely.

'I am so delighted that we may continue our interrupted acquaintance, Lady Rutherford,' he said, continuing to pat her hand. 'Allow me to compliment you on your appearance in the fashionable world. You looked charmingly at the opera the other night! My companion Lady Hartleigh agreed with me heartily! '

Suddenly furious, Meg glared up at him. 'Perhaps you should limit your attentions to your companion! And the stage!'

He laughed softly. 'Dear me, how very unfashionable! Coming from a lady whom I observe to be most fashionable.' His eyes raked her suggestively, 'From her gowns, to her…marriage.'

All of a sudden Meg felt that she could scarcely breathe. She managed a polite smile for Lady Castlereagh who waved to her from a barouche.

Winterbourne continued smoothly, 'And I always like to be fashionable, my dear.'

The oily endearment mocked her. Marcus had once called her that. She took a shaky breath at the remembered tenderness in his voice…he hadn't meant it either. Oh, God, that was Lady Gwdyr, looking dreadfully haughty. She must pull herself together, she'd nearly cut the icy peeress.

'We could be fashionable together, don't you think, Lady Rutherford?' From his voice you'd have thought he was suggesting an outing to Almack's, thought Meg dazedly. Instead of which his eyes, roving over her body, were suggesting something quite different, something of which the mere thought sent shudders of revulsion through her very soul.

Help came from a most unexpected quarter.

'Why, Lady Rutherford! How delightful. I have been longing to further our acquaintance.' The arch tones of Lady Hartleigh were as welcome as manna from heaven. No doubt, thought Meg ironically, as her brain started to function again, she is annoyed with me for purloining another of her lovers.

Lady Hartleigh showed all the skill of a prize collie bitch as she cut Meg out neatly and appropriated Winterbourne's arm. She chattered without ceasing of this person and that, of the scandalous price of candles and the outrageous way in which her dressmaker was dunning her.

'Too dreadful!' she said mournfully. And flashed a quick glance at Meg. 'Tell me, do they dun you, Lady Rutherford?'

'Er…no,' admitted Meg. There was no opportunity for that. Cousin Samuel's training had been far too thorough.

'Outrageous,' said Lady Hartleigh. 'Here am I, a poor widow, who cannot in the least afford to be dunned, being pestered to within an inch of my life, and the Countess of Rutherford, with one of the wealthiest men in the land to husband, doesn't get a single one!' She shook her head sadly at the injustice of such a thing.

Meg stared at her suddenly. Why, she was mocking *herself*! Why should she do such a thing? Then, as Sir Blaise stepped away momentarily to respond to the greeting of a friend, the green eyes flashed towards Meg. 'Stay away from Winterbourne, Lady Rutherford.'

Nothing more. The brilliant eyes were veiled instantly and Meg could not decide whether she had been given a warning or a threat.

Later that evening in the privacy of her carriage Lady Hartleigh said casually to her escort, 'The Countess of Rutherford seems to be making quite a hit in certain quarters.'

'Quite so, my dear,' he responded suavely. 'One must grant that Rutherford's taste is, on the whole, impeccable.'

She nodded thoughtfully. 'And, of course, it coincides so neatly with your own.' There was a faint hint of speculation in the lilting voice.

'But of course, my dear.' Sir Blaise smiled. 'No doubt you are feeling his unexpected marriage to be an unfortunate lapse of taste.'

She shrugged her slim shoulders, elegant in their low-cut gown. 'What should I care?'

'Oh, merely for the loss of a fortune and a title.'

A mocking laugh rippled from her. 'You forget, Sir Blaise. I have a title and…sufficient money for my wants.'

'It is always pleasant to have a little more than is sufficient,' he suggested.

'Very pleasant,' she agreed. 'But what is done is done. I see no way of altering the facts. Do you?'

'It is *always* possible to alter the facts, my dear Althea,' he assured her. 'Perhaps you might like to give me some assistance. For which, of course, you would be suitably…er…rewarded.'

Another ripple of laughter eddied through the darkness of the carriage, this time laced with triumph. 'Behold me, Sir Blaise. All ears, I do assure you!'

Chapter Thirteen

Lady Rutherford gazed nervously around Almack's crowded assembly rooms as she waltzed with Jack Hamilton and wondered why she had ever let Marcus persuade her that she would enjoy London. True she had made friends and met with more kindness than she would have believed possible. Yet she felt totally alone. Of all her acquaintance only one seemed to suspect that Lady Rutherford was merely a disguise.

Jack Hamilton would not let Meg hide when they were alone. He was the one person she could relax with slightly, but not even to Jack could she explain what was the matter. She could have told Marc, but she had not seen him for a long time. Only Marcus, Lord Rutherford, who greeted her politely, bought occasional gifts to adorn his countess, and had never attempted to come near her again after that dreadful morning in the library. Meg told herself proudly that she didn't care. Every single night as she cried herself to sleep.

But that wasn't the only problem. The reason she was scanning the rooms so anxiously was because Sir Blaise Winterbourne, ever since escorting her in the park, had made her the object of his attentions. He never missed

a chance to approach her, soliciting her to dance in sit-
uations where she could not possibly refuse him. Only
when Rutherford was present did he avoid her, and, as
Rutherford so rarely escorted his countess to parties,
Winterbourne had ample opportunity to further his pur-
suit of the lovely Lady Rutherford.

So Meg hid behind her mask, never allowing him to
see her fear, deflecting his gallantries as she did those
of a dozen others. And dreaded sleep. Sleep, which
should have been a haven of respite from her growing
unhappiness, but had become a nightmare in itself.
Night after night she woke terrified, longing for Marc,
but having found him missing that first time and having
been informed that it was not her place to come seeking
him, she forced herself to remain in her own room. If
he were not home, but had gone to take his pleasure
with a woman he did not find distasteful, she did not
wish to know it. And besides, she had sworn never to
be in the position of poor relation ever again, never to
beg for anything. Especially not from her own husband
with whom she had made a very clear bargain.

Through the silken swirl of dancers she caught a
glimpse of Winterbourne's mocking eyes. Every muscle
in her body seized and she stumbled slightly as Jack
whirled her through a turn. The feeling of dizzy sickness
that had swept over her without warning so often in the
last two or three weeks was worse than ever as panic
ripped through her. She felt Jack's hand tighten on hers,
his arm like iron about her waist as he steadied her.

'Whoops,' he said unemotionally. They continued
back up the room, Meg deathly pale and Jack thoughtful.

He made it a practice never to interfere between a
couple but he was sorely tempted to break this rule and

take Marc by the scruff of his immaculate neck and shake some sense into him! Meg, he thought, was starting to look like a ghost. And, unless Jack missed his guess, it was not just the unsatisfactory state of affairs between Marc and Meg. Winterbourne had something to do with it.

There he was now! Watching her through the swirl of dancers. And, judging by the way Meg had stiffened in his arms, she had seen him too. No doubt he would claim Meg for the next waltz, after which she would be as glittering and unapproachable as ever. Well, this time he was going to do something about it!

Staking everything on one throw, he said softly, 'You know, you don't have to dance with him, Meg. When he approaches you, tell him you have the headache and that you are about to leave. I'll escort you home.'

She stared up at him in shock. 'What…what are you talking about, Jack?' she faltered.

'I don't know, Meg,' he answered honestly. 'You will not confide in me. Which is fair enough, I am not your husband. But whatever is wrong between you and Marc, you should tell him about Winterbourne.'

'There is nothing to tell,' she said. Her heart quailed at the thought of confiding in Marcus. Belatedly she realised that she had not denied Jack's assumption that she and Marcus were at odds.

'Just that he upsets you and will not leave you alone when Marc is not present,' said Jack, tightening his arm as he whirled her around.

She rallied. 'No more so than half a dozen others. All of whom, Di warns me, are husbands who would dearly like to be able to serve Marc as he served them!' There was a sting of angry contempt in her voice.

'True enough,' he said with a chuckle. 'But don't

blame it entirely on the philandering of Marc's bachelor days. With most of 'em, your own charms have just as much to do with it!'

She snorted, ignoring the last part of his comment. 'You speak as though my lord's philandering days were all in the past!'

The bitterness in her voice got through at once. Jack stared down at her. At last! The mask had dropped completely. He said slowly, 'Take my word for it, Meg, they are. And believe me, I would know if they weren't!'

Aware that she had slipped, Meg recovered quickly. 'My dear Jack, you are Marc's closest friend. I would not expect you to betray him. Nor should you think I mind. It is a marriage of convenience, after all.'

Deliberately he said, 'I might not betray Marc, but neither would I tell *you* an outright lie by assuring you that if Marc has sought any other woman since marrying you, then he is keeping it very dark. And, if you are refining on that unfortunate meeting in the park weeks ago, then I think you have between you made a mountain out of a molehill.'

Shaken, she said, 'But he said—'

'Meg, I don't know, or wish to know, what damnfool things Marc has said in a temper,' said Jack firmly as the music drew to a close. 'But Marc has no more sought consolation elsewhere than you have. Unless you count sparring at Jackson's, engaging in more curricle races than ever before, consuming far too much brandy and generally behaving like a bear with a sore head!'

'You mean I'm making him unhappy?' Meg was horrified. She had thought Marc was entirely happy to be free to pursue his own hedonistic life. He must be! He had exactly what he had asked for.

Jack nodded, adding, 'But no more so than he's making you unhappy. You're just better at hiding it from the world.' She was, too. He was willing to bet that, if it hadn't been for Winterbourne, he might never have realised that she was unhappy. Her next words, though, stunned him.

'But he finds me distasteful!' It came out in a stricken whisper.

Jack stared at her and said, 'Meg, he's really not *that* stupid! If he gave you that impression it was in sheer self-defence. You two are as bad as each other!'

She would have protested further but Lady Jersey came up just then, full of wickedly malicious gossip, and Meg was claimed by Sir Toby. He never danced, but often claimed Meg to sit out for the more energetic reels on the basis that she was family and would afford him protection from actually having to perform.

He was quite open about this as he steered her to a chair and, when she threatened teasingly to make him dance, he simply said, 'No, no, my dear! Think of the scandal if I expired on the floor in your arms! And Di is far too young for widowhood!'

Truth to tell, Meg was only too happy to sit out with him for half an hour. He was kind and undemanding to converse with and she was finding that she tired more and more easily in the last couple of weeks. And she felt sick so often; throwing up in the mornings and feeling queasy at the sight of food. Doubtless she was not getting enough sleep, but even the appalling paroxysms of vomiting with which she was afflicted were better than nightmares.

So she acquiesced to Sir Toby's plan for her entertainment with a certain relief. Apart from a chance to rest, it gave her the opportunity to think. Something she had resolutely avoided for some time.

Jack's blunt advice had cleared her head appreciably. If he said Marc was not…amusing himself elsewhere, then he probably wasn't. Jack wouldn't lie to her. But the question remained, why wasn't he? She had, albeit accidentally, refused him her bed. It would have been fair enough if he had sought consolation. Then that morning in the library…had he thought *she* was disgusted with *him*? If that were so he would never approach her…

Oh, God! What a mess she had made of everything! If only she had had the courage to tell him how she felt and assure him that she would still abide by their agreement, then it would all be much easier. At least they would have understood each other.

She bestowed half of her attention on Sir Toby's description of the excellencies of his favourite spaniel bitch and the litter she was nursing.

'Lovely dog, Meg. Must ask Marc if he'd like one of the pups…'

By the end of their peaceful half-hour Meg was feeling much better and Sir Toby was wondering just what Meg was thinking about. Something was bothering her, but he rather suspected that Jack had the matter in hand. Probably safer if he didn't interfere.

'Ah! A family affair! How cosy. My dance, I believe, Lady Rutherford.' Winterbourne's smooth tones broke in upon them. Sir Toby looked at him disapprovingly. Couldn't stand Winterbourne. Oily sort of chap. You practically skidded every time he opened his mouth. Still, the ladies seemed to like him and it was no business of his who Meg danced with. He might just mention it to Jack, though.

So he bowed gracefully to Meg and said, 'Thank you,

m'dear. Let Marc know about the pup. He can have one if he's a mind to it.'

He was gone into the crowd, leaving Meg to face Winterbourne.

Made bold by Jack's advice Meg went on the attack, ignoring the choking fear. She had run for long enough! 'Really, Mr Winterbourne, I am at a loss to explain your predilection for my company.'

Seeing his raised eyebrows, she said, 'Oh, dear! How clumsy of me. I have so much trouble remembering your high degree.'

'I'm sure you do, Lady Rutherford. I always thought that given a little schooling you would turn out quite creditably. And as for my predilection, as you call it, for your charming company...let us say that I always finish what I set out to do.'

White with anger now more than fear, Meg said sweetly, 'How sad not to know when to give up. Especially when someone else has already achieved the goal ahead of you.'

'My dear Lady Rutherford, I am not one to measure my...er...achievements against those of another man.'

'Just as well!' she said with a glittering smile.

'Quite so,' he said. 'Ah, here is our dear Cousin Henrietta.' He acknowledged her with a sweeping bow. 'How do you do?'

'Dear Sir Blaise, and Marguerite. I am very well,' cooed Henrietta. 'How charming a couple you make. I was just saying to Lady Jersey how much pleasure it gives me to see my two cousins so happy in each other's company.'

Meg's nausea rose and she forced herself to breathe deeply. Jack was right—she had to tell Marc. What was Sir Blaise saying now?

'A moment earlier and I should not have known whom to solicit to dance. As it is, I am promised to Lady Rutherford for this waltz. Pray excuse us, Cousin.'

'But of course, dear Blaise. Good evening, Marguerite. I shall call upon you in the next day or so to arrange a little alfresco entertainment. Perhaps to Richmond with Sir Blaise. Just a family affair, of course.'

Meg murmured a polite rejoinder, all the while vowing mentally to have a full calendar for the next month. Head held high, she permitted Winterbourne to lead her towards the dance floor. Glancing back at her cousin, she saw that Lady Fellowes was watching them go with a faint smile twisting her thin lips. A smile of triumph. Meg's dark brows snapped together as a sudden suspicion flickered through her head. Could Henrietta possibly know what had happened? Could she be egging Winterbourne on? Hoping that Winterbourne would ruin the Countess of Rutherford and justify her refusal to house her husband's orphaned cousin? No! Surely not! It was too base! She shook her head to clear it. There was a more immediate problem to deal with. She had to get rid of Winterbourne.

She was damned if she would submit to his persecution any longer! Going on the attack had given her courage and she was on the look out for an opportunity to turn the tables on her persecutor. It presented itself in the large form of Jack Hamilton who strayed into their path with seeming innocence.

Meg took her chance at once, saying clearly for all to hear, 'Ah, Jack, here you are! Mr Winterbourne...I mean, Sir Blaise has been good enough to escort me to you. I have the headache and would be vastly obliged if you would take me home.' She turned to Winterbourne. 'I thank you, sir, for your escort and your most informative conversation. Be sure I will bear it in mind. Good night.'

'The biter bit,' said Winterbourne, acknowledging her appropriation of his own method of forcing her compliance.

She met his eyes and said, 'As you see, sir, I am an apt pupil.'

He bowed and said smoothly, 'You relieve my mind enormously, Lady Rutherford.'

Meg placed her hand on Jack's arm and allowed him to lead her away, heaving a sigh of relief. She should have turned on Winterbourne weeks ago instead of trying to avoid him and dodging him through the fashionable crushes of London's hostesses. It never paid to run away from your fears, she reflected. And that was precisely what she had been doing, both with Winterbourne and Marc.

Jack had forced her to voice her unhappiness about Marc and by doing so she had found out the truth. Now that she had faced Winterbourne and served him with his own sauce, she no longer felt as though he were dominating her life. She was still afraid of him, but she was not afraid of being afraid, which had been crippling.

Jack called a chair for her and walked back to Grosvenor Square beside it, conversing with her companionably. He did not allude to their earlier conversation and, although tired and a little abstracted, Meg found his presence very soothing.

Meg opened the front door with her latch key, saying, 'Shall you come in, Jack? I don't doubt that the servants are abed but there will be brandy in the library if you would care for it.'

A discreet cough informed her that Delafield at least was not in bed. 'Good evening, my lady, Mr Hamilton. Can I fetch you anything?'

'Oh, Delafield, how nice,' said Meg. 'Yes. Some tea in the library for me if you please. Jack?'

'The brandy will be enough,' he said, preceding Meg to the door.

Marcus, arriving home early from Cribb's Parlour, headed straight for the library as had become his habit. He tended to put off going to bed these days. He was not sure if he dreaded more finding Meg in his bed or not finding her in his bed. Not that there was much chance of finding her in his bed again. His own curst pride had ensured that. It bothered the hell out of him.

And her growing friendship with Jack continued to terrify him. He couldn't bear to think that they might... fall in love. The unspoken words seared themselves into his soul. And the thought of Meg giving herself to Jack as she had to him. It appalled him but he had made a bargain. A contract. And he hadn't given her much cause to wish to renegotiate the terms of their marriage. But that was what he wanted. To cancel that sordid transaction and start again. Offer her his love. His adoration. And pray to God that she would forgive him and accept it.

His hand was on the latch when he heard voices within. He stopped dead, listening. A delightful ripple of feminine laughter bubbled up...that was Meg... followed by deeper tones... Good God! It couldn't be! Surely Jack would not...had he behaved so badly to Meg that things had already gone this far? The thought was like a knife twisting inside him. For a moment he hesitated.

And then scorching, jealous rage ignited inside him. He had told Meg that she was welcome to her amusements, need not fear his wrath…so long as she was discreet—and there was no discretion about this, dammit all! And then, on a blinding flash of realisation; he would not permit it anyway! She was *his* wife and it was about time she was reminded of it!

He flung open the door and stalked in, expecting to find them in each other's arms. Instead of which he found Jack standing in front of the fire, nursing a glass of brandy and Meg at the sofa-table, pouring herself a cup of tea from a very elegant basaltware teapot. He had to admit that if this *was* a seduction, then it was like none that he had ever participated in. Brandy, yes. But *tea*?

Neither did their reaction remotely suggest that they were concerned at his unexpected entry. His wife, damn her, simply smiled and offered him brandy, which Jack moved to pour. All of which served to make him even angrier.

Despite the fact that he didn't really believe they had been intending to betray him, he said coldly, 'I'll thank you to conduct yourself with more discretion, my lady. Entertaining a gentleman alone at this hour is not at all the thing.'

Meg was silent as colour flooded her cheeks and drained away, leaving her strangely white. For a long moment their eyes held and Marcus could see the wound he had dealt her reflected in them. He couldn't speak. Horror that he could have said something so despicable to Meg held him speechless. How utterly brutal he had been! And she was looking as though he had struck her! What the hell was wrong with him these days? He couldn't remember ever feeling this bad tempered for so long at a stretch. It had to stop!

At last she broke the silence. 'No doubt my lack of discretion bothers you more than my supposed infidelity.' For all its soft tone her voice shook with suppressed pain and the cup and saucer rattled in her hand as she set it down.

He didn't quite know what to say but Jack saved him the trouble. 'Meg, why don't you take that cup of tea up to bed with you and leave me to chat with Marc? It was good of you to offer to wait with me but, since he's home now, you need not scruple to go up. Goodnight, my dear.'

Marcus flushed. If he could see that look of frozen pain on her face, then so could Jack. No doubt he was trying in his chivalrous way to protect her. From her own husband! Shame lashed him that his best friend could possibly think Meg needed protection from him. Suddenly he was flooded with relief that she had had Jack to turn to in her misery. But enough was enough. He had to reassure her, could not let her go thinking he believed her capable of betraying him.

He went straight to her and picked up the cup and saucer. 'I beg your pardon, Meg. That was infamous of me. And quite unwarranted.' He eyed her closely. 'You look exhausted. Go to bed, my dear. I'll see you in the morning.' She nodded and held out her hand for the tea cup, again the calm Lady Rutherford who had held him at bay for the past month. He winced. She had accepted the apology at face value, but every line of her body was tautened to breaking point. She would not willingly drop her barriers again. And he could not force the issue in front of Jack.

So, shackling his urge to sweep her into his arms and

kiss her into surrender and oblivion, he smiled. 'I'll take it for you.' And he escorted her to the door, opening it for her before giving her the cup. 'Goodnight, Meg.'

He bent to kiss her gently on the cheek.

Her eyes widened in shock and instinctively her hand lifted to touch the spot lingeringly, as revealing as the sudden vulnerability in her eyes. Marcus felt an iron band tighten inexorably around his heart. Was that all he had needed to do? Could it possibly be as simple, as difficult, as that? Had he only needed to show her a little unashamed tenderness to breach her defences?

'Goodnight my lord…M…Marc.' Her voice was little more than a whisper and then she was gone.

Steeling himself, he shut the door behind her and turned to face Jack.

'Very well. You don't need to say it. I insulted both of you comprehensively. Your intelligence! Our friendship! Her virtue! You name it, I insulted it!'

'You forgot your own intelligence,' said Jack mildly. 'I had not thought you could possibly be such a codshead!' He didn't think it was the moment to admit that he had been aiming for this outcome. 'You really are a sapskull, Marc!'

Marcus groaned and said, 'For God's sake, give me that brandy! What brings you here at this hour? I'll accept that it wasn't Meg's charms.'

'I escorted her home from Almack's,' said Jack. He hesitated and then said, 'Since you are here, there's something I wanted to say. Ask you actually.'

'Mmm?' Marcus took a reviving sip of his brandy. He supposed Jack was going to tell him what a fool he was making of himself.

'Why is Meg so scared of Blaise Winterbourne? Did you or Di warn her about him? Because if you did, I think you overstated the case a trifle. The poor girl is terrified of him. And surely he wouldn't dare—?'

'What?' Marcus practically dropped his brandy. 'Did she tell you she is scared of him?'

Jack's amazement was writ large in his stunned demeanour. 'She didn't have to tell me, Marc,' he said. 'It's obvious every time he approaches her or dances with her. At least it is to me. Probably would be to you too—if you were ever there, that is.'

Marcus felt sick. 'He's been dancing with her? And she let him?'

'How can she refuse?' asked Jack reasonably. 'Although I think he makes quite sure she is in no position to do so, without calling attention to herself. She managed it tonight—that's how I came to bring her home. And I hate to say it, but his attentions are beginning to be noticed. That cousin of Meg's is doing her best to draw everyone's attention to it.'

'That bastard!' Marcus exploded. 'I swear I'll kill him!' His eyes narrowed to slits of icy rage, his fists clenched as though ready to strike. He began to pace like an enraged tiger. Raking strides took him back and forth across the room, his whole body alive with a searing anger not even Jack had ever seen.

Eventually he calmed down enough to say, 'This must go no further, Jack. I'd prefer Meg didn't even know I've told you.' Briefly he told Jack what had happened on his wedding night, finishing with, 'I let him go because I thought the risk to Meg of any scandal was too great.'

'He tried to rape her?' Sick horror sounded in Jack's voice.

'Came damn close too,' said Marcus, shuddering as he remembered how close.

'My God!' said Jack. 'It's miracle she hasn't collapsed from the strain! Why the hell didn't she tell you?'

'Because,' said Marcus evenly, 'I impressed it upon her that we were to lead separate lives, were not to tease each other and we have been doing just that. But not any more.'

'Well, thank God for that!' said Jack in relief. 'You two have been at cross purposes for quite long enough. I was getting quite depressed at watching the pair of you make a mull of your marriage.' He added thoughtfully, 'Interfering did give me something to do, though.'

Taking himself upstairs half an hour after seeing Jack out, Marcus castigated himself for not realising that Meg's façade hid unhappiness, for not forcing the issue when he had seen she looked unwell. He felt shamed that she could possibly have tried to carry such a burden alone, that she had been too hurt by his coldness to come to him. Never again, he vowed as he changed into his nightshirt. I'll see her in the morning and put this right.

He would have liked to go to her then and there, but she was probably asleep. And if he got into bed with her he would not answer for his behaviour…still, it would do no harm to peep through the door quietly. If she were asleep he could go away again…if not…

Accordingly he took a candle and padded through the bathroom, trying not to think about the night he had found her in the bath. He tapped very gently on the door. She would hear it if she were awake. There was no reply.

He was halfway back to his bedchamber when a muffled cry of fright pierced through him. In a flash he was across the bathroom and through the door.

A small lamp was burning on the nightstand and by its light he saw Meg sitting up in bed, obviously dazed and shaken, clutching the bedclothes in trembling fingers as she shuddered convulsively.

'Meg!'

She turned to him, her eyes wide and unseeing as the nightmare held her in its lingering grip. For how long, he wondered, had she been having these nightmares? Days? Weeks? No wonder she had been looking ill! He strode across the room and sat down on the edge of the bed to take her in his arms. She was not really awake, but she seemed to settle as he held her and murmured comfort in her ear. He silently cursed his pride that had blinded him to her sadness. He had thought she looked unwell because she was indulging her social ambitions, when all the time she had probably been plagued by nightmares.

He had let himself believe that she was, after all, no different from any other woman who would have married him for his money. Despite the fact that she had refused to accept his charity and had only accepted his name when he persuaded her that it would be a fair bargain. No doubt if he could hide his hurt under a surfeit of pleasure-seeking, so could she. He should have gone to her the morning after she had refused him her bed and had it out with her. Instead he had indulged his pride and left the hurt to fester, in both of them, it seemed.

She moved slightly in his arms, murmuring in distress.

'Meg, sweetheart. It's just me, Marc,' he soothed her. 'You're safe now. Nothing can hurt you. Go to sleep.'

'Marc?' She sounded barely awake.

'Yes, love.' The endearment slipped out unconsciously. He froze as he heard it on his lips.

'Not Lord Rutherford…just Marc.' And with an odd
little sigh she suddenly relaxed completely in his arms
and fell deeply asleep.

What the hell did she mean? *Not Lord Rutherford…just Marc.* It made no sense. They were the same
person, weren't they? Or were they? He thought about
it as he climbed over her and settled down with her in
his arms. She had called him Marc when she was ill,
when she was relaxed with him, when he had made love
to her. Ever since their quarrel he had been *my lord* and
she had been *madam* or *my lady*. It did make sense. The
man she had called Marc was a far cry from Lord
Rutherford. She hadn't even tried to tell *him* about
Winterbourne.

Then it dawned on him. That night he had found her
in his bed—she had asked to see him the next morning.
She had started to say something about Winterbourne,
about coming to find him. The realisation of what he
had done exploded through him. She *had* come to him.
And he had turned her away, had not bothered to listen.
Instead he had indulged his pride again, spouting arrogant nonsense about his rights, making it impossible for
her ever to confide in him, or indeed approach him at
all.

With the result that she had suffered a month of sheer
hell that would have broken most other women. Not
only had she had to endure Winterbourne's attentions,
but she had endured them in the belief that the one
person whom she might have expected to protect her,
was the one person she could not tell. She had endured
it in the belief that he would not, in fact, give a damn.

She stirred slightly as his arms tightened unconsciously. A small sigh of content breathed from her. Marcus rested his face against the silken locks. His little Meg. Somehow he would have to make quite sure she knew that Lord Rutherford was gone for good. Somehow he had to convince her that Meg was safe with Marc and would not need to hide within Lady Rutherford any more. Not with him, anyway.

Chapter Fourteen

Meg woke quite early feeling more refreshed after her night's sleep than she had in weeks. She lay in a contented doze. Her dreams last night had not been so terrible as they usually were. Somehow, at the last minute, the vileness that was Winterbourne had transformed into Marc, whose strong arms had banished the strangling terror, whose voice had comforted her.

Gradually she became aware of a heavy weight across her waist and another one pinning her legs to the bed. Puzzled, she turned her head and encountered her husband's sleeping face, strangely relaxed and gentle in slumber, with the cold eyes hidden. Fascinated she stared at it. The straight aristocratic nose, the square chin with the veriest suspicion of stubble. With a delightful shiver she remembered how sensuously it had rasped across her tender breasts when he made love to her. He had chuckled at her shocked reaction the first time, a deep seductive rumble and had promptly done it again…and again.

Somewhat belatedly she wondered why he was in her bed. Did this mean that he had come to claim his rights and had been too considerate to awaken her? Suddenly she remembered her dream, that Winterbourne had been transformed or rather had been banished by Marc. Had it been a dream? Or had Marc heard her? She knew she had woken up crying out several times in the past weeks.

His eyes opened, putting an end to her speculations. For they were warm and tender and he smiled at her, a glorious, beckoning smile as he whispered, 'I'm a bloody fool, Meg. Will you forgive me?' The arm lying over her waist tightened, an iron band drawing her to him.

She went willingly, her soft curves yielding to the hard strength of his body and felt him stir against her.

'Forgive *you*? Oh, Marc, I'm so sorry!' Tears trickled down her cheeks. 'I didn't mean all those awful things I said!'

He kissed the tears away and said in a light tone belied by the depth of tenderness in his eyes, 'Didn't you? Well, you should have, because I deserved the lot of them!' And then desire took over for both of them, rendering all the extended apologies they had intended utterly obsolete.

Over a month's abstinence had Marcus straining at the bit like a half-wild stallion and Meg discovered that her hitherto gentle husband could be fiercely possessive and demanding in his lovemaking and that having her nightgown ripped off by the right man was really quite exhilarating. And Marcus found that his shy, inexperienced bride could, with the right encouragement, become quite inventive in her efforts to please him.

Afterwards they slept again, wrapped in each other's arms in the blissful exhaustion of utter fulfilment.

* * *

Meg woke again later to find herself alone and a note on her pillow.

Dear Meg,
I have something to see to this morning. It will not take long. If you like, after that I could take you for a drive or stroll in the park. Which reminds me, we have not yet arranged a riding horse for you or a suitable carriage if you would like to drive yourself.

Marc

With a happy sigh Meg sat up and swung her legs out of bed. Only to be assailed with a wave of dizzying nausea. In her joy at being reconciled to Marc, she had quite forgotten to get up carefully and slowly, ring for a cup of tea and get straight back into bed before the nausea could really take hold. Frantically she dived for the nightstand and was copiously and comprehensively sick into the wash basin.

Feeling extremely plain and quite unlike the seductive siren who had so thoroughly pleasured, and been pleasured by, her husband an hour or so earlier, Meg rang the bell and got back into bed to wait for Lucy.

Meg had in the end decided to keep Lucy as her maid without asking anyone's advice. She liked Lucy and didn't give a damn what anyone thought anyway. But she did wish Lucy did not seem quite so delighted by her puzzling bouts of sickness. She even seemed to think Meg ought to be delighted. Oh, well, as long as she brought hot water to make a pot of tea, Meg was prepared to overlook her ill-concealed delight at this fresh evidence of Lady Rutherford's weakness.

Perhaps, thought Meg hopefully, now that she and

Marc were sharing a bed again, the nightmares would stop. She was sure the sickness was only because she hadn't been getting enough sleep. Even when he was cross with her, Marc had said she would make herself ill if she didn't let up.

It turned out to be one of her worst mornings. The cup of tea helped only marginally and the thought of breakfast revolted her. Lucy, more than usually heartless, brought up some dry toast and insisted that she eat it. Mrs Crouch, she said, had insisted it was just the thing for a lady who was feeling a mite poorly and the mistress was to eat it up and no nonsense.

Meg did as she was bid, thinking that Di had been quite right in her prophecy that the staff would accept her. Lucy and Mrs Crouch were as kind as Agnes Barlow could have been.

Marcus whipped through his accounts that morning with only a cursory blink of amazement at the trivial nature of the bills with which Meg had presented him. Despite Di's encouragement, Meg had spent very little on herself. Except, he noted with a rueful grin, at Hatchard's. The bill from there did make him raise his eyebrows a trifle. Obviously Jack, whom he knew to have taken her there the first time, had been far more successful than Di in persuading her to extravagance.

He already knew that she kept a careful eye on the household accounts. Mrs Crouch had indicated that the mistress was doing just as she ought, learning the ways of a fashionable London household and then making shrewd suggestions where necessary. He snorted. No doubt Great-uncle Samuel would be proud of her now.

When he had finally ascertained that he had dealt

with all the bills for the last month he gave his secretary directions for settling them and ordered his curricle to be brought around.

He returned an hour later with an oddly shaped parcel under his arm and a spring in his step as he went in search of Meg. Delafield informed him that he believed the mistress to be in the drawing room.

Upon entering the drawing room, Marcus thought that either Delafield must have made a mistake or that Meg had left the room. It appeared to be empty at first glance. He was about to leave when an odd circumstance caught his eye. The crimson drapery on the pedestal table was half off. Startled, he went to investigate.

And found Meg lying unconscious behind the table, half-covered in the drape, her face white. For a moment he was frozen in shock and then with a strangled groan he dropped the parcel on the table and knelt beside her, gathering her into his arms. He lifted her effortlessly and carried her to the sofa to lay her down upon it as though she might break.

Chafing her hand, he said, 'Meg, sweetheart. What's wrong? Meg?'

Her eyelids fluttered open. 'Where...what happened?' She looked completely dazed, her eyes unfocused.

'Are you all right, Meg?' He held her comfortingly against his shoulder.

'Y...yes. I felt so strange...and then...I was looking out the window and I turned to hold on to the table...' She sounded very puzzled.

'You must have fainted,' he said worriedly. She just wasn't getting enough sleep, he thought. And what about the nightmares? 'Meg...' He was very hesitant. After all, they had only just made up their differences—

at least, he hoped they had. 'Meg, how much sleep have you been getting? Have you been having nightmares, apart from the one you had last night?'

Her sigh of relief breathed through them both. 'Every night,' she whispered, with an involuntary shudder.

His arm tightened protectively as his eyes closed in pain at the thought of her waking up alone and scared, unable to come to him for comfort. 'The night you came to find me—'

'Yes. That was the first one.' She began to cry softly. 'I tried to bear it, Marc. But in the end I was so frightened to sleep that I just tried to avoid it as much as I could. Put off coming home…read…anything… anything but sleep…'

'You'll sleep in my bed from now on,' he said quietly. She stirred in his arms. 'No, don't argue. There is nothing for *you* to be ashamed of. If I hadn't been such a bloody fool that morning, this wouldn't have happened. In fact, if I hadn't been too top-heavy to think straight when I came up to bed that night I would have just got into bed with you. Instead of which I went back down to the library and spent a damnably uncomfortable night on the sofa!'

She twisted around to look at him. 'You did *what*?' Stunned disbelief echoed in her voice, all her tears suspended.

Shamefaced, he nodded. 'Told you I was a bloody fool. The crick in my neck lasted for days!'

'You mean you didn't…you just let me think…'

He nodded again. 'So, you see, I did deserve all the things you said to me. Even if not for quite the reasons you thought I deserved them for.'

They sat quietly for a while until Marcus bethought himself of the forgotten parcel and fetched it.

With a teasing smile he said, 'I have something here for you, my sweet.'

She stared up at him, her heart pounding. He had something for her, for Meg. With hands that trembled, she took the package and unwrapped it on her lap. The coverings fell away and she sat dazed, staring at a silver teapot.

Lifting her eyes to his, she said huskily, 'But we have lots of teapots…' Her voice cracked with emotion.

His sounded wobbly too. 'But this is for you, Meg. Just for you.'

Tears flooded her eyes. 'For Meg? Not for Lady Rutherford?' she whispered. And flushed scarlet. He'd think she'd lost her wits.

But with a groan he caught her into his arms, teapot and all, and said harshly, 'It's for Meg—from Marc.' She could feel his lips on her hair, his arms warm and hard, holding her safely. It was just for her—for Meg, from Marc. Not something the Earl of Rutherford thought his countess ought to have to present a good appearance. She would not need to hide any longer.

As if he had read her thoughts he said, 'Lady Rutherford may throw as much dust in the eyes of the *ton* as she can, but I want Meg.' He held her at arm's length and looked deep into her eyes.

'Oh, Marc! I…' Her heart nearly tore apart with the torrent of love that poured through it. The words were nearly out, when she remembered. He didn't want to love. And despite all he'd said, he hadn't said he loved her. She choked the words back. Forced them into submission. He was her friend again, her lover in only one sense.

'Meg?' His fingers had tightened on her shoulders. His eyes burnt into hers.

She forced herself to smile. 'Then…then we are friends again?'

In his turn Marcus forced a smile. 'Friends.' He pulled her back into his arms and stared despairingly over her head. *Friends*. For a moment he had thought, had hoped, that she loved him. But she had drawn back. As he must. It was too soon to tell her how much he cared. He'd have to show her first, regain her trust.

Belatedly he remembered he'd suggested a drive in the park and reminded her of it.

'Just the thing to bring some colour back to your cheeks,' he said firmly, overriding her protest that she really didn't feel at all the thing. 'Fresh air will help,' he insisted. 'We'll go to the Park. If we take Burnet, he can look after the horses while we have a gentle stroll.'

Meg argued no more. The thought that Marc wanted to spend time with her out of bed was too wonderful to be gainsaid. She vowed that this time she would do nothing to disturb the happiness she had been granted. It was too fragile.

Half an hour later in Marcus's curricle, Meg was regretting profoundly that she had not been more assertive over her qualms about taking carriage exercise that morning. The rocking of the well-sprung vehicle on the cobbles was making her dreadfully queasy. Her stomach roiled in protest and she felt cold and clammy. Determinedly she gritted her teeth and tried to think of something, anything else. Marc, thank God, had his eyes on his horses and had noticed nothing amiss. If they could but reach the Park so that she could get down!

Finally, just as they turned into the Park, she could

control herself no longer and gasped, 'My lord... Marc...stop! Please! I must get down...'

Marcus glanced down at her and swore. She looked about as green as the grass. There was a barouche directly behind them; he could not possibly stop in the gateway. Frantically he drove in and pulled his team over.

Before Marcus could so much as open his mouth, Burnet had let go of the straps, leapt from his perch and was at the wheelers' heads. But Meg was even faster. The horses's hooves had not stilled before she was on the carriageway, retching violently.

Marcus was beside her in a trice. 'Meg! Why did you not say you felt so unwell?' Dear God, was she really ill? Was it more than just a lack of sleep and unhappiness? And she had not told him!

Recovering slightly, Meg said, 'Oh, Marc! I'm so sorry...in front of everyone!'

'Damn and blast everyone!' he said, to the intense delight of the Ladies Castlereagh and Sefton, who passed by in a barouche at that moment. 'It's *you* I'm worried about!' He dragged a handkerchief from his pocket and wiped her mouth gently.

Despite looking distinctly green, she smiled at him radiantly. 'I shall be all right. I am always much better after lunch for some reason.'

He stared at her in disbelief as the implications of what she had said crashed in on him. *Always much better after lunch.* He could remember his mother being affected the same way—when she was increasing!

'How...how long have you been feeling sick in the mornings, Meg?' he asked very quietly.

She thought carefully. 'A couple of weeks, maybe three.'

'And you didn't think perhaps you should mention this to me?' He couldn't believe that she would not have told him something of *this* magnitude. Even if they had been at odds! Exultation warred with shame that she had not told him.

'Tell you I felt a bit sick in the mornings? Why?' Meg was puzzled. Belatedly Marc remembered; in her experience, gentlemen were never interested when one was unwell. Samuel had never bothered with her, even when she broke an arm, and now she raised questioning eyes to his face. But it went further than that…she was not in the least flustered, just puzzled. Puzzled, for God's sake!

And Marcus realised, with a lurch of his heart, that his innocent, uninformed bride had absolutely no idea of the significance of her bouts of sickness. That she had never had anyone to tell her these things, had never thought that she would need to know them. Instead of her coming to him, beaming with shy pride in her news, *he* was going to have to tell *her* she was probably pregnant. Looking around wildly for help, he caught his tiger's sapient eye.

'Took my old ma the same way, every blessed time,' offered that worthy in a helpful spirit that made Marcus long to brain him. 'Goes off after a bit usually.' He seemed quite unsurprised.

'Thank you, Burnet,' said Marcus drily, wondering if everyone in the household except himself and Meg knew the truth. He hoped to God his staff was as discreet as he had always thought. If this got out, they would be twitted by their entire acquaintance. He pushed these thoughts to the back of his mind. For now he had to get Meg home, preferably without further mishap.

'I think, my dear, that I had better take you home,' he said in as restrained a tone as he could manage. He wanted to explode with his joy, to shout his triumph to the blue skies with their lamb's-wool clouds. A child! His child! Meg's child! He didn't give a damn if it were a boy or a girl! He had better tell Meg first. Privately!

'A baby?' Meg could not believe her ears. 'You think I'm having a baby?'

Marcus nodded. 'It's quite likely you know, sweetheart. It is a common result of sharing a bed…or—' his eyes twinkled wickedly '—a bath, for that matter.'

Meg would have blushed had she not been scarlet already. After marching her into the library and settling her on the sofa, Marc had proceeded to ask her a series of the most embarrassingly intimate questions imaginable, on a subject she had never dreamed a gentleman would know anything about.

He had actually asked her when she had last had her monthly courses, and upon hearing that it was before their wedding, had asked her how long before. Flustered at such a personal question, she had had to rack her brain for ages before remembering that it had been about a fortnight before. As if that were not enough, he had actually asked her if she were generally regular.

Upon being informed in an embarrassed mutter that she was, he had told her very gently that he thought she was going to have a baby.

A baby. A baby of her own. Marc's baby. She sat in stunned silence, unable to speak for the wave of joy that flooded her heart. She would have a baby to love and nurse. Someone who would love her, depend upon her. Someone who needed Meg. And Marc had given her this priceless gift.

Concerned at her long silence, Marcus spoke her name very softly. 'Meg?' What was she thinking? Was she frightened at what lay before her. Childbirth? Suddenly Marcus was frightened. It overwhelmed his joy. Women died in childbirth…frequently…as his mother had done. His guts twisted into a hard knot of fear at the memory. What if he lost Meg? Resolutely he thrust the idea away.

'Meg, are you all right?' She was so silent, her head bowed. He put a hand under her chin and lifted it gently and met such a blaze of joy in the blue-grey eyes that his own knot of fear began to dissolve in the face of it.

'All right?' Her voice was breathless. 'All right? Oh, Marc! Thank you!' She flung her arms around him and hugged him. He held her tightly, stroking the nape of her neck, his fingers teasing and seductive, and felt her quiver responsively. Not quite the usual way of doing things, he thought ruefully. She should have told him! Come to think of it, shouldn't he be thanking her? Nothing, he realised, absolutely nothing about this marriage fitted in with his expectations.

After a light meal Meg retired to her room for a nap and Marcus headed for the library to do some much-needed thinking. All this was more than he had bargained for. He had glibly told Meg that he was marrying for children. Expected her to produce an heir or three.

With a sickening sense of shame, he realised that in making his cold-blooded bargain, he had accorded her less respect than he would one of his brood mares. He had not expected to feel this chilling, bone-shaking fear at the thought of Meg in childbirth.

Or had he? Was that why he had tried to choose a wife he would not care about? Except, of course, in a friendly, detached sort of way. Women died all the time in childbirth. Vibrant, affectionate, *loving* women. Women like his mother, for example.

For the first time in years Marcus allowed himself to think about his mother's death and the baby brother who had died with her. He knew that the one unhappiness in his parents' marriage had been that they only had two children. It had not been a desire for a back-up heir that had worried them. They had simply wanted children and there had been several miscarriages in the fifteen years between his own birth and the pregnancy that had killed her.

He remembered his parents' happiness during those last school holidays. The buzz of excitement in the household. They were ecstatic. The pregnancy had gone so well. And five weeks later he'd been summoned to his housemaster's study where the news had been broken to him. He remembered thinking that the gods had been jealous of so much happiness, and he determined to guard against it. What you didn't have, no one, not even the gods, could take away. His father's agony of guilt and remorse had only confirmed him in his opinion. Better not to care if loss could destroy a man so totally.

And now he cared. Without ever intending such a thing, he had fallen in love with Meg after making a bargain with her that now shamed his soul with its sordid assumptions. And she had accepted it. Not because she was after his money or title, but because she had been desperate and had had nowhere else to go—and because she had been too innocent and unsophisticated to see it for the insult it was. With a groan he realised that he had taken advantage of her as surely as Winterbourne had attempted to.

And now she was pregnant, radiant with joy. Had thanked him as though he had bestowed a priceless gift upon her, when what he had given could prove to be a death sentence. He wanted to go to her and tell her he loved her. Beg her to start over with him. Let him court her and woo her as he should have done.

But even if it now revolted him, they had made a bargain. He had promised not to make demands on Meg, not to interfere with her. Just because he no longer wanted the freedom he had reserved for himself was not a sufficient reason to break his word. She had accepted his word in good faith. How was she supposed to understand that his proposal had been an attempt to hide his own fears, when even he had not realised that?

And even if she did agree, even if she did come to love him in return…it would be to tempt the gods, make them look too closely at his joy, make them look with jealousy on his little Meg. The thought stabbed through him like a cold, shining lance, piercing his entrails with chilly, merciless terror. To voice his love would be to offer Meg as a hostage to fortune.

But he could not go on the way he had been. Even if he did not dare to ask for her love, they would have to be friends if she were to be happy. He could not bear to think that she might ever be too proud, or scared of him, to ask for his help. And perhaps if the gods could see his despair, they might think he was already miserable enough and overlook his little Meg.

As she dressed for dinner Meg was conscious of a warm glow of happiness. She was having a baby and she was going to see Marc at dinner. He had tucked her up for her nap and said so.

Until dinner, my sweet.

The endearment rested safely in her heart, a buffer against all possible harm. She was going to see Marc. Even if it was across fifty feet of over-polished mahogany. All right then, twenty feet! But it might as well be fifty for all the conversation you could have down its length. Still, if that was how Marc preferred it… It was his house, after all, and she had promised not to tease him.

She floated down to dinner, far happier than she had been in weeks. Marcus was awaiting her in the library and smiled as she came in. She felt her heart leap in a wild dance of joy as he came to her and kissed her tenderly.

'Did you sleep well?' he asked as he released her.

'Oh, yes,' she said, rubbing her cheek against his shoulder.

Marcus felt a stab of joy. She looked so much better, less pale and wan. And her eyes had lost that haunted look he had seen in them lately. She was again the confiding, trusting woman he had married. Just what he had done to deserve such a blessing he didn't know, but he was damned if he'd endanger it again.

And he was definitely not going to risk exposing her to Winterbourne again. Which brought him to a problem. He really had to go to Yorkshire to oversee some of the improvements that he had set in train and he was definitely not prepared to leave Meg alone in London. But how would she cope with the journey if she were feeling unwell?

As he escorted her to the dining room, he asked, 'How would you feel about a trip to Yorkshire in a couple of weeks?'

Her eyes flew to his. 'You'd take me?'

He nearly died. She could still think he'd leave her behind? After what she'd told him?

With Delafield in the hall he couldn't do a thing except press the small hand on his arm and say, 'I won't *not* take you. We'll travel in easy stages, any way you like, by chaise or my curricle. And we'll stop as often as you like. I need to go up to see to a few things, but there's no hurry. We'll go when you feel you can manage it, not before.'

He wanted her with him. It took a moment to sink in, that he didn't want to be without her, even for a short time. Her heart swelled. Surely, even if he never loved her as she loved him, she could be happy with what she had now?

To her surprise at the end of dinner, when the covers had been removed and the footmen dismissed, Marcus beckoned to Delafield and said, 'Now that you have demonstrated to your mistress that the staff can provide a formal dinner, do you think we could have it set out in the library when we dine alone or just have one or two intimate guests?' It was said with the sweetest of smiles, but there was no mistaking the authority in that voice.

Delafield seemed shocked. 'My lord, what is suitable for a bachelor establishment cannot be right for my lady—'

'My lady,' said Marcus inflexibly, 'would prefer not to have to shout across twenty feet of mahogany to address a simple remark to me. You know what Shakespeare says…''Her voice was ever gentle, sweet and low, an excellent thing in a woman''…I do feel, Delafield, that we should preserve your mistress's excellences where possible.'

Meg practically choked in her napkin in her efforts to stifle her giggles. Master and servant turned their attention to her at once.

'I beg your pardon, my lady,' said Marcus. 'I hope this meets with your approval.'

She nodded, the lower part of her face still hidden behind the napkin, bright eyes gleaming with fun. It was so lovely to have her tender, caring Marc back. To be able to share a joke…and a bed.

'Good. Bring your wine glass with you and we'll both go to the library.' He rose and held out his arm with a very wicked smile. A smile which suggested he was pleased to be sharing a bed again. Blushing, she went to him and placed her hand on his arm.

As they left the room she was moved to inquire, 'Why *do* women have to leave the room for the gentlemen to finish their wine?'

Marcus grinned as he caught a warning glare from Delafield who was holding the door for them. 'Tradition, my dear, dictates that the gentlemen are supposed to sit over their wine and recount…er…stories in somewhat dubious taste…if you follow my meaning.'

He observed his wife's comprehensive blush with marked satisfaction.

'Oh,' said Meg weakly.

Marcus promptly pressed his advantage. 'Dining alone with one's wife, of course, has obvious benefits,' he pronounced urbanely as he allowed his gaze to rest appreciatively on Meg's low-cut neckline.

'It does?' Meg was only sure of one thing. He was going to say something absolutely outrageous.

'Mmm. I always prefer to follow up such stories with action!'

Chapter Fifteen

Sitting before a roaring fire in the cosy library of Rutherford House, wrapped in what appeared to be every cashmere shawl in London, with a hot brick at her feet on a very fine day in late spring, Meg was wondering if she could deal with another seven months of this nearly terminal boredom. She was seriously considering telling Marc that it was all a false alarm and she had had her monthly courses after all. According to Mrs Crouch it would be a while before she started to show. Perhaps by then Marc would have calmed down a trifle.

Even being back in the same bed was driving her insane, because he wouldn't touch her! Not since the night he'd told Delafield to reduce the dining table. After telling her a couple of what she suspected were relatively tame post-dinner stories, he'd seduced her on the library floor in front of the fire and since then he'd behaved as though he'd taken a vow of celibacy! He just about had a seizure if she so much as sneezed and she had not been allowed to attend a single party in the last week. He had given it out that she was indisposed and unable to see anyone. And unfortunately Di had been out of town for a few days.

Meg had been understandably shy about telling anyone she was pregnant. But in the face of Marc's overreaction she had to do something! Which was why she had meekly acquiesced in his plan for her morning: to whit, sitting in front of the fire doing nothing except wait for Di, who had returned last night. The moment Marc's back had been turned she had scribbled a quick note and dispatched one of the footmen with it.

There was something odd about Marc's reaction to her pregnancy. At first she had not doubted that he was delighted, but increasingly he looked worried. She had caught him looking at her as though he were guilty of some heinous crime. And when she asked him if something was wrong, he lied. Badly.

And he was cosseting her to death. Sending her to bed early. Keeping her in bed late, which would have been fine if he had joined her. But the wretched man came to bed long after she was asleep and was invariably out of bed by the time she awoke. She usually awoke to discover him making her a cup of tea, having shamelessly intercepted Lucy at the door in his nightrail.

In the face of his behaviour, she could not doubt his concern, could not doubt that he cared for her personally, but she could not break through his iron control. And she wasn't quite sure what to do about it. Or even if she should do something about it. Perhaps Marc was afraid that if they made love the baby might drop out or something. After having been told by her husband that she was pregnant, Meg was not prepared to confess to even more ignorance of her bodily functions to him.

So, when in doubt, ask an expert. Di had four healthy

and mischievous children and that made her the obvious choice.

She came in unannounced. 'Goodness, Meg! Are you really sick? It's simply boiling in here.'

Her keen glance took in the voluminous shawls and the look of resignation on Meg's perspiring face as she sat down on the sofa beside her. 'Whatever is the matter? You know, dear, if you're a trifle warm, I should take off one of those shawls. Or maybe even five of them.'

Meg hesitated for a moment and then said baldly, 'Marc seems to think I'm increasing.'

'Marc! What the devil would he know about it?' asked Di.

'Well, he certainly knows more than I do!' confessed Meg shamefacedly and told Di what had happened.

To her everlasting credit Di succeeded in maintaining a straight face until the end of Meg's recital.

'You were sick?' There was an expression of respectful awe on her face as she regarded her sister-in-law. 'In Hyde Park?'

'On the carriage way.'

'During the morning promenade?'

Meg nodded.

At first it was just a twitch at the corner of her mouth, which rapidly progressed to a broad grin. Finally Di gave up the unequal struggle and succumbed to peals of laughter. Meg, who had spent the entire week cooped up with a husband in low spirits, joined in heartily.

'Oh, dear,' gasped Di, when she could speak. 'I should love to have seen his face! His high and mighty lordship, the Earl of Rutherford! How utterly splendid! Why, oh, *why*, did I have to be away? But tell me, why is Marc looking so glum? I saw him from the carriage as I drove up and he doesn't look happy at all. And why on earth are you sitting tucked up in front of the fire on such a lovely day? Are you feeling sick?'

'Not now,' said Meg. 'I'm always fine by late morning. As for why I'm sitting here—Marc won't let me so much as set foot out of the house. He was delighted at first, I think, but now he seems…I don't know… pleased, but…angry.'

'Oh.' Di was silent for a few moments. 'Maman. I never thought of that.'

'Pardon?'

'Maman. Our mother,' said Di slowly. 'Did Marc never tell you anything about her?'

Meg shook her head. What on earth could her mother-in-law have to do with it?

Di told her. 'Maman died in childbirth when I was twenty and Marc was fifteen. No. He wouldn't tell you. Stupid question. He never talks about her much. He was shattered by her death and our father's reaction didn't help. You see, Papa blamed himself and his desire for more children. He spent the rest of his life flailing around in his own guilt. Which was silly, because Maman wanted the baby as much as he did.'

She sighed and then went on, 'So Marc, while doubtless *aux anges* in one respect, is also shaking with terror in case you should suffer the same fate. At least, I suppose that is the problem. And it certainly explains his over-protectiveness. He practically drove me crazy the first couple of times I was increasing, so I hate to imagine how he'd feel about you.'

The thought of death had not occurred to Meg. She had been so excited at the thought of a baby that the risks involved had not sunk in. She had just thought Marc was concerned about her feeling sick.

Swallowing hard, she turned to Di and said, 'But do you think—?'

Di interrupted her briskly. 'What I think is that Marc is making a cake of himself! Now, get rid of these ridiculous shawls and come and take a stroll in the park with me. It will be very much better for you if you stay active and healthy. Take my word for it, giving birth needs lots of energy and if you sit around worrying about Marc's idiocy for the next six months you'll go mad. Come along, I can tell you all about it as we go.'

'There's just one other thing, Di.' Meg definitely didn't want to ask this question either on the way to, or in, the park. 'Is it safe to…to…well, to make love when you are increasing?'

Di simply stared at her. 'Is it safe? Why ever wouldn't it be?'

Meg blushed. Maybe Marc just wasn't interested. had only ever wanted her because he needed an heir. 'I just thought…well…Marc won't touch me!'

'Marc,' said the absent Earl's sister, not mincing matters, 'is the biggest idiot I know!' She stopped just short of informing Meg that, although he might not have used such stratagems himself, Marc Langley certainly knew there was nothing to fear in making love to a pregnant woman. A pregnant wife, in fact, was one of many a rake's preferred targets.

Instead she opted for practical suggestions. 'Now, here's what you should do…' And she proceeded to give a piece of scandalously detailed advice that brought a very naughty twinkle to Meg's eyes, and an even naughtier smile to her lips.

'*That* should settle *him*!' concluded Lady Diana confidently.

Lady Rutherford thought there could be no doubt of that.

By dint of some extremely devious questioning of the servants, Meg had ascertained that Marc was taking his bath during the late afternoon when she was supposedly tucked up safely in bed. No doubt he thought he was being excessively clever, she mused with unbecoming smugness, as she nestled down into her silken bedclothes for a sleep after her stroll with Di.

Her sister-in-law had been full of information and advice about pregnancy, childbirth and babies. She hadn't bothered about toddlers. 'Time enough for that. They are revolting little angels. That's all you need to know about them for now.'

And, 'Once you stop feeling quite so sick, get Marc to take you down to Alston Court. Fresh air and gentle walks in the country will be much better for you than town... He's taking you already? After going to Yorkshire? Humph! At least he's showing *some* evidence of rational thought!'

Meg had felt as though she were being advised by a loving mother or elder sister as they walked.

'Of course women die, my love. I can't deny that. But to be worrying about it now is nonsensical. You can do nothing about it except stay as well and happy as you can.

'Wet nurses may be fashionable, but you feed him, or her, yourself. Marc won't mind and it is the loveliest feeling you can imagine. So cuddly!'

And later, 'I'll come down to Alston Court for your confinement naturally—' She stopped short as Meg stared in amazement. 'Well, only if you want me to...'

'Want you?' Meg's eyes were shimmering with tears.

The one thing really scaring her had been facing the ordeal without a mother or sister. The thought of Cousin Henrietta attending the birth was not to be borne. 'Would you really come? Oh, Di!'

'Of course I'm coming!' said Di indignantly. 'Now dry your eyes. You can't possibly *cry* in the middle of Hyde Park. Throwing up here was outrageous enough!' Then, in tones of inspiration, she added, 'You know, dear, if I were you, I should bring that nice, sensible Mrs Barlow you told me about, back from Yorkshire. I'm sure Marc would think it a good idea.'

Now, as Meg dozed off, she clung to the idea that Di was treating her as though she were truly family, not just Marc's accidental bride. Briefly she thought of the dangers in childbirth. Di was right. She should concentrate on staying happy and healthy. And Di had promised to have a tactful word with Marc. Tactful for Di, anyway. So she went off to sleep, content in the knowledge that Lucy had promised faithfully to awaken her at four o'clock.

Marcus relaxed back in his bath and shut his eyes with a sigh of relief. He'd had a busy morning and Di's message demanding his immediate presence had taken him completely by surprise. She didn't do that often, so he had gone and received an earful of sisterly candour that had left him stunned.

He really hadn't meant to scare Meg with his behaviour, but he could see now that he had been just a shade over-protective. And of course he didn't think she needed to spend the next seven months incarcerated on a sofa…it was just that—

Just that he was an ignorant, addlepated male, who

shouldn't be allowed out without a leash, Di had finished for him.

He had apologised and promised to atone. And she'd had one or two brilliant ideas; such as taking the Barlows down to Alston Court. But when it came to his own sister informing him that making love to his wife would not cause the baby any harm, he drew the line. Frostily he had told Diana to mind her own business. He had left almost at once, but the dignity of his grand exit was totally ruined by Di escorting him downstairs and shamelessly telling him, in front of her fascinated butler and two openly amused footmen, that reformed rakes were all the same—the world's biggest prudes when it came to their own wives.

She was right, of course, he admitted to himself in the sanctity of his bath. He was being an idiot. He couldn't help himself where Meg was concerned. His erstwhile cynical and rational brain seemed to dissolve into a liquefied mess of panic just thinking about her in childbirth. And of course he didn't think that making love would endanger the baby, or not in the way Di meant. It was just that stupid, illogical idea that to be too happy was courting disaster. That he was terrified to tell Meg that he loved her. And that he knew he would never be able to make love to her again without telling her. He hadn't explained that to Di. It sounded mawkish in the extreme, even to him and he didn't dare think what Di would have to say!

Perhaps, he thought, it would be better to accept the joy he had now and leave the future to take care of itself. It made far more sense really. He wondered why he hadn't thought of it before. Probably because you don't think at all when Meg's around, an annoying internal voice informed him. Any fool who could think that she and Jack would have had an affair is clearly unhinged!

His decision made, he stretched, luxuriating in the warmth of his bath and in the delightful intention of taking his wife to bed. Early. For the express purpose of having his scandalously wicked way with her. His loins tightened painfully at the thought. After which he was going to tell her just how much he loved her. If he could find the words…if they even existed…

A faint click behind him informed him that he was not alone. Startled he swung around and there was Meg, draped—dressed would definitely have been an over-statement—in a flimsy silk peignoir. Its shimmering, pink folds clung and shifted in the most tantalising way, affording glimpses of long silky limbs which made him wonder if the incendiary heat charging his body would cause the bath to boil over. His mouth suddenly dry, he stared at her, noting the darker pink of her nipples which peeped shyly through the diaphanous fabric and that darker shadow at the top of her thighs… He swallowed hard. Hell! She looked like a siren in that thing, ripe, seductive.

'Oh, hullo, Marc. Am I disturbing you?' The slight curve at the corner of her mouth told him that she knew perfectly well he was extremely disturbed. In a very basic, male way. And her voice! It sounded so husky. What the hell was she thinking of? The answer came at once. His sweet little Meg was thinking of exactly the same thing he was.

As if in confirmation of this, she smiled at him with heart-stopping slowness and glided across the floor to one of the niches. Unhurriedly she allowed the peignoir to slither with a seductive hushing off her shoulders on to the bench and, wearing nothing but that smile and her rippling, tumbling curls, she came and sat down on the edge of the bath beside him. Ostensibly to trail her legs in the water.

'Will you be long in the bath?'

Marc looked up and met the blandest query in her eyes. The hunter, he realised belatedly, had become the hunted...and was enjoying it immensely. His shy bride had turned out to be an unprincipled little hussy.

'How long would you like me to be?' he drawled. Two could play this game.

'Oh, take your time,' she responded.

That went without saying, thought Marc, as one silken leg grazed his shoulder in seeming innocence. He would be only too pleased to take his time with her. Within reason, of course, he amended, as that leg slid past again.

Casually he stretched and slid one wet, powerfully muscled arm behind her bottom to scoop her off the edge and into the bath. She came unresistingly and met his fiery gaze with a becoming blush. He smiled wickedly. So, she was not quite as calm as she was pretending to be. Good.

Keeping his voice light, despite the screaming demands of his body, Marcus enquired, 'Just what do you think you are doing?'

'What do *you* think I'm doing?' countered Meg, a trifle breathlessly as he manoeuvred her with one compelling hand in the small of her back to straddle his hips. The other hand was lazily caressing one puckered and aching nipple. She gasped in pleasure, her eyes widening in shock at the novelty of her position.

Marcus did not reply at once. Her response was so spontaneous, so lovely, he just wanted to watch her, adore her with his eyes and hands.

But at last he said, 'Seducing me?' The hand at her breast trailed down her stomach, leaving a track of fire, and slid between her thighs. The hand at her back drew her closer and she felt his mouth close possessively on first one breast and then the other. She pressed small, moist kisses on his nape, under his ear and sobbed with desire as he loved her, gently, thoroughly.

In a voice husky with passion she asked, 'Do you mind being seduced?' She had a feeling that the tables were well and truly turned now anyway.

A little laugh shook him as he lifted her to ease her against his throbbing body. 'Does it feel as though I mind?' He gave her no chance to reply, reaching up to tangle his long fingers in her silken tresses, and taking her mouth in a kiss of raw, unfettered passion as he brought her quivering body down to meet his possessive thrust in absolute mastery.

Meg's last coherent thought was that if he did mind, he was certainly going to a great deal of effort to disguise the fact. They hadn't even made it to the sofa-bed this time.

Meg lay nestled safely in Marc's arms, wondering dreamily if they ought to get up and dress for dinner. It felt so lovely just to lie here with his hard, warm body pressed against her, his gentle, knowing hands caressing her shoulder and the occasional pressure of his lips as he dropped a light kiss on her still-damp hair.

Marc had dried her so tenderly after they had finally left the bath and somehow they had ended up in his bed making love again. And now they lay together in a tender intimacy which nearly broke her heart. At times like this it was so easy to pretend that he loved her, know that she loved him... The words welled up in her heart, straining, desperate to escape. She held them back, not wishing to destroy the fragile joy of the moment. Instead she turned her face slightly and pressed a kiss on the hard wall of his chest, revelling in the contrast of smooth skin and underlying steel of muscle, drinking in the warm, musky scent of his body.

His arms tightened to iron around her and she heard a soft groan deep in his throat. And then his voice, inexpressibly tender, 'Meg, dearest, loveliest Meg. My little love…'

She couldn't bear it. The endearment shattered her joy into fragments which pierced her heart like a storm of arrows. For a moment she just froze, trying to ignore her pain, but it was impossible to pretend any longer. Her eyes filled with tears which spilt over in a flood of grief. 'Don't…please, Marc…don't say that,' she whispered.

The words nearly tore his heart out. It was too late, he thought despairingly as he turned her gently to face him. She didn't want his love. He had hurt her too badly, confused her with his contradictory behaviour. Then, as he saw the tear-drowned eyes and the trembling mouth, hope surged in him. *'Don't say it?'* he asked. 'Why not, my darling?'

She saw him through a blur of tears. 'I can't bear it,' she said brokenly. 'Not…not unless you love me.' Oh, God, what had she said? He didn't want her love. No one had ever wanted her love. Numbly, she waited for the inevitable rejection, for him to tell her gently that he could not love her, that he was sorry, but he was just fond of her. His very kindness would make it the worst rejection of all.

His voice was barely recognisable, tearing with emotion. 'Then you love me, Meg?'

'Yes,' she whispered. 'I'm sorry, Marc…I can't help it.' She tried to pull away from him, but found that his arms were drawing her back, cradling her against him as he kissed the tears away.

'I think we need to renegotiate our bargain then, my little love,' he said, shakenly. 'Something along the lines of *a heart for a heart*. Mine was yours long ago, even if I was too proud to admit it and ask for yours in return. As I do now.'

Her heart completely overflowed in its frantic joy. 'Oh, Marc,' she sobbed. 'It was always yours. I knew when you asked me to marry you that I would love you. You were always so kind to me…looked after me, but you never seemed to *pity* me. Even when you offered to marry me, you offered a bargain between equals. Always before people either despised me or pitied me. You were the only one who ever accepted me and didn't care about my family.'

A surge of shame ripped through him. That vile bargain he had struck with her! All these weeks it had kept them apart, tormenting him, nearly destroying Meg. Yet she had continued to love him and he, fool that he was, had never seen it.

'And you never told me.' He kissed her gently. 'Because of our stupid bargain. And because I shut you out.'

She shook her head. 'No. Not just that. I was too scared anyway. You see, when I went to Yorkshire I thought that Cousin Euphemia and Cousin Samuel had sent for me because they cared about me. But they…they didn't. And Henrietta had told me I was a disgrace. So…I…I couldn't tell you. Why on earth would you, of all people, want me to love you? No one else did.'

'Because I can't live without it, Meg,' he said passionately. And lowered his mouth to hers in a kiss of total possession and dedication.

Chapter Sixteen

Gala Night at Vauxhall Gardens was always enjoyable, thought Meg. She had attended several times before in company with Di and Toby, who included her in their parties as a matter of course. Jack Hamilton had been her escort on these occasions. Handsome, kind, attentive to her every need, he was an escort any lady might preen herself on. But nothing, thought Meg, could possibly rival the delight of wandering the groves in the company of her absurd and over-protective husband. Unless it was waltzing with him, pressed to his body in a way that made every nerve tingle as his powerful thighs moved intimately against hers as they danced.

Her eyes, raised to his, shone with her love and Marcus had to bring every vestige of self-discipline to bear not to bend and accept the invitation of her softly parted lips. His arm tightened appreciably around her, drawing her even closer. He was aware that quite a number of persons were watching them in scandalised amusement. He couldn't have cared less. She was his! And he wanted the whole world to know it!

And in a couple of days he'd have her all to himself. Her morning sickness was so much better, now she was getting enough sleep, that they were leaving for Yorkshire. After that he'd take her straight down to Alston Court. The thought of seeing Meg in the place he'd always thought of as home sent a warm glow right through him. She'd never had a proper home, one full of love and happiness. And of late years, he'd known deep down that Alston Court was crying out for a mistress, to be the happy home it had been in his mother's day. Seeing Meg there would finally lay that ghost to rest as well.

Watching them as he chatted casually to Di, Jack thought that, until now, even he had never seen the real Meg. Oh, he had seen past the glittering façade of Lady Rutherford, but he had never seen the glowing, adoring girl who was circling the floor in Marc's arms.

Di was saying something of the sort about Marc. 'Such a change in the pair of them! Oh, Jack, I've not seen Marc like this since he was a boy.' Consideringly she said, 'Not even then! No boy could look like that!'

She was right, thought Jack. Finally surrendering to love in his mid-thirties, Marc was mature enough to know the value of what he had been granted. He had seen Marc with enough women to recognise the difference. For the first time ever Marc was letting his feelings show and obviously didn't give a damn who saw it.

'And Meg!' continued Di, with an almost maternal pride. 'I vow she is lovelier than ever. Such a bloom!' She stopped short, and Jack waited with a slightly quirked eyebrow.

Taking pity on her sudden embarrassment, he said smoothly, 'Better start thinking of christening presents, hadn't we? I understand you and Toby and I have to do our duty early next year.'

'Oh, good!' said Di, in relieved accents. 'I'm so glad they asked you as well. Now I must get back to our box. Aunt Regina will be grilling poor Toby mercilessly.' She rustled away after giving him an affectionate pat on the arm.

Jack stayed to watch the dancers as they swirled past him in a scented whirl of silk and superfine. A discreet cough at his elbow drew his attention. He turned and blinked in surprise. Lady Hartleigh stood just behind him, her gaze fixed on a tall, tawny-headed figure as he whirled his laughing partner through a turn.

Without looking at Jack, she said in amusement, 'He never danced with me like that.'

'Did you want him to?' asked Jack curiously. And then thought, what a tactless question!

But Althea Hartleigh gave a genuine laugh. 'No, Mr Hamilton, I did not. Heavens! Only think of the *scandal* had he done so!' Then with a faint smile she added, 'As you so rightly thought, I wanted Rutherford's money and his title.' She paused for a moment and added, 'And his, shall we say, physical prowess.'

Whatever answer he had expected, it hadn't been that! 'You're very honest,' he said gently, wondering if she had been hurt by Marc's defection.

She shrugged. 'Not my worst enemy could accuse me of deluding myself. And it did not occur to me that Marcus wanted more. Well, he didn't, did he? Not from me.' She was silent for a moment and then said deliberately, 'Any more than I wished to give it.'

'I'm sorry—' began Jack.

He was interrupted at once. 'Don't be. We would not have been happy. I thought Marcus as cold and calculating as myself. Had I known he could be like this, I should have run a mile!' There was no mistaking the sincerity in her voice.

There was a moment's silence and then she said, 'Tell Marcus to watch his bride. Winterbourne is out of town at the moment but when he gets back... I have heard some things that worried me about Lady Rutherford and Blaise Winterbourne. And he watches her all the time. Both he and Henrietta Fellowes are out to do the chit a mischief.'

Jack stiffened and she laughed harshly. 'Don't be a fool, Hamilton! I can see what's under my nose. That child is as much in love with Marcus as he is with her. But that would not deter Winterbourne. As a woman, I cannot stand by and acquiesce in what he would do to her. And I have as much affection for Marcus as for any man—I do not wish to see him hurt. Warn them for me. I cannot approach either without causing trouble.' She smiled up at him with something of her old glimmer in the green eyes. 'As I did that day in the park! Add to your kindness by apologising to Lady Rutherford for my tactlessness and wishing her happy for me. I took a liking to her that day. Unlike most wives, she was furious with her husband, not me. I found it a refreshingly honest perspective.' She drew a sharp breath. 'The dance is over. I must rejoin my party.'

Before Jack could do more than nod in assent she was gone, lost in the fashionable crowd coming off the dance floor.

Marcus had Meg's hand tucked securely in his arm. He felt as though he were still floating in a haze of music and silk. Slanting a glance down at her, he found her soft eyes raised to his face. This was the real Meg, warm, giving, vibrant. The mask was gone for good.

Thank God he had finally had the sense and courage to accept the joy he had been offered.

'I love you, sweetheart,' he murmured.

'I…I…' Her breath failed her totally. Despite the fact that he hadn't lost a single opportunity in the last week to tell her how much he loved her, it still reduced her to jelly. And the last thing she had expected was that he would say it in the middle of a crowded dance floor. Dammit all, she couldn't even speak! The words she longed to say could not make it past the lump in her throat, but lodged there quivering, useless. But her eyes, shimmering with sudden tears, said enough for Marcus.

Understandingly he caressed the small hand clutching his sleeve. 'A terrible place to make a declaration, my darling. I'll make it again later in more appropriate surroundings.' Probably several times, he mused. Now that the words were out, he suspected that he might never be tired of saying them. Especially if they were going to bring that look into her eyes.

'Time to rejoin the others for supper,' said Jack as they came up to him. He would have to try to get Marc alone to pass on Althea's message. No point in alarming Meg. Not in her condition. He grinned at her, 'Come and draw Lady Grafton's fire, Meg. She's grilling Toby at the moment, apparently.'

Marcus grinned. 'Poor chap must be exhausted. Aunt Regina won't just sit there and let him chunter on about his dogs. Come along, Meg. Do your duty!'

There was a teasing twinkle in his eye, which deepened as Meg said naughtily, 'Dear me, how is it that such a small word as *duty*, can encompass such a *varied* multitude of tasks?'

'You, my lady, are a baggage!' her husband informed her. 'Furthermore, you are embarrassing Jack.'

'Behold my blush,' said Jack laconically.

Back at the box Marcus had hired for the evening, Jack found it worse than impossible to drop a quiet word in his host's ear. The formidable Lady Grafton was intent on giving both Meg and her iniquitous nephew the once over. Persuaded by Di to return from Bath and give the union her blessing, she was determined not to do so without first enjoying herself.

And after supper she insisted that her nephew escort her for a brief stroll and then to view the fireworks, taking as an insult his suggestion that she might find it too much.

'Hmph! I'm not in my winding sheet yet, Rutherford. Nor likely to be after a stroll around the gardens.' She paused to consider. 'Not but what the scandalous behaviour of most of your generation is enough to send anyone to their grave!'

The party, accordingly, got up. Sir Toby claimed Meg's escort, saying to Jack in an undertone, 'Exhausted, dear boy! You take Di. Couldn't cope with any more of the Langley women tonight.'

The fireworks were magnificent and Meg, who never tired of them, was utterly entranced. But she found that standing still for so long was far more tiring than walking. In fact, she began to feel slightly unwell due to the warmth of the crush of people and an overpowering aroma of scent.

Before she could say anything, Sir Toby, experienced in the ways of ladies in delicate condition, remarked, 'I say, m'dear, it's getting a trifle crowded. Shall we take a stroll?'

Marcus heard this and turned around in time to see Meg's relieved face as she assented. He cocked his head at her in an unspoken question and she smiled back reassuringly. A stroll, she thought, would be lovely. No need to annoy Lady Grafton by dragging Marc away.

There were innumerable walks in the gardens, which were lit by well over thirty thousand lamps. Meg and Sir Toby wandered up and down, meeting very few other couples. Those they did see seemed perfectly content to lose themselves in a fashion Meg did not doubt Lady Grafton would label as scandalous with unconvincing righteousness.

As they strolled in companionable silence Meg reflected on her new happiness. During the past week since their reconciliation she and Marc had gradually come to a full understanding. At last Meg could see why he had been so confused. Why, even when he fell in love, he had been so reluctant to tell her. Their bargain had just been an excuse, for both of them. He had hidden his fear and pain over his mother's death behind its terms and she had used it to disguise her fear of rejection.

Now the pretences were over, leaving them free to acknowledge the truth. That they loved each other and would take the joy offered with both hands.

Her mind was brought back to earth by an audible snap as her garter gave way.

'Oh, bother!' she said, as, with a disconcerting slither, her silk stocking came down.

'Eh?' Sir Toby was rather startled.

'My garter,' she said with a blush. 'It's broken… Would you mind…could you…?'

'Oh, certainly, m'dear,' said Sir Toby cheerfully. 'I'll just pop around the corner and wait for you.' He bowed elegantly and took himself off.

Meg battled with the garter for several moments before deciding to give up and just stuff the offending item, along with her stocking, into her reticule.

Just as she straightened up an amused voice said, 'How very convenient. That will be one less article to strip from you. And I don't even have to draw off that dolt Carlton.'

She whirled to meet Sir Blaise Winterbourne's cruel eyes. Shock rendered her speechless for a moment and then she opened her mouth to scream.

Sir Blaise was too fast. He moved like lightning and had one arm twisted behind her back while his free hand was clamped mercilessly over her mouth. She could do nothing as he forced her away, the pain in her arm was making her dizzy. She barely noticed the pearl bracelet she had been wearing snap and drop to the ground.

'Do not think that Rutherford will be able to save you this time, my dear,' he mocked. 'He is at the other end of the gardens. And even if you tell him you went with me unwillingly, our dear mutual cousin Henrietta will assure the world that she saw us leaving together via the water gate, a most happy couple.' His voice was light as he continued. 'So you see, you are ruined anyway. It remains only to be seen whether you will drag your husband's name in the mud or submit to your fate quietly.'

Sheer terror held Meg in its relentless grip. She had been right, then, that evening at Almack's. No doubt Henrietta would be delighted to see her ruined and be able to say, *Like mother, like daughter!* And if Marc, knowing the truth, stood by her, then his proud name would be ruined as well. Not for one moment did Meg doubt that he would stand by her.

The pain in her arm grew worse as Sir Blaise, enjoying his triumph, twisted it harder. The dim walk seemed to swirl and tilt before her eyes. They had reached an unfrequented part of the grounds. He turned her to face him, still with her arm twisted cruelly. She could not doubt that he meant to ravish her, but suddenly her terror and pain scorched into sheer flaming rage. She would *not* tamely submit and let him destroy her and Marc. Furiously she began to squirm and wriggle, stamping at his feet, striking at him with her free hand.

He caught it and laughed. 'Remember, my dear, if you scream, your cousin will swear you came willingly.'

And then she remembered something: Agnes Barlow's gruff tones as she advised Nellie Bates, one afternoon in the kitchen at Fenby, on how to deal with a suitor who'd become too forward for Nellie's liking. She couldn't for the life of her see what use it would be, but Agnes had seemed quite sure.

She jerked her knee upwards—hard.

After some ten minutes Sir Toby succumbed to his concern about the inordinate length of time his sister-in-law was taking over a mere broken garter. Strolling back around the corner, he was most surprised to find her gone.

'Extraordinary,' he said to himself. It was most unlike the chit. She ought not to be wandering about alone. If Marc found out he'd be fit to be tied. Or had Marc come to find her? Just as he was pondering the likelihood of this, his eye was caught by something half hidden under a bush. Pink and shiny, it shimmered in the lamplight.

Suddenly his air of languor dropped from him as he strode over to pick it up. Meg's reticule! At least it looked like hers. He opened it and, sure enough, there was a silk stocking with a broken garter on top.

For a moment he was undecided, but then he saw something else on the ground a few yards away. With an oath he sprang forward. Meg might have dropped her reticule and forgotten it, but she would not have dropped that bracelet! Without the least hesitation he began to run back towards the boxes.

'She said *what*?' Marcus had gone absolutely white at Jack's information. He felt as though someone had just ripped out his heart. Looking around frantically, he said in a shaking voice, 'Where's Meg?'

'Calm down, man!' said Jack. 'She's with Toby. He's quite capable of looking after her. And Althea Hartleigh says that Winterbourne is out of—'

'Hamilton!'

They swung around to see Lady Hartleigh.

She gripped Jack's sleeve. 'Winterbourne is here! Have you told—?' She glanced at Marcus's face. 'You did. He chatted briefly to Henrietta Fellowes and then disappeared off after Lady Rutherford and Carlton. You'd better hurry. That bitch looked as though she'd been left with a juicy bone.'

Marcus was gone, running in the direction taken by Toby and Meg half an hour ago. The thought that Winterbourne might try to abduct Meg terrified him. The fury he had felt on his wedding night was as nothing to the rage and panic he felt now. Then he had scarcely known Meg. Now she was his, the most precious thing in his life. No fear of scandal would save Winterbourne this time. Marcus would kill him if he tried to lay hands on Meg!

Dimly he realised that Jack had come with him. He slowed down—they were at the junction of the Grand

Walk and the Grand Cross Walk and he had no idea where to go.

'Marc, this is crazy!' expostulated Jack. 'She's safe enough with Toby. He'd never leave her alone here, you know—'

He stopped abruptly as a relieved yell came to their ears.

'Thank God!' Toby was running towards them from the Dark Walk. He came up, panting. 'Meg's disappeared. Garter broke, so I stepped away to let her deal with it. You know, just around the corner. Came back and found these!' He held up the reticule and broken bracelet.

Marcus took them in hands that shook uncontrollably.

His eyes met Jack's in anguish. 'Winterbourne. This time I'm going to kill him.' The deadly quiet of his tones startled Jack and Toby more than an explosion of rage would have done.

'What?' Sir Toby was considerably taken aback. In the twenty years he had known Marcus he had never seen him like this. Had never suspected that he could feel anything this deeply.

'Where were you, Toby?' Marcus forced himself to act logically. He could not help Meg by running in circles.

'Follow me.'

Meg felt her knee crash into her tormentor with satisfying force. And stared in stupefaction at the result.

Winterbourne's hands dropped from her, all their brutal strength dissolved as though it had never been. He doubled over with a wheezing moan and collapsed in a shuddering heap, practically sobbing in agony.

Agnes's voice echoed in her memory. *That'll settle 'im an' give you time to run.*

Meg ran blindly. She had no idea where she was going precisely, but she knew she didn't want to be there. What she wanted was Marc…his arms around her, secure and warm, banishing her fear. She had not taken more than a dozen strides before she hit a solid wall.

A solid wall with arms that tightened around her and a voice that broke as it said, 'Meg! Oh, thank God! Are you safe?'

She'd never felt safer. And Jack and Toby were there as well, patting her shoulders and reassuring her.

At first Marc felt as though nothing mattered but having Meg back safely in his arms, apparently unharmed. He held her to him tightly, his cheek pressed to her hair as she clung to him. His hands stroked her gently, soothingly until he felt her shuddering ease, felt her relax against him. Then he spared a glance for Winterbourne, still wheezing painfully on the ground. Dimly he was aware of surprise—surprise that he could feel not the slightest twinge of masculine sympathy for a man in that situation.

Then rage took over. He caught Jack's eye and said, 'Look after Meg for me, Jack. There is something I have to do.' He put her into Jack's arms very gently, saying, 'Stay with Jack, my love.' He caught Jack's eye. 'Try not to let her watch.'

He strode over to Winterbourne's gasping form.

'Get up, you cur!' he snarled. 'This time I'm going to give you what you deserve.'

Winterbourne stayed where he was.

Marcus waited a moment, and then said in biting accents, 'Toby, go out to the carriages and borrow a whip.

If anyone asks what you want with it, you may tell them, with my compliments, that I need it to thrash Winterbourne, who is too cowardly to stand and face me. He has only enough courage to assault a woman!'

Winterbourne staggered to his feet, still clutching his midriff. 'Think...scandal,' he gasped.

'*Your* scandal,' said Marcus. 'There are enough witnesses, including Lady Hartleigh, to prove that you assaulted my wife! And if you try it, I'll have nothing to lose by putting a bullet straight through you! I don't think either the law or society will find my actions unforgivable. You can tell Henrietta Fellowes that with my compliments.'

He waited a moment, taking a savage satisfaction in Winterbourne's pain. 'If you have that flask of yours, Toby, give him some. You can always have the scullery maid boil it before you drink from it again. Or I'll buy you a new one.'

Toby obliged and Winterbourne gulped at the brandy gratefully. Slightly recovered, he looked around uncertainly, all his urbanity fled. He glanced at the flask and then at Sir Toby.

'Keep it,' said Toby coldly. 'I've too much respect for my scullery maid to soil her with anything you've touched!'

'Now,' said Marcus, from between clenched teeth, 'now, Winterbourne, I have something to say to you.'

The right hook he delivered to Winterbourne's nose sent the baronet reeling. He followed it with a savage uppercut which snapped his head back and Winterbourne staggered backwards into a tree. Marcus followed him, but Winterbourne slithered to the ground again with a moan.

'Good God! What on earth has Rutherford done to

Winterbourne?' A startled, feminine, voice brought Marc up short.

Coldly and deliberately, Marc turned his head. Lady Jersey and her lord stood staring in rampant curiosity.

'Really, Marc! Do you think this is a suitable venue for you to pursue your quarrel with Winterbourne?' Lady Jersey appeared to feel deeply over this unseemly fracas.

'Good evening, Sally,' said Marc, very politely. 'While it may not be the venue I would have chosen, since Winterbourne considered it a suitable venue for attempted rape, I was, shall we say, constrained?'

'What?' Sally Jersey's eyes flew to Meg, still supported by Jack. 'Dear God. Meg, are you all right?' Horrified sympathy rang in her voice as she rushed across to Meg.

The Earl of Jersey spoke thoughtfully. 'Sorry to interrupt you, Rutherford. If your arm gets tired, let me know. Be happy to take a turn.'

His wife turned sharply from comforting Meg. 'Oh, for goodness sake! What if someone else comes along? The last thing Meg needs is for anyone to know about this. Not that anyone will blame her, but for such a thing to get about…it would be intolerable for the poor girl!'

She cast a contemptuous glance at Winterbourne and spoke in tones of shuddering disgust. 'Rest assured that if he ever attempts to enter Almack's again, he will be thrown out. Trust me. And I'll make it quite plain that he is not to be received by anyone!' Her eyes glittered venomously. 'I won't need to say why. No one will question me.'

No one, least of all Winterbourne, doubted her. The Countess of Jersey's word was law. If she decreed that

Winterbourne could not be received, then he was finished as far as the ladies were concerned.

'I'll deal with the clubs,' offered Lord Jersey, sealing Winterbourne's ruin. 'Better if you keep out of it, Marc. Someone might guess the truth. Leave it to Sally and myself.' He held out his arm to his countess. 'Come along, my love. Before I am tempted to assist Marc in murdering that filth. Evening, all.' He led his wife away inexorably.

Disgustedly Marcus stepped back, throttling the temptation to send Toby for a whip. Sally was right. If anyone else appeared…

'Marc? Could we…could we go home now?'

He turned and looked at Meg. She still stood in the circle of Jack's arm, but her eyes said clearly that she wanted him. He cast a lingering glance down at Winterbourne. There probably wasn't much point in sending for the whip. After what Meg had done to him, he wouldn't even feel it.

He walked over to Meg and took her from Jack, dragging her into his arms. 'Oh God, Meg! Will you never do anything the way you're meant to?' His voice was rough with passion. 'I expected a fashionable wife who would run up astronomical bills at the dressmakers. The only bill you have run up is at Hatchard's! I thought I wanted a marriage of convenience and fell in love with you instead! Now I come racing to rescue you and find that you have rescued yourself!' He held her tightly.

'Do you you mind?' asked Meg as she nestled against him. Here in his arms she was safe from everything.

A strange sound, half-groan and half-laugh, was ripped from deep inside Marcus at her question. Mind? *Mind?* How could he possibly mind having his life turned upside down and his heart turned inside out? He hadn't even been alive before he met Meg!

'Not a bit, my love,' he vowed, dropping a kiss on her hair. 'Although you will need to order some new clothes soon. Perhaps then you may fulfil at least *one* of my expectations!'

'I've got plenty of clothes,' she reassured him.

'Really?' He ran his hands over her still-flat belly, in tender appreciation. 'Not for long you haven't!' He brought his mouth down on hers, crushing it mercilessly in his relief.

Jack and Toby turned away tactfully. The latter's eye fell on Winterbourne, still slumped, whimpering, at the foot of the tree, oblivious to anything beyond his own battered body.

A disgusted snort escaped him. 'Stinking cur! Didn't even try to defend himself!'

'After what Meg did to him?' Jack sounded faintly amused.

Sir Toby shifted uncomfortably. 'Yes, well. Y'know, Jack, never thought I'd say this—but the bastard deserved it!'

Epilogue

Seven months later Marcus Langley, Earl of Rutherford, stood gazing adoringly down at his pale, exhausted wife who held his son and heir nestled against her soft breast. The baby whimpered and nuzzled hungrily as his parents smiled at each other.

Marcus dropped to one knee beside the bed. 'Darling Meg, you're all right?' His voice shook uncontrollably. It had been the worst nine hours of his life. His hand gripped hers and he raised it to his mouth, turning it to press a kiss into the soft palm.

'She's fine, Marc,' came an astringent voice behind him. 'Now, why don't you get out of the way so Agnes and I can show her how to feed the baby?'

The thought of Meg nursing his son sent a wave of sheer joy surging through Marcus. Completely ignoring Diana and the openly grinning Agnes Barlow, he leaned over and kissed his wife gently. Then he bent and placed a very careful salute on top of the fuzzy head at her breast.

A soft whisper reached his ear. 'I love you, Marc.'

His heart swelled as he stood and looked down at the two of them. His wife and son. His family. He was complete now, and each new addition would add to that fulfilment. That was the odd thing about love—having surrendered to it, there didn't seem to be any limit on how much he could give...or receive.

GET SWEPT AWAY BY THESE HANDSOME HEROES FROM HARLEQUIN HISTORICALS

On Sale July 2004

THE DUTIFUL RAKE
by Elizabeth Rolls

The Earl of Rutherford
Renowned rogue

FULK THE RELUCTANT
by Elaine Knighton

Fulk de Galliard
Honored knight

On Sale August 2004

A SCANDALOUS SITUATION
by Patricia Frances Rowell

Robert Armstrong
Gentleman protector

THE WIDOW'S BARGAIN
by Juliet Landon

Sir Alex Somers
Raider of castles—and hearts

Visit us at www.eHarlequin.com

HARLEQUIN HISTORICALS®

HHMED37

Savor the breathtaking
romances and thrilling adventures
of Harlequin Historicals

On sale September 2004

THE KNIGHT'S REDEMPTION by Joanne Rock

A young Welshwoman tricks Roarke Barret into marriage
in order to break her family's curse—of spinsterhood.
But Ariana Glamorgan never expects to fall for the
handsome Englishman who is now her husband....

PRINCESS OF FORTUNE by Miranda Jarrett

Captain Lord Thomas Greaves is assigned to guard Italian
princess Isabella di Fortunaro. Sparks fly and passions flare
between the battle-weary captain and the spoiled, beautiful
lady. Can love cross all boundaries?

On sale October 2004

HIGHLAND ROGUE by Deborah Hale

To save her sister from a fortune hunter, Claire Talbot offers
herself as a more tempting target. But can she forget the
feelings she once had for Ewan Geddes, a charming
Highlander who once worked on her father's estate?

THE PENNILESS BRIDE by Nicola Cornick

Home from the Peninsula War, Rob Selbourne discovers
he must marry a chimney sweep's daughter to
fulfill his grandfather's eccentric will. Will Rob
find true happiness in the arms of
the lovely Jemima?

www.eHarlequin.com

HARLEQUIN HISTORICALS®

HHMED38

eHARLEQUIN.com

For great romance books at great prices,
shop www.eHarlequin.com today!

GREAT BOOKS:
- **Extensive selection** of today's hottest books, including **current** releases, **backlist** titles and new **upcoming** books.
- **Favorite authors:** Nora Roberts, Debbie Macomber and more!

GREAT DEALS:
- **Save every day:** enjoy great savings and special online promotions.
- *Exclusive* **online offers:** FREE books, bargain outlet savings, special deals.

EASY SHOPPING:
- Easy, secure, **24-hour shopping** from the comfort of your own home.
- **Excerpts, reader recommendations** and our **Romance Legend** will help you choose!
- **Convenient shipping and payment methods.**

**Shop online
at www.eHarlequin.com today!**

INTBB2

eHARLEQUIN.com

The eHarlequin.com online community is *the* place to share opinions, thoughts and feelings!

- Joining the community is easy, fun and **FREE!**

- Connect with **other romance fans** on our message boards.

- Meet your **favorite authors** without leaving home!

- **Share opinions** on books, movies, celebrities…and *more!*

Here's what our members say:

"I love the friendly and helpful atmosphere filled with support and humor."
—Texanna (eHarlequin.com member)

"Is this the place for me, or what? There is nothing I love more than 'talking' books, especially with fellow readers who are reading the same ones I am."
—Jo Ann (eHarlequin.com member)

Join today by visiting
www.eHarlequin.com!

INTCOMM

eHARLEQUIN.com

The Ultimate Destination for Women's Fiction

For **FREE online reading**, visit
www.eHarlequin.com now and enjoy:

Online Reads
Read **Daily** and **Weekly** chapters from
our Internet-exclusive stories by your
favorite authors.

Interactive Novels
Cast your vote to help decide how these
stories unfold...then stay tuned!

Quick Reads
For shorter romantic reads, try our
collection of Poems, Toasts, & More!

Online Read Library
Miss one of our online reads?
Come here to catch up!

Reading Groups
Discuss, share and rave with other
community members!

For great reading online,
visit www.eHarlequin.com today!

INTONL04